Harding's Luck

Harding's Luck

By

E. Nesbit

With illustrations by

H.R. Millar

NEW YORK

Books of Wonder

1998

TO

ROSAMUND PHILIPPA PHILIPS

WITH

E. NESBIT'S LOVE

First published by Macmillan & Co. 1909

8/01 – B+T – $13.95.

First published in this edition 1998 by

Books of Wonder

16 West 18th Street

New York, NY 10011

Design and typography © 1998 by Ozma, Inc.

Printed in the U.S.A.

ISBN 0-929605-91-8 (hardcover)

ISBN 0-929605-90-X (paperback)

1 2 3 4 5 6 7 8 9

List of Chapters

Tinkler and the Moonflower

Dickie lived at New Cross. At least the address was New Cross, but really the house where he lived was one of a row of horrid little houses built on the slope where once green fields ran down the hill to the river, and the old houses of the Deptford merchants stood stately in their pleasant gardens and fruitful orchards. All those good fields and happy gardens are built over now. It is as though some wicked giant had taken a big brush full of yellow ocher paint, and another full of mud-color, and had painted out the green in streaks of dull yellow and filthy brown; and the brown is the roads and the yellow is the houses. Miles and miles and miles of them, and not a green thing to be seen except the cabbages in the greengrocers' shops, and here and there some poor trails of creeping-jenny drooping from a dirty window-sill. There is a little yard at the back of each house; this is called "the garden," and some of these show green—but they only show it to the houses' back windows. You cannot see it from the street. These gardens are green because green is the color that most pleases and soothes men's eyes; and however you may shut people up between bars of yellow and mud color, and however hard you may make them work, and however little wage you may pay them for working, there will always be found among those people some men who are willing to work a little longer, and for no wages at all, so that they may have green things growing near them.

But there were no green things growing in the garden at the back of the house where Dickie lived with his aunt. There were stones and bones, and bits of brick, and dirty old dishcloths matted together with grease and mud, worn-out broomheads and broken shovels, a bottomless pail, and the moldy remains of a hutch where once rabbits had lived. But that was a very long time ago, and Dickie had never seen the rabbits. A boy had brought a brown rabbit to school once, buttoned up inside his jacket, and he had let Dickie hold it in his hands for several minutes before the teacher detected its presence and shut it up in a locker till school should be over. So Dickie knew what rabbits were like. And he was fond of the hutch for the sake of what had once lived there.

And when his aunt sold the poor remains of the hutch to a man with a barrow who was ready to buy anything, and who took also the pails and the shovels, giving threepence for the lot, Dickie was almost as unhappy as though the hutch had really held a furry friend. And he hated the man who took the hutch away, all the more because there were empty rabbit-skins hanging sadly from the back of the barrow.

It is really with the going of that rabbit-hutch that this story begins. Because it was then that Dickie, having called his aunt a Beast, and hit at her with his little dirty fist, was well slapped and put out into the bereaved yard to "come to himself," as his aunt said. He threw himself down on the ground and cried and wriggled with misery and pain, and wished—ah, many things.

"Wot's the bloomin' row now?" the Man Next Door suddenly asked; "been hittin' of you?"

"They've took away the 'utch," said Dickie.

"Well, there warn't nothin' in it."

"I diden want it took away," wailed Dickie.

"Leaves more room," said the Man Next Door, leaning on his spade. It was Saturday afternoon and the next-door garden was one of the green ones. There were small grubby daffodils in it, and dirty-faced little primroses, and an arbor beside the water-butt, bare at this time of he year, but still a real arbor. And an elder-tree that in the hot weather had flat, white flowers on it big as tea-plates. And a lilac-tree with brown buds on it. Beautiful. "Say, matey, just you chuck it! Chuck it, I say! How in thunder can I get on with my digging with you 'owlin' yer 'ead off?" inquired the Man Next Door. "You get up and peg along in an' arst yer aunt if she'd be agreeable for me to do up her garden a bit. I could do it odd times. You'd like that."

"Not 'arf!" said Dickie, got up, and went in.

"Come to yourself, eh?" sneered the aunt. "You mind, and let it be the last time you come your games with me, my beauty. You and your tantrums!"

Dickie said what it was necessary to say, and got back to the "garden."

"She says she ain't got no time to waste, an' if you 'ave she don't care what you does with it."

"There's a dirty mug you've got on you," said the Man Next Door, leaning over to give Dickie's face a rub with a handkerchief hardly cleaner. "Now I'll come over and make a start." He threw his leg over the fence. "You just peg about an' be busy pickin' up all them fancy articles, and nex' time yer aunt goes to Buckingham Palace for the day we'll have a bonfire."

"Fifth o' November?" said Dickie, sitting down and beginning to draw to himself the rubbish that covered the ground.

"Fifth of anything you like, so long as *she* ain't about," said he, driving in the spade. "'Ard as any old doorstep it is. Never mind, we'll turn it over, and we'll get some little seedses and some little planteses and we shan't know ourselves."

"I got a 'apenny," said Dickie.

"Well, I'll put one to it, and you leg 'long and buy seedses. That's wot you do."

Dickie went. He went slowly, because he was lame. And he was lame because his "aunt" had dropped him when he was a baby. She was not a nice woman, and I am glad to say that she goes out of this story almost at once. But she did keep Dickie when his father died, and she might have sent him to the workhouse. For she was not really his aunt, but just the woman of the house where his father had lodged. It was good of her to keep Dickie, even if she wasn't very kind to him. And as that is all the good I can find to say about her, I will say no more. With his little crutch, made out of a worn-out broom cut down to his little height, he could manage quite well in spite of his lameness.

He found the cornchandler's—a really charming shop that smelt like stables and had deep dusty bins where he should have liked to play. Above the bins were delightful little square-fronted drawers, labelled Rape, Hemp, Canary, Millet, Mustard, and so on; and above the drawers pictures of the kind of animals that were fed on the kind of thing that the shop sold. Fat, oblong cows that had eaten Burley's Cattle Food, stout pillows of wool that Ovis's Sheep Spice had fed, and, brightest and best of all, an incredibly smooth-plumaged parrot, rainbow-colored, cocking a black eye bright with the intoxicating qualities of Perrokett's Artistic Bird Seed.

"Gimme," said Dickie, leaning against the counter and pointing a grimy thumb at the wonder—"gimme a pennorth o' that there!"

"Got the penny?" the shopman asked carefully.

Dickie displayed it, parted with it, and came home nursing a paper bag full of rustling promises.

"Why," said the Man Next Door, "that aint' seeds. It's parrot food, that is."

"It said the Ar-something Bird Seed," said Dickie, downcast; "I thought it 'ud come into flowers like birds—same colors as wot the poll parrot was, dontcherknow?"

"G<small>IMME</small>," <small>SAID</small> D<small>ICKIE</small>—"G<small>IMME A PENN'ORTH O' THAT THERE.</small>"

"And so it will like as not," said the Man Next Door comfortably. "I'll set it along this end soon's I've got it turned over. I lay it'll come up something pretty."

So the seed was sown. And the Man Next Door promised two more pennies later for *real* seed. Also he transplanted two of the primroses whose faces wanted washing.

It was a grand day for Dickie. He told the whole story of it that night when he went to bed to his only confidant, from whom he hid nothing. The confidant made no reply, but Dickie was sure this was not because the confidant didn't care about the story. The confidant was a blackened stick about 5 inches long, with little blackened bells to it like the bells on a dog's collars. Also a rather crooked bit of something whitish and very hard, good to suck, or to stroke with your fingers, or to dig holes in the soap with. Dickie had no idea what it was. His father had given it to him in the hospital where Dickie was taken to say goodbye to him. Goodbye had to be said because of father having fallen off the scaffolding where he was at work and not getting better. "You stick to that," father had said, looking dreadfully clean in the strange bed among all those other clean beds; "it's yourn, your very own. My dad give it to me, and it belonged to his dad. Don't you let anyone take it away. Some old lady told the old man it 'ud bring us luck. So long, old chap."

Dickie remembered every word of that speech, and he kept the treasure. There had been another thing with it, tied on with string. But Aunt Maud had found that, and taken it away "to take care of," and he had never seen it again. It was brassy, with a white stone and some sort of pattern on it. He had the treasure, and he had not the least idea what it was, with its bells that jangled such pretty music, and its white spike so hard and smooth. He did not know—but I know. It was a rattle—a baby's old-fashioned rattle—or, if you would rather call it that, a "coral and bells."

"And we shall 'ave the fairest flowers of hill and dale," said Dickie, whispering comfortably in his dirty sheets, "and green sward. Oh! Tinkler dear, 'twill indeed be a fair scene. The gayest colors of the rainbow amid the Ague Able green of fresh leaves. I do love the Man Next Door. He has indeed a 'art of gold."

That was how Dickie talked to his friend Tinkler. You know how he talked to his aunt and the Man Next Door. I wonder whether you know that most children can speak at least two languages, even if they have never had a foreign nurse or been to foreign climes—or whether you think that you are the only child who can do this?

Believe me, you are not. Parents and guardians would be surprised to learn that dear little Charlie has a language quite different from the one he uses to them—a language in which he talks to the cook and the housemaid. And yet another language—spoken with the real accent too—in which he converses with the boot-boy and the grooms.

Dickie, however, had learned his second language from books. The teacher at his school had given him six—"Children of the New Forest," "Quentin Durward," "Hereward the Wake," and three others—all paper-backed. They made a new world for Dickie. And since the people in books talked in this nice, if odd, way, he saw no reason why he should not—to a friend whom he could trust.

I hope you're not getting bored with all this?

You see, I must tell you a little about the kind of boy Dickie was and the kind of way he lived, or you won't understand his adventures. And he had adventures—no end of adventures—as you will see presently.

Dickie woke, gay as the spring sun that was trying to look in at him through his grimy windows.

"Perhaps he'll do some more to the garden today!" he said, and got up very quickly.

He got up in the dirty, comfortless room and dressed himself. But in the evening he was undressed by kind, clean hands, and washed in a big bath half-full of hot, silvery water, with soap that smelt like the timber yard at the end of the street. Because, going along to school, with his silly little head full of Artistic Bird Seeds and flowers rainbow-colored, he had let his crutch slip on a banana-skin and had tumbled down, and a butcher's cart had gone over his poor lame foot. So they took the hurt foot to the hospital, and of course he had to go with it, and the hospital was much more like the heaven he read of in his books than anything he had ever come across before.

He noticed that the nurses and the doctors spoke in the kind of words that he had found in his books, and in a voice that he had not found anywhere; so when on the second day a round-faced, smiling lady in a white cap said, "Well, Tommy, and how are we today?" he replied—

"My name is far from being Tommy, and I am in Lux Ury and Af Fluence, I thank you, gracious lady."

At which the lady laughed and pinched his cheek.

When she grew to know him better, and found out where he had learned to talk like that, she produced more books. And from them he learned more new words. They were very nice to him at the hospital, but when they sent him home they put his lame foot into a thick boot with a horrid, clumpy sole and iron things that went up his leg.

His aunt and her friends said, "How kind!" but Dickie hated it. The boys at school made game of it—they had got used to the crutch—and that was worse than being called "Old Dot-and-go-one," which was what Dickie had got used to—so used that it seemed almost like a pet name.

And on that first night of his return he found that he had been robbed. They had taken his Tinkler from the safe corner in his bed where the ticking was broken and there was a soft flock nest for a boy's best friend.

He knew better than to ask what had become of it. Instead he searched and searched the house in all its five rooms. But he never found Tinkler.

Instead he found next day, when his aunt had gone out shopping, a little square of cardboard at he back of the dresser drawer, among the dirty dusters and clothes pegs and string and corks and novelettes.

It was a pawnticket—"Rattle. One shilling."

Dickie knew about pawntickets. You, of course, don't. Well, ask some grown-up person to explain; I haven't time. I want to get on with the story.

Until he had found that ticket he had not been able to think of anything else. He had not even cared to think about his garden and wonder whether the Artistic Bird Seeds had come up parrot-colored. He had been a very long time in the hospital, and it was August now. And the nurses had assured him that the seeds must be up long ago—he would find everything flowering, you see if he didn't.

And now he went out to look. There was a tangle of green growth at the end of the garden, and the next garden was full of weeds. For the Man Next Door had gone off to look for work down Ashford way, where the hop-gardens are, and the house was to let.

A few poor little pink and yellow flowers showed stunted among the green where he had sowed the Artistic Bird Seed. And, towering high above everything else—oh, three times as high as Dickie himself—there was a flower—a great flower like a sunflower, only white.

"Why," said Dickie, "it's as big as a dinner-plate."

It was.

It stood up, beautiful and stately, and turned its cream-white face towards the sun.

"The stalk's like a little tree," said Dickie; and so it was.

It had great drooping leaves, and a dozen smaller white flowers stood out below it on long stalks, thinner than that needed to support the moonflower itself.

"It is a moonflower, of course," he said, "if the other kind's sunflowers. I love it! I love it! I love it!"

He did not allow himself much time for loving it, however; for he had business in hand. He had, somehow or other, to get a shilling. Because without a shilling he could not exchange that square of cardboard with "Rattle" on it for his one friend, Tinkler. And with the shilling he could. (This is part of the dismal magic of pawntickets which some grown-up will kindly explain to you.)

"I can't get money by the sweat of my brow," said Dickie to himself; "nobody would let me run their errands when they could get a boy with both legs to do them. Not likely. I wish I'd got something I could sell."

He looked round the yard—dirtier and nastier than ever now in the parts that the Man Next Door had not had time to dig. There was certainly nothing there that anyone would want to buy, especially now the rabbit-hutch was gone. Except... why, of course—the moonflowers!

He got the old worn-down knife out of the bowl on the back kitchen sink, where it nestled among potato peelings like a flower among foliage, and carefully cut half a dozen of the smaller flowers. Then he limped up to New Cross Station, and stood outside, leaning on his crutch, and holding out the flowers to the people who came crowding out of the station after the arrival of each train—thick, black crowds of tired people, in too great a hurry to get home to their teas to care much about him or his flowers. Everybody glanced at them, for they were wonderful flowers, as white as water-lilies, only flat—the real sunflower shape—and their centers were of the purest yellow and color.

"Pretty, ain't they?" one black-coated person would say to another. And the other would reply—

"No. Yes. I dunno! Hurry up, can't you?"

It was no good. Dickie was tired, and the flowers were beginning to droop. He turned to go home, when a sudden

"IT *IS* A MOONFLOWER, OF COURSE," HE SAID.

thought brought the blood to his face. He turned again quickly and went straight to the pawnbroker's. You may be quite sure he had learned the address on the card by heart.

He went boldly into the shop, which had three handsome gold balls hanging out above its door, and in its window all sorts of pretty things—rings, and chains, and brooches, and watches, and china, and silk handkerchiefs, and concertinas.

"Well, young man," said the stout gentleman behind the counter, "what can we do for you?"

"I want to pawn my moonflowers," said Dickie.

The stout gentleman roared with laughter, and slapped a stout leg with a stout hand.

"Well, that's a good 'un!" he said, "as good a one as ever I heard. Why, you little duffer, they'd be dead long before you came back to redeem them, that's certain."

"You'd have them while they were alive, you know," said Dickie gently.

"What are they? Don't seem up to much. Though I don't know that I ever saw a flower just like them, come to think of it," said the pawnbroker, who lived in a neat villa at Brockley and went in for gardening in a gentlemanly, you -needn't-suppose-I-can't-afford-a-real-gardener-if-I-like sort of way.

"They're moonflowers," said Dickie, "and I want to pawn them and then get something else out with the money."

"Got the ticket?" said the gentleman, cleverly seeing that he meant "get out of pawn."

"Yes," said Dickie; "and it's my own Tinkler that my daddy gave me before he died, and my aunt Missa Propagated it when I was in hospital."

The man looked carefully at the card.

"All right," he said at last; "hand over the flowers. They are not so bad," he added, more willing to prize them now that they were his (things do look different when they are your own, don't they?). "Here, Humphreys, put these in a jug of water till I go home. And get this out."

"Here, Humphreys, put these in a jug of water till I go home"

A pale young man in spectacles appeared from a sort of dark cave at the back of the shop, took flowers and ticket, and was swallowed up again in the darkness of the cave.

"Oh, thank you!" said Dickie fervently. "I shall live but to repay your bounteous generosity."

"None of your cheek," said the pawnbroker, reddening, and there was an awkward pause.

"It's not cheek; I meant it," said Dickie at last, speaking very earnestly. "You'll see, some of these days. I read an interesting Nar Rataive about a Lion the King of Beasts and a Mouse, that small and Ty Morous animal, which if you have not heard it I will now Pur seed to relite."

"You're a rum little kid, I don't think," said the man. "Where do you learn such talk?"

"It's the wye they talk in books," said Dickie, suddenly returning to the language of his aunt. "You bein' a toff I thought you'd unnerstand. My mistike. No 'fence."

"Mean to say you can talk like a book when you like, and cut it off short like that?"

"I can Con-vers like Lords and Lydies," said Dickie, in the accents of the gutter, "and your noble benefacteriness made me seek to express my feelinks with the best words at me Command."

"Fond of books?"

"I believe you," said Dickie, and there were no more awkward pauses.

When the pale young man came back with something wrapped in a bit of clean rag, he said a whispered word or two to the pawnbroker, who unrolled the rag and looked closely at the rattle.

"So it is," he said, "and it's a beauty too, let alone anything else."

"Isn't he?" said Dickie, touched by this praise of his treasured Tinkler.

"I've got something else here that's got the same crest as your rattle."

"Crest?" said Dickie; "isn't that what you wear on your helmet in the heat and press of the Tower Nament?"

The pawnbroker explained that crests no longer live exclusively on helmets, but on all sorts of odd things. And the queer little animal, drawn in fine scratches on the side of the rattle, was, it seemed, a crest.

"Here, Humphreys," he added, "give it a rub up and bring that seal here."

The pale young man did something to tinkler with some pinky powder and a brush and a wash-leather, while his master fitted together the two halves of a broken white cornelian.

"It came out of a seal," he said, "and I don't mind making you a present of it."

"Oh!" said Dickie, "you are a real rightern." And he rested his crutch against the counter expressly to clasp his hands in ecstasy as boys in books did.

"My young man shall stick it together with cement," the pawnbroker went on, "and put it in a little box. Don't you take it out till tomorrow and it'll be stuck fast. Only don't go trying to seal with it, or the sealing-wax will melt the cement. It'll bring you luck, I shouldn't wonder."

(It did; and such luck as the kind pawnbroker never dreamed of. But that comes further on in the story.)

Dickie left the shop without his moonflowers, indeed, but with his Tinkler now whitely shining, and declared to be "real silver, and mind you take care of it, my lad," his white cornelian seal carefully packed in a strong little cardboard box with metal corners. Also a broken-backed copy of "Ingoldsby Legends" and one of "Mrs. Markham's English History," which had no back at all. "You must go on trying to improve your mind," said the pawnbroker fussily. He was very pleased with himself for having been so kind. "And come back and see me—say next month."

"I will," said Dickie. "A thousand blessings from a grateful heart. I will come back. I say, you are good! Thank you, thank you—I will come back next month, and tell you everything I have learned form the Perru Sal of your books."

"Perusal," said the pawnbroker—"that's the way to pernounce it. Goodbye, my man, and next month."

But next month found Dickie in a very different place from the pawnbroker's shop, and with a very different person from the pawnbroker who in his rural retirement at Brockley gardened in such a gentlemanly way.

Dickie went home—his aunt was still out. His books told him that treasure is best hidden under loose boards, unless of course your house has a secret panel, which his had not. There was a loose board in his room, where the man "saw to" the gas. He got it up, and pushed his treasures as far in as he could—along the rough, crumbly surface of the lath and plaster.

Not a moment too soon. For before the board was coaxed quite back into its palace the voice of the aunt screamed up.

"Come along down, can't you? I can hear you pounding about up there. Come along down and fetch me a ha'porth o'wood—I can't get the kettle to boil without a fire, can I?"

When Dickie came down his aunt slightly slapped him, and he took the halfpenny and limped off obediently.

It was a very long time indeed before he came back. Because before he got to the shop with no window to it, but only shutters that were put up at night, where the wood and coal were sold, he saw a Punch and Judy show. He had never seen one before, and it interested him extremely. He longed to see it unpack itself and display its wonders, and he followed it through more streets than he knew; and when he found that it was not going to unpack at all, but was just going home to its bed in an old coach-house, he remembered the firewood;

and the halfpenny clutched tight and close in his hand seemed to reproach him warmly.

He looked about him, and knew that he did not at all know where he was. There was a tall, thin, ragged man lounging against a stable door in the yard where the Punch and Judy show lived. He took his clay pipe out of his mouth to say—

"What's up, matey? Lost your way?"

Dickie explained.

"It's Lavender Terrace where I live," he ended—"Lavender Terrace, Rosemary Street, Deptford."

"I'm going that way myself," said the man, getting away from the wall. "We'll go back by the boat if you like. Ever been on the boat?"

"No," said Dickie.

"Like to?"

"Don't mind if I do," said Dickie.

It was very pleasant with the steamboat going along in such a hurry, pushing the water out of the way, and puffing and blowing, and something beating inside it like a giant's heart. The wind blew freshly, and the ragged man found a sheltered corner behind the funnel. It was so sheltered, and the wind had been so strong that Dickie felt sleepy. When he said, "'Ave I bin asleep?" the steamer was stopping at a pier at a strange place with trees.

"Here we are!" said the man. "'Ave you been asleep. Not 'alf! Stir yourself, my man; we get off here."

"Is this Deptford?" Dickie asked. And the people shoving and crushing to get off the steamer laughed when he said it.

"Not exactly," said the man, "but it's all right. This 'ere's where we get off. You ain't had yer tea yet, my boy."

It was the most glorious tea Dickie had ever imagined. Fried eggs and bacon—he had one egg and the man had three—bread and butter —and if the bread was thick, so was the butter—and as many cups of tea as you liked to say thank you for. When it was over the man asked Dickie if he could walk a little way, and when Dickie said he could they set out in the most friendly way side by side.

"I like it very much, and thank you kindly," said Dickie presently. "And the tea and all. An' the egg. And this is the prettiest place ever I see. But I ought to be getting 'ome. I shall catch it a fair treat as it is. She was waitin' for the wood to boil the kettle when I come out."

"Mother?"

"Aunt. Not me real aunt. Only I calls her that."

"She any good?'

"Ain't bad when she's in a good temper."

"That ain't what she'll be in when you gets back. Seems to me you've gone and done it, mate. Why, it's hours and hours since you and me got acquainted. Look! the sun's just going."

It was, over trees more beautiful than anything Dickie had ever seen, for they were now in a country road, with green hedges and green grass growing beside it, in which little roundfaced flowers grew—daisies they were—even Dickie knew that.

"I got to stick it," said Dickie sadly. "I'd best be getting home."

"I wouldn't go 'ome, not if I was you," said the man. "I'd go out and see the world a bit, I would."

"What—me?" said Dickie.

"Why not? Come, I'll make you a fair offer. Ye come alonger me an' see life! I'm agoin' to tramp as far as Brighton and back, all alongside the sea. Ever seed the sea?"

"No," said Dickie. "Oh, no—no, I never."

"Well, you come alonger me. I ain't 'it yer, have I, like what yer aunt do? I give yer a ride in a pleasure boat, only you went to sleep, and I give you a tea fit for a hemperor. Ain't I?"

"You 'ave that," said Dickie.

"Well, that'll show you the sort of man I am. So now I make you a fair offer. You come longer me, and be my little un, and I'll be your daddy, and a better dad, I lay, nor if I'd been born so. What do you say, matey?"

The man's manner was so kind and hearty, the whole adventure was so wonderful and new ...

"Is it country where you going?" said Dickie, looking at the green hedge.

"All the way, pretty near," said the man.

"We'll tramp it, taking it easy, all round the coast, where gents go for their outings. They've always got a bit to spare then. I lay you'll get some color in them cheeks o' yours. They're like putty now. Come, now. What you say? Is it a bargain?"

"It's very kind of you," said Dickie, "but what call you got to do it? It'll cost a lot—my victuals, I mean. What call you got to do it?"

The man scratched his head and hesitated. Then he looked up at the sky and then down at the road—they were resting on a heap of stones.

At last he said, "You're a sharp lad, you are—bloomin' sharp. Well, I won't deceive you, matey. I want company. Tramping alone ain't no beano to me. An' as I gets my living by the sweat of charitable ladies an' gents it don't do no harm to 'ave a little nipper alongside. They comes down 'andsomer if there's a nipper. An' I like nippers. Some blokes don't, but I do."

Dickie felt that this was true. But—"We'll be beggars, you mean?" he said doubtfully.

"Oh, don't call names," said the man; "we'll take the road, and if kind people gives us a helping hand, well, so much the better for all parties, if wot they learnt me at Sunday School's any good. Well, there it is. Take it or leave it."

The sun shot long golden beams through the gaps in the hedge. A bird paused in its flight on a branch quite close and clung there swaying. A real live bird. Dickie thought of the kitchen at home, the lamp that smoked, the dirty table, the fender full of ashes and dirty paper, the dry bread that tasted of mice, and the water out of the broken earthenware cup. That would be his breakfast, when he had gone to bed crying after his aunt had slapped him.

"I'll come," said he, "and thank you kindly."

"Mind you," said the man carefully, "this ain't no kidnapping. I ain't 'ticed you away. You come on your own free wish, eh?"

"Oh, yes."

"Can you write?"

"Yes," said Dickie, "if I got a pen."

"I got a pencil—hold on a bit." He took out of his pocket a new envelope, a new sheet of paper, and a new pencil ready sharpened by machinery. It almost looked, Dickie thought, as though he had brought them out for some special purpose. Perhaps he had.

"Now," said the man, "you take an' write—make it flat agin the sole of me boot." He lay face downward on the road and turned up his face downward on the road and turned up his boot, as though boots were the most natural writing-desks in the world.

"Now write what I say: 'Mr. Beale. Dear Sir. Will you please take me on tramp with you? I 'ave no father nor yet mother to be uneasy' (Can you spell 'uneasy'? That's right—you are a scholar!), 'an' I asks you let me come alonger you.' (Got that? All right, I'll stop a bit till you catch up. Then you say) 'If you take me along I promise to give you all what I earns to get anyhow, and be a good boy and do what you say. And I shall be very glad if you will. Your obedient servant—' What's your name, eh?"

"Dickie Harding."

"Get it wrote down, then. Done? I'm glad I wasn't born a table to be wrote on. Don't it make yer legs stiff, either!"

He rolled over, took the paper and read it slowly and with difficulty. Then he folded it and put it in his pocket.

HE LAY FACE DOWNWARD ON THE ROAD AND TURNED UP HIS BOOT

"Now we're square," he said. "That'll stand true and legal in any police-court in England, that will. And don't you forget it."

To the people who live in Rosemary Terrace the words "police-court" are very alarming indeed. Dickie turned a little paler and said, "Why police? I ain't done nothing wrong writin' what you tilled me?"

"No, my boy," said the man, "you ain't done no wrong; you done right. But there's bad people in the world—police and such—as might lay it up to me as I took you away against your will. They could put a man away for less than that."

"But it ain't again my will," said Dickie; "I want to!"

"That's what *I* say," said the man cheerfully. "So now we're agreed upon it, if you'll step it we'll see about a doss for tonight; and tomorrow we'll sleep in the bed with the green curtains."

"I see that there in a book," said Dickie, charmed. "He Reward the Wake, the last of the English, and I wunnered what it stood for."

"It stands for laying out," said the man (and so it does, though that's not at all what the author of "Herward" meant it to mean)—"laying out under a 'edge or a 'aystack or such and lookin' up at the stars till you goes by-by. An' jolly good business, too, fine weather. An' then you 'oofs it a bit and resties a bit, and someone gives you something to 'elp you along the road, and in the evening you 'as a glass of ale at the Publy Kows, and finds another set o' green bed curtains. An' on Saturday you gets in a extra lot of prog, and a Sunday you stays where you be and washes of your shirt."

"Do you have adventures?" asked Dick, recognizing in this description a rough sketch of the life of a modern knight-errant.

"'Ventures? I believe you!" said the man. "Why, only last month a brute of a dog bit me in the leg, at a back door Sutton way. An, once I see a elephant."

"Wild?" asked Dickie, thrilling.

"Not azackly wild—with a circus 'e was. But big! Wild ones ain't 'alf the size, I lay! And you meets soldiers, and parties in red coats ridin' on horses, with spotted dawgs, and motors as run you down and take your 'ead off afore you know you're dead if you don't look alive. Adventures? I should think so!"

"Ah!" said Dickie, and a full silence fell between them.

"Tired?" asked Mr. Beale presently.

"Just a tidy bit, p'raps," said Dickie bravely, "but I can stick it."

"We'll get summat with wheels for you tomorrow," said the man, "if it's only a sugarbox; an' I can tie that leg of yours up to make it look like as if it was cut off."

"It's this 'ere nasty boot as makes me tired," said Dickie.

"Hoff with it," said the man obligingly; "down you sets on them stones and hoff with it! T'other too if you like. You can keep to the grass."

The dewy grass felt pleasantly cool and clean to Dickie's tired little foot, and when they crossed the road where a watercart had dripped it was delicious to feel the cool mud squeeze up between your toes. That was charming; but it was pleasant, too, to wash the mud off on the wet grass. Dickie always remembered that moment. It was the first time in his life that he really enjoyed being clean. In the hospital you were almost too clean; and you didn't do it yourself. That made all the difference. Yet it was the memory of the hospital that made him say, "I wish I could 'ave a bath."

"So you shall," said Mr. Beale; "a reg'ler wash all over—this very night. I always like a wash meself. Some blokes think it pays to be dirty. But it don't. If you're clean they say 'Honest Poverty,' an' if you're dirty they say 'Serve you right.' We'll get a pail or something this very night."

"You are good," said Dickie. "I do like you."

Mr. Beale looked at him through the deepening twilight—rather queerly, Dickie thought. Also he sighed heavily.

"Oh, well—all's well as has no turning; and things don't always— What I mean to say, you be a good boy and I'll do the right thing by you."

"I know you will," said Dickie, with enthusiasm. "*I* know 'ow good you are!"

"Bless me!" said Mr. Beale uncomfortably. "Well, there. Step out, sonny, or we'll never get there this side Christmas."

*   *   *   *   *

Now you see that Mr. Beale may be a cruel, wicked man who only wanted to get hold of Dickie so as to make money out of him; and he may be going to be very unkind indeed to Dickie when once he gets him away into the country, and is all alone with him—and his having that paper and envelope and pencil all ready looks odd, doesn't it? Or he may be a really benevolent person. Well, you'll know all about it presently.

*   *   *   *   *

"And—here we are," said Mr. Beale, stopping in a side-street at an open door from which yellow light streamed welcomingly. "Now mind you don't contradict anything wot I say to people. And don't you forget you're my nipper, and you got to call me daddy."

"I'll call you farver," said Dickie. "I got a daddy of my own, you know."

"Why," said Mr. Beale, stopping suddenly, "you said he was dead."

"So he is," said Dickie; "but 'e's my daddy all the same."

"Oh, come on," said Mr. Beale impatiently. And they went in.

Burglars

Dickie fell asleep between clean, coarse sheets in a hard, narrow bed, for which fourpence had been paid.

"Put yer clobber under yer bolster, likewise yer boots," was the last instruction of his new friend and "father."

There had been a bath—or something equally cleansing—in a pail near a fire where ragged but agreeable people were cooking herrings, sausages, and other delicacies on little gridirons or pans that they unrolled from the strange bundles that were their luggage. One man who had no gridiron cooked a piece of steak on the kitchen tongs. Dickie thought him very clever. A very fat woman asked Dickie to toast a herring for her on a bit of wood; and when he had done it she gave him two green apples.

He laid in bed and heard jolly voices talking and singing in the kitchen below. And he thought how pleasant it was to be a tramp, and what jolly fellows the tramps were; for it seemed that all these nice people were "on the road," and this place where the kitchen was, and the good company and the clean bed for fourpence, was a Tramps' Hotel—one of many that are scattered over the country and called "Common Lodging Houses."

The singing and laughing went on long after he had fallen asleep, and if, later in the evening, there were loud-voiced arguments, or quarrels even, Dickie did not hear them.

Next morning, quite early, they took the road. From some mysterious source Mr. Beale had obtained an old double perambulator, which must have been made, Dickie thought, for very fat twins, it was so broad and roomy. Artfully piled on the front part was all the furniture needed by travellers who mean to sleep every night at the Inn of the Silver Moon. (That is the inn where they have the beds with the green curtains.)

"What's all that there?" Dickie asked, pointing to the odd knobbly bundles of all sorts and shapes tied on to the perambulator's front.

"All our truck what we'll want on the road," said Beale.

"And that pillowy bundle on the seat."

"That's our clothes. I've bought you a little jacket to put on o' nights if it's cold or wet. An' when you want a lift—why, here's your carriage, and you can sit up 'ere and ride like the Lord Mayor, and I'll be yer horse; the bundles'll set on yer knee like a fat baby. Tell yer what, mate—looks to me as if I'd took a fancy to you."

"I 'ave to you, I know that," said Dickie, settling his crutch firmly and putting his hand into Mr. Beale's. Mr. Beale looked down at the touch.

"Swelp me!" he said helplessly. Then, "Does it hurt you—walking?"

"Not like it did 'fore I went to the orspittle. They said I'd be able to walk to rights if I wore that there beastly boot. But that 'urts worsen anythink."

"Well," said Mr. Beale, "you sing out when you get tired and I'll give yer a ride."

"Oh, look," said Dickie—"the flowers!"

"They're only weeds," said Beale. They were, in fact, convolvuluses, little pink ones with their tendrils and leaves laid flat to the dry earth by the wayside, and in a water-meadow below the road level big white ones twining among thick-growing osiers and willows.

Dickie filled his hands with the pink ones, and Mr. Beale let him.

"They'll die directly," he said.

"But I shall have them while they're alive," said Dickie, as he had said to the pawnbroker about the moonflowers.

It was a wonderful day. All the country sights and sounds, that you hardly notice because you have known them every year as long as you can remember, were wonderful magic to the little boy from Deptford. The green hedge, the cows looking over them; the tinkle of sheep-bells; the "baa" of the sheep; the black pigs in a sty close to the road, their breathless rooting and grunting and the shiny, blackleaded cylinders that were their bodies; the stubbly fields where barley stood in sheaves—real barley, like the people next door but three gave to their hens; the woodland shadows and the lights of sudden water; shoulders of brown upland pressed against the open sky; the shrill thrill of the skylark's song, "like canary birds got loose"; the splendor of distance—you never see distance in Deptford; the magpie that perched on a stump and cocked a bright eye at the travellers; the thing that rustled a long length through dead leaves in a beech coppice, and was, it appeared, a real live snake—all these made the journey a royal progress to Dickie of Deptford. He forgot that he was lame, forgot that he had run away—a fact that had cost him a twinge or two of fear or conscience earlier in the morning. He was happy as a prince is happy, new-come to his inheritance, and it was Mr. Beale, after all, who was the first to remember that there was a carriage in which a tried little boy might ride.

"In you gets," he said suddenly; "you'll be fair knocked. You can look about you just as well a sittin' down," he added, laying the crutch across the front of the perambulator. "Never see such a nipper for noticing, neither. Hi! there goes a rabbit. See 'im? Crost the road there? See him?"

Dickie saw, and the crown was set on his happiness. A rabbit. Like the ones that his fancy had put in the moldering hutch at home.

"It's got loose," said Dickie, trying to scramble out of the perambulator; "let's catch 'im and take 'im along."

"''E ain't loose—'e's wild," Mr. Beale explained; "'e ain't never bin caught. Lives out 'ere with 'is little friendses," he added after a violent effort of imagination—"in 'oles in the ground. Gets 'is own meals and larks about on 'is own."

"How beautiful!" said Dickie, wriggling with delight. This life of the rabbit, as described by Mr. Beale, was the child's first glimpse of freedom. "I'd like to be a rabbit."

"You much better be my little nipper," said Beale. "Steady on, ate. 'Ow'm I to wheel to bloomin' pram if you goes on like as if you was bag of eels?"

They camped by a copse for the midday meal, sat on the grass, made a fire of sticks, and cooked herrings in a frying-pan, produced from one of the knobbly bundles.

"It's better'n Fiff of November," said Dickie; "and I do like you. I like you nexter my own daddy and Mr. Baxter next door."

"That's all right," said Mr. Beale awkwardly. It was in the afternoon that, half-way up a hill, they saw coming over the crest a lady and a little girl.

"Hout yer gets," said Mr. Beale quickly; "walk as 'oppy as you can, and if they arsts you you say you ain't 'ad nothing to eat since las' night and then it was a bit o' dry bread."

"Right you are," said Dickie, enjoying the game.

"An' mind you call me father."

"Yuss," said Dickie, exaggerating his lameness in the most spirited way. It was acting, you see, and all children love acting.

Mr. Beale went more and more slowly, and as the lady and the little girl drew near he stopped altogether and touched his cap. Dickie, quick to imitate, touched his.

"Could you spare a trifle, mum," said Beale, very gently and humbly, "to 'elp us along the road? My little chap, 'e's lame like wot you see. It's a 'ard life for the likes of 'im, mum."

"He ought to be at home with his mother," said the lady.

Beale drew his coat sleeve across his eyes.

"'E ain't got no mother," he said; "she was took bad sudden—a chill it was, and struck to her innards. She died in the infirmary. Three months ago it was, mum. And us not able even to get a bit of black for her."

Dickie sniffed.

"Poor little man!" said the lady; "you miss your mother, don't you?"

"Yuss," said Dickie sadly; "but farver, 'es very good to me. I couldn't get on if it wasn't for farver."

"Oh, well done, little un!" said Mr. Beale to himself.

"We lay under a 'aystack last night," he said aloud, "and where we'll lie tonight gracious only knows, without some kind soul lends us a 'elping 'and."

The lady fumbled in her pocket, and the little girl said to Dickie—

"Where are all your toys?"

"I ain't got but two," said Dickie, "and they're at 'ome; one of them's silver—real silver—my grandfarver 'ad it when 'e was a little boy."

"But if you've got silver you oughtn't to be begging," said the lady, shutting up her purse. Beale frowned.

"It only pawns for a shilling," said Dickie, "and farver knows what store I sets by it."

"A shilling's a lot, I grant you that," said Beale eagerly; "but I wouldn't go to take away the nipper's little bit o' pleasure, not for no shilling I wouldn't," he ended nobly, with a fond look at Dickie.

"You're a kind father," said the lady.

"Yes, isn't he, mother?" said the little girl. "May I give the little boy my penny?"

The two travellers were left facing each other, the richer by a penny, and oh—wonderful good fortune—a whole half-crown. They exchanged such glances as might pass between two actors as the curtain goes down on a successful dramatic performance.

"You did that bit fine," said Beale—"fine, you did. You been there before, ain't ye?"

"No," I never," said Dickie; "'ere's the steever."

"You stick to that," said Beale, radiant with delight; "you're a fair masterpiece, you are; you earned it honest if ever a kid done. Pats on the napper, she does, and out with 'arf a dollar! A bit of all right, I call it!"

They went on up the hill as happy as any one need wish to be.

They had told lies, you observe, and had by these lies managed to get half a crown and a penny out of the charitable; and far from being ashamed of their acts, they were bubbling over with merriment and delight at their own cleverness. Please do not be too shocked. Remember that neither of them knew any better. To the elder tramp lies and begging were natural means of livelihood. To the little tramp the whole thing was a new and entrancing game of make-believe.

By evening they had seven-and-sixpence.

"Us'll 'ave a fourpenny doss outer this," said Beale. "Swelp me Bob, we'll be ridin' in our own moty afore we know where we are at this rate."

"But you said the bed with the green curtains," urged Dickie.

"Well, p'rhaps you're right. Lay up for a rainy day, eh? Which this ain't, not by no means. There's a 'aystack a bit out of the town, if I remember right. Come on, mate."

And Dickie for the first time slept out of doors. Have you ever slept out of doors? The night is full of interesting little sounds that will not, at first, let you sleep—the rustle of little wild things in the hedges, the barking of dogs in distant farms, the chirp of crickets and the croaking of frogs. And in the morning the birds wake you, and you curl down warm among

"IT ONLY PAWNS FOR A SHILLIN'," SAID DICKIE.

the hay and look up at the sky that is growing lighter and lighter, and breathe the chill, sweet air, and go to sleep again wondering how you have ever been able to lie of nights in one of those shut-up boxes with holes in them which we call houses.

The new game of begging and inventing stories to interest the people from whom it was worth while to beg went on gaily, day by day and week by week; and Dickie, by constant practice, grew so clever at taking his part in the acting that Mr. Beale was quite dazed with admiration.

"Blessed if I ever see such a nipper," he said, over and over again.

And when they got nearly to Hythe, and met with the red-whiskered man who got up suddenly out of the hedge and said he'd been hanging off and on expecting them for nigh on a week, Mr. Beale sent Dickie into a field to look for mushrooms—which didn't grow there—expressly that he might have a private conversation with the red-whiskered man—a conversation which began thus—

"Couldn't get 'ere afore. Couldn't get a nipper."

"'E's 'oopy, 'e is; 'e ain't no good."

"No good?" said Beale. "That's all you know! 'E's a wunner, and no bloomin' error. Turns the ladies round 'is finger as easy as kiss yer 'and. Clever as a train dawg 'e is—an' all outer 'is own 'ead. And to 'ear the way 'e does the patter to me on the road. It's as good as a gaff any day to 'ear 'im. My word! I ain't sure as I 'adn't better stick to the road, and keep away from old 'ands like you, Jim."

"Doin' well, eh?" said Jim.

"Not so dusty," said Mr. Beagle cautiously; "we mugger along some'ow. An' 'e's got so red in the face, and plumped out so, they'll soon say 'e doesn't want their dibs."

"Starve 'im a bit," said the red-whiskered man cheerfully.

Mr. Beale laughed. Then he spat thoughtfully. Then he said—

"It's rum—I likes to see the little beggar stokin' up, for all it spoils the market. If 'e gets a bit fat 'e makes it up in cleverness. You should 'ear 'im!" and so forth and so on, till the red-whiskered man said quite crossly—

"Seems to me you're a bit dotty about this 'ere extry double nipper. I never knew you took like it afore."

"Fact is," said Beale, with an air of great candor, "it's 'is cleverness does me. It ain't as I'm silly about 'im—but 'e's that clever."

"I 'ope 'e's clever enough to do wot 'e's told. Keep 'is mug shut—that's all."

"He's clever enough for hanythink," said Beale, "and close as wax. 'E's got a silver toy 'idden away somewhere—it only pops for a bob—and d'you think 'e'll tell me where it's stowed? Not 'im, and us such pals as never was, and 'is jaw wagging all day long. But 'e's never let it out."

"Oh stow it!" said the other impatiently; "I don't want to 'ear no more about 'im. If 'e's straight 'e'll do for me, and if he ain't I'll do for 'im. See? An' now you and me'll have a word or two particler, and settle up about this 'ere job. I got the plan drawed out. It's a easy job as ever I see. Seems to me Tuesday's as good a day as any. Tip-topper—Sir Edward Talbot, that's 'im—'e's in furrin parts for 'is 'ealth, 'e is. Comes 'ome end o' next month. Little surprise for 'im, eh? You'll 'ave to train it. Abrams for 'im, eh? You'll 'ave to train it. Abrams 'e'll be there Monday. And see 'ere..." He sank his voice to a whisper.

When Dickie came back, without mushrooms, the red-whiskered man was gone.

"See that bloke just now?" said Mr. Beale.

"Yuss," said Dickie.

"Well, you never see 'im. If anyone arsts you if you ever see 'im, you never set eyes on 'im in all your born—not to remember 'im. Might a passed 'im in a crowd—see?"

"Yuss," said Dickie again.

"'Tasn't been 'arf a panto neither! Us two on the road," Mr. Beale went on.

"Not 'arf!"

"Well, now we're agoin' in the train like dooks—an' after that we're agoin' to 'ave a rare old beano. I give you *my* word!"

Dickie was full of questions, but Mr. Beale had no answers for them. "You jes' wait;" "hold on a bit;" "them as lives longest sees mot"— these were the sort of remarks which were all that Dickie could get out of him.

It was not the next day, which was a Saturday, that they took the train like dukes. Nor was it Sunday, on which they took a rest and washed their shirts, according to Mr. Beale's rule of life.

They took the train on Monday, and it landed them in a very bright town by the sea. Its pavements were of red brick and its houses of white stone, and its bow-windows and balconies were green, and Dickie thought it was the prettiest town in the world. They did not stay there, but walked out across the downs, where the skylarks were singing, and on a dip of the downs came upon great stone walls and towers very strong and grey.

"What's that there?" said Dickie.

"It's a carstle—like wot the King's got at Windsor."

"Is it a king as lives 'ere, then?" Dickie asked.

"No! Nobody don't live 'ere, mate," said Mr. Beale. "It's a ruin, this is. Only howls and rats lives in ruins."

"Did anyone ever live in it?"

"I shouldn't wonder," said Mr. Beale indifferently. "Yes, course they must 'ave, come to think of it. But you learned all that at school. It's what they call 'ist'ry."

Dickie, after some reflection, said, "D'jever 'ear of Here Ward?"

"I knowed a Jake Ward wunst."

"Here Ward the Warke. He ain't a bloke you'd know—e's in 'istry. Tell you if you like."

The tale of Hereward the Wake lasted till the jolting perambulator came to anchor in a hollow place among thick furze bushes. The bare, thick stems of the furze held it up like a roof over their heads as they sat. It was like a little furze house.

Next morning Mr. Beale shaved, a thing he had not done since they left London. Dickie held the mug and the soap. It was great fun, and, afterward, Mr. Beale looked quite different. That was great fun too. And he got quite a different set of clothes out of his bundles, and put them on. And that was the greatest fun of all.

"Now, then," he said, "we're agoin' to lay low 'ere all d'y, we are. And then come evening we're agoin' to 'ave our beano. That red-'eaded chap wot you never see 'e'll lift you up to a window what's got bars to it, and you'll creep through, you being so little, and you'll go soft's a mouse the way I'll show you, and undo the side-door. There's a key and a chain and a bottom bolt. The top bolt's cut through, and all the others is oiled. That won't frighten you, will it?"

"No," said Dickie. "What should it frighten me for?"

"Well, it's like this," said Mr. Beale a little embarrassed. "Suppose you was to get pinched?"

"What ud pich me? A dawg?"

"There won't be no dawg. A man, or a lady, or somebody in the 'ouse. Supposen they was to nab you—what 'ud you say?"

Dickie was watching his face carefully.

"Whatever you tells me to say," he said.

The man slapped his leg gently.

"If that ain't the nipper all over! Well, if they was to nab you, you just say what I tells you to. And then, first chance you get, you slip away from 'em and go to the station. An' if they comes arter you, you say you're agoin' to your father at

Dover. And first chance you get you slip off, and you come to that 'ouse where you and me slep' at Gravesend. I've got the dibs for yer ticket done up in this 'ere belt I'm a goin' to put on you. But don't you let on to anyone it's Gravesend you're a coming to. See?"

"An' if I don't get pinched?"

"Then you just opens the door and me and that red-headed bloke we comes in."

"What for?" asked Dickie.

"To look for some tools 'e mislaid there a year ago when 'e was on a plumbing job—and they won't let 'im 'ave them back, not by fair means, they won't. That's what for."

"Rats!" said Dickie briefly. "I ain't a baby. It's burgling, that's what it is."

"You'll a jolly sight too fond of calling names," said Beale anxiously. "Never mind what it is. You be a good boy, matey, and do what you're told. That's what you do. You know 'ow to stick it on if you're pinched. If you ain't you just lay low till we comes out with the ... the plumber's tools. See?"

"And if I'm nabbed, what is it I am to say?"

"You must let on as a strange chap collared you on the road, a strange chap with a black beard and a red 'ankercher, and give you a licking if you didn't go and climb in at the window. Say you lost your father in the town, and this chap said he knew where 'e was, and if you see me you don't know me. Nor yet that red-headed chap wot you never see." He looked down at the small, earnest face turned up to his own. "You *are* a little nipper," he said affectionately. "I don't know as I ever noticed before quite wot a little un you was. Think you can stick it? You shant go without you wants to, matey. There!"

"It's splendid!" said Dickie; "it is an adventure for a bold knight. I shall feel like Here Ward when he dressed in the potter's clothes and went to see King William."

He spoke in the book voice.

"There you go," said Mr. Beale, "but don't you go and talk to 'em like that if they pinches you; they'd never let you loose again. Think they'd got a marquis in disguise, so they would."

Dickie thought all day about this great adventure. He did not tell Mr. Beale so, but he was very proud of being so trusted. If you come to think of it, burgling must be a very exciting profession. And Dickie had no idea that it was wrong. It seemed to him a wholly delightful and sporting amusement.

While he was exploring the fox-runs among the thick stems of the grass Mr. Beale lay at full length and pondered.

"I don't more'n 'arf like it," he said to himself. "Ho yuss. I know that's wot I got him for—all right. But 'e's such a jolly little nipper. I wouldn't like anything to 'appen to 'im, so I wouldn't."

Dickie took his boots off and went to sleep as usual, and in the middle of the of the night Mr. Beale woke him up and said, "It's time."

There was no moon that night, and it was very, very dark. Mr. Beale carried Dickie on his back for what seemed a very long way along dark roads, under dark trees, and over dark meadow. A dark bush divided itself into two parts and one part came surprisingly towards them. It turned out to be the red-whiskered man, and presently from a ditch another man came. And they all climbed a chill, damp park-fence, and crept along among trees and shrubs along the inside of a high park wall. Dickie, still on Mr. Beale's shoulders, was astonished to find how quietly this big, clumsy-looking man could move.

Through openings in the trees and bushes Dickie could see the wide park, like a spread shadow, dotted with trees that were like shadows too. And on the other side of it the white face of a great house showed only a little paler than the trees about it. There were no lights in the house.

They got quite close to it before the shelter of the trees ended, for a little wood lay between the wall and the house.

Dickie's heart was beating very fast. Quite soon, now, his part in the adventure would begin.

"Ere—catch 'old," Mr. Beale was saying, and the red-whiskered man took Dickie in his arms, and went forward. The other two crouched in the wood.

Dickie felt himself lifted, and caught at the window-sill with his hands. It was a damp night and smelt of earth and dead leaves. The window-will was of stone, very cold. Dickie knew exactly what to do. Mr. Beale had explained it over and over again all day. He settled himself on the broad window-ledge and held on to the iron window-bars while the red-whiskered man took out a pane of glass, with treacle and a handkerchief so that there should be no noise of breaking or falling glass. Then Dickie put his hand through and unfastened the window, which opened like a cupboard door. Then he put his feet through the narrow space between two bars and slid through. He hung inside with his hands holding the bars, till his foot found the table that the had been told to expect just below, and he got from that to the floor.

"Now I must remember exactly which way to go," he told himself. But he did not need to remember what he had been told. For quite certainly, and most oddly, he *knew* exactly where the door was, and when he had crept to it and got it open he found that he now knew quite well which way to turn and what passages to go along to get that little side-door that he was to open for the three men. It was exactly as though he had been there before, in a dream. He went as quietly as a mouse, creeping on hands and knee, the lame foot dragging quietly behind him.

I will not pretend that he was not frightened. He was, very. But he was more brave than he was frightened, which is the essence of bravery, after all. He found it difficult to breathe quietly, and his heart beat so loudly that he felt almost sure that if any people were awake in the house they would hear it, even upstairs in their beds. But he got to the little side-door, and feeling with sensitive, quick fingers found the well-oiled bolt, and shot it back. Then the chain—holding the loose loop of it in his hands so that it should not rattle, he slipped its ball from the socket. Only the turning of the key remained, and Dickie accomplished that with both hands, for it was a big key, kneeling on his one sound knee. Then very gently he turned the handle, and pulled—and the door opened, and he crept from behind it and felt the cool, sweet air of the night on his face.

It seemed to him that he had never known what silence was before—or darkness. For the door opened into a close box arbor, and no sky could be seen, or any shapes of things. Dickie felt himself almost bursting with pride. What an adventure! And he had carried out in part of it perfectly. He had done exactly what he had been told to do, and he had done it well. He stood there, on his one useful foot, clinging to the edge of the door, and it was not until something touched him that he knew that Mr. Beale and the other men were creeping through the door that he had opened.

And at that touch a most odd feeling came to Dickie—the last feeling he would have expected—a feeling of pride mixed with a feeling of shame. Pride in his own cleverness, and another kind of pride that made that cleverness seem shameful. He had a feeling, very queer and very strong, that he, Dickie, was not the sort of person to open doors for the letting in of burglars. He felt as you would feel if you suddenly found your hands covered with filth, not good honest dirt, but slimy filth, and would not understand how you could have let it get there.

He caught at the third shape that brushed by him.

"Father," he whispered, "don't do it. Go back, and I'll fasten it all up again. Oh! don't, father."

"Shut your mug!" whispered the red-whiskered man. Dickie knew his voice even in that velvet-black darkness. "Shut your mug, or I'll give you what for!"

"Don't, father," said Dickie, and said it all the more for that threat.

"I can't go back on my pals, matey," said Mr. Beale; "you see that, do't yer?"

Dickie did see. The adventure was begun: it was impossible to stop. It was helped and had to be eaten, as they say in Norfolk. He crouched behind the open door, and heard the soft pad-pad of the three men's feet on the stones of the passage grow fainter and fainter. They had woollen socks over their boots, which made their footsteps sound no louder than those of padded pussy-feet. Then the soft rustle-pad died away, and it was perfectly quiet, perfectly dark. Dickie was tired; it was long past his proper bedtime, and the exertion of being so extra clever had been very tiring. He was almost asleep when a crack like thunder brought him stark, staring awake—there was a noise of feet on the stairs, boots, a blundering, hurried rush. People came rushing past him. There was another sharp thunder sound and a flash like lightning, only much smaller. Someone tripped and fell; there was a clatter like pails, and something hard and smooth hit him on the knee. Then another hurried presence dashed past him into the quiet night. Another—No! there was a woman's voice.

"Edward, you shan't! Let them go! You shan't—no!"

And suddenly there was a light that made one wink and blink. A tall lady in white, carrying a lamp, swept down the stairs and caught at a man who sprang into being out of the darkness into the lamplight.

"Take the lamp," she said, and thrust it on him. Then with unbelievable quickness she bolted and chained the door, locked it, and, turning, saw Dickie.

"What's this?" she said. "Oh, Edward, quick—here's one of them!... Why—it's a child—"

Some more people were coming down the stairs, with candles and excited voices. Their clothes were oddly bright. Dickie had never seen dressing-gowns before. They moved in a very odd way, and then began to go round and round like tops.

The next thing that Dickie remembers is being in a room that seemed full of people and lights and wonderful furniture, with someone holding a glass to his lips, a little glass, that smelt of public-houses, very nasty.

"No!" said Dickie, turning away his head.

"Better?" asked a lady; and Dickie was astonished to find that he was on her lap.

"Yes, thank you," he said, and tried to sit up, but lay back again because that was so much more pleasant. He had had no idea that anyone's lap could be so comfortable.

"Now, young man," said a stern voice that was not a lady's, "just you tell us how you came here, and who put you up to it."

"I got in," said Dickie feebly, "through the butler's pantry window," and as he said it he wondered how he had known that it was the butler's pantry. It is certain that no one had told him.

"What for?" asked the voice, which Dickie now perceived came from a gentle man in rumpled hair and a very loose pink flannel suit, with cordy things on it such as soldiers have.

"To let—" Dickie stopped. This was the moment he had been so carefully prepared for. He must think what he was saying.

"Yes," said the lady gently, "it's all right—poor little chap, don't be frightened—nobody wants to hurt you!"

"I'm not frightened," said Dickie—"not now."

"To let—?" reminded the lady, persuasively.

"To let the man in."

"What man?"

"I dunno."

"There were three or four of them," said the gentleman in pink; "four or five—"

"What man, dear?" the lady asked again.

"The man as said 'e knew w'ere my farver was," said Dickie, remembering what he had been told to say; "so I went along of 'im, an' then in the wood 'e said 'e'd give me a dressing down if I didn't get through the winder and open the door; 'e said 'e'd left some tools 'ere and you wouldn't let 'im 'ave them."

"You see," said the lady, "the child didn't know. He's perfectly innocent." And she kissed Dickie's hair very softly and kindly.

Dickie did not understand then why he suddenly felt as though he were going to burst. His ears grew very hot, and his hands and feet very cold.

"I know'd right enough," he said suddenly and hoarsely; "an' I needn't a gone if I 'adn't wanted to."

"He's feverish," said the lady, "he doesn't know what he's saying. Look how flushed he is."

"I wanted to," said Dickie; "I thought it 'ud be a lark, And it was too."

He expected to be shaken and put down. He wondered where his crutch was. Mr. Beale had had it under his arm. How could he get to Gravesend without a crutch? But he wasn't shaken or put down; instead, the lady gathered him up in her arms and stood up, holding him.

"I shall put him to bed," she said; "you shan't ask him any more questions tonight. There's time enough in the morning."

She carried Dickie out of the drawing-room and away from the other people to a big room with blue walls and blue and grey curtains and beautiful furniture. There was a high four-post bed with blue silk curtains and more pillows than Dickie had ever seen before. The lady washed him with sweet-smelling water in a big basin with blue and gold flowers on it, dressed him in a lace-trimmed nightgown, which must have been her own, for it was much too big for any little boy.

Then she put him into the soft, warm bed that was like a giant's pillow, tucked him up and kissed him. Dickie put thin arms round her neck.

"I do like you," he said, "but I want farver."

"Where is he? No, you must tell me that in the morning. Drink up this milk"—she had it ready in a glass that sparkled in a pattern—"and then go sound asleep. Everything will be all right, dear."

"May Heavens," said Dickie, sleepily, "bless you, generous Bean Factress!"

*　　*　　*　　*　　*

"A most extraordinary child," said the lady, returning to her husband. "I can't think who it is that he reminds me of. Where are the others?"

"I packed them off to bed. There's nothing to be done," said her husband. "We ought to have gone after those men."

"They didn't get anything," she said.

"No—dropped it all when I fired. Come on, let's turn in. Poor Eleanor, you must be worn out."

"Edward," said the lady, "I wish we could adopt that little boy. I'm sure he comes of good people—he's been kidnapped or something."

"Don't be a dear silly one!" said Sir Edward.

*　　*　　*　　*　　*

That night Dickie slept in sheets of the finest linen, scented with lavender. He was sunk downily among pillows, and over him lay a down quilt covered with blue-flowered satin. On the footboard of the great bed was carved a shield and a great dog on it.

Dickie's clothes lay, a dusty, forlorn little heap, in a stately tapestry-covered chair. And he slept, and dreamed of Mr. Beale, and the little house among the furze, and the bed with the green curtains.

The Escape

When Lady Talbot learned over the side of the big bed to awaken Dickie Harding she wished with all her heart that she had just such a little boy of her own; and when Dickie awoke and looked in her kind eyes he felt quite sure that if he had had a mother she would have been like this lady.

"Only about the face," he told himself, "not the way she's got up; nor yet her hair nor nuffink of that sort."

"Did you sleep well?" she asked him, stroking his hair with extraordinary gentleness.

"A fair treat," said he.

"Was your bed comfortable?"

"Ain't it soft, neither," he answered. "I don't know as ever I felt of anythink quite as soft without it was the geese as 'angs up along the Broadway Christmas-time."

"Why, the bed's made of goose-feathers," she said, and Dickie was delighted by the coincidence.

"'Ave you got e'er a little boy?" he asked, pursuing his first waking thought.

"No, dear; if I had I could lend you some of his clothes. As it is, we shall have to put you into your own." She spoke as though she were sorry.

Dickie saw no matter for regret. "My father 'e bought me a little coat for when it was cold of a night lying out."

"Lying out? Where?"

"In the bed with the green curtains," said Dickie. This led to Here Ward, and Dickie would willingly have told the whole story of that hero in full detail, but the lady said after breakfast, and now it was time for our bath. And sure enough there was a bath of steaming water before the fireplace, which was in quite another part of the room, so that Dickie had not noticed the cans being brought in by a maid in a pink print dress and white cap and apron.

"Come," said the lady, turning back the bed-clothes.

Somehow Dickie could not bear to let that lady see him crawl clumsily across the floor, as he had to do when he moved without his crutch. It was not because he thought she would make fun of him; perhaps it was because he knew she would not. And yet without his crutch, how else was he to get to that bath? And for no reason that he could have given he began to cry.

The lady's arms were round him in an instant.

"What is it, dear? Whatever is it?" she asked; and Dickie sobbed out—

"I ain't got my crutch, and I can't go to that there barf without I got it. Anything 'ud do—if 'twas only an old broom cut down to me 'eighth. I'm a cripple, they call it, you see. I can't walk like wot you can."

She carried him to the bath. There was a scented soap, there was a sponge, and a warm, fluffy towel.

"I ain't had a barf since Gravesend," said Dickie, and flushed at the indiscretion.

"Since *when*, dear?"

"Since Wednesday," said Dickie anxiously.

He and the lady had breakfast together in a big room with long windows that the sun shone in at, and, outside, a green garden. There were a lot of things to eat in silver dishes, and the very eggs had silver cups to sit in, and all the spoons and forks had dogs scratched on them like the one that was carved on the footboard of the bed upstairs. All except the little slender spoon that Dickie had to eat his egg with. And on that there was no dog, but something quite different."

"Why," said he, his face brightening with joyous recognition, "my Tinkler's got this on it—just the very moral of it, so 'e 'as."

Then he had to tell all about the Tinkler, and the lady looked thoughtful and interested; and when the gentleman came in and kissed her, and said, How were we this morning, Dickie had to tell about Tinkler all over again; and then the lady said several things very quickly, beginning with, "I told you so, Edward," and ending with "I knew he wasn't a common child."

Dickie missed the middle part of what she said because of the way his egg behaved, suddenly bursting all down one side and running over into the salt, which, of course, had to be stopped at all costs by some means or other. The tongue was the easiest.

The gentleman laughed. "Weh! don't eat the eggcup," he said. "We shall want it again. Have another egg."

But Dickie's pride was hurt, and he wouldn't. The gentleman must be very stupid, he thought, not to know the difference between licking and eating. And as if anybody could eat an eggcup, anyhow! He was glad when the gentleman went away.

After breakfast Dickie was measured for a crutch—that is to say, a broom was held up beside him and a piece cut off its handle. Then the lady wrapped flannel around the hairy part of the broom and sewed black velvet over that. It was a beautiful crutch, and Dickie said so. And he showed his gratitude by inviting the lady to look "'ow spry 'e was on 'is pins," but she only looked a very little while, and then turned and gazed out of the window. So Dickie had a good look at

the room and the furniture—it was all different from anything
he ever remembered seeing, and yet he couldn't help thinking
he had seen them before, these high-backed chairs covered
with flowers, like on carpets; the carved bookcases with rows
on rows of golden-beaded books; the bow-fronted, shining
sideboard, with handles that shone like gold, and the corner
cupboard with glass doors and china inside, red and blue and
goldy. It was a very odd feeling. I don't think that I can
describe it better than by saying that he looked at all these
things with a double pleasure—the pleasure of looking at new
and beautiful things, and the pleasure of seeing again things
old and beautiful which he had not seen for a very long time.

His limping survey of the room ended at the windows,
when the lady turned suddenly, knelt down, put her hand
under his chin and looked into his eyes.

"Dickie," she said, "how would yo like to stay here and be
my little boy?"

"I'd like it right enough," said he, "only I got to go back
to father."

"But if father says you may?"

"'E won't," said Dickie, with certainty, "an' besides,
there's Tinkler."

"Well, you're to stay here and be *my* little boy till we find
out where father is. We shall let the police know. They're sure
to find him."

"The pleece!" Dickie cried in horror. "Why, father, 'e ain't
done nothing."

"No, no, of course not," said the lady in a hurry; "but the
police know all sorts of things—about where people are, I
know, and what they're doing—even when they haven't *done*
anything."

"The pleece knows a jolly sight too much," said Dickie, in
gloom.

And now all Dickie's little soul was filled with one
longing; all his little brain awake to one only thought: the

police were to be set on the track of Beale, the man whom he called father; the man who had been kind to him, had wheeled him in a perambulator for miles and miles through enchanted country; the man who had bought him a little coat "to put on o' nights if it was cold or wet"; the man who had shown him the wonderful world to which he awakens who has slept in the bed with the green curtains.

The lady's house was more beautiful than anything he had ever imagined—yet not more beautiful than certain things that he almost imagined that he remembered. The lady was better than beautiful, she was dear. Her eyes were the eyes to which it is good to laugh—her arms were the arms in which it is good to cry. The tree-dotted parkland was to Dickie the Land of Heart's Desire.

But father—Beale—who had been kind, whom Dickie loved!...

The lady left him alone with a book, beautiful beyond his dreams—three great volumes with pictures of things that had happened and been since the days of Hereward himself. The author's charming name was Green, and recalled curtains and nights under the stars.

But even those beautiful pictures could not keep Dickie's thoughts from Mr. Beale: "father" by adoption and love. If the police were set to find out "where he was and what he was doing?" ... Somehow or other Dickie must get to Gravesend, to that house where there had been a bath, or something like it, in a pail, and where kindly tramp-people had toasted herrings and given apples to little boys who helped.

He had helped then. And by all the laws of fair play there ought to be someone now to help him.

The beautiful book lay on the table before him, but he no longer saw it. He no longer cared for it. All he cared for was to find a friend who would help him. And he found one. And the friend who helped him was an enemy.

The smart, pink-frocked, white-capped, white-aproned maid, who, unseen by Dickie, had brought the bath-water and the bath, came in with a duster. She looked malevolently at Dickie.

"Shovin' yourself in," she said rudely.

"I ain't," said he.

"If she wants to make a fool of a kid, ain't I got clever brothers and sisters?" inquired the maid, her chin in the air.

"Nobody says you ain't, and nobody ain't makin' a fool of me," said Dickie.

"Ho no. Course they ain't," the maid rejoined. "People comes 'ere without e'er a shirt to their backs and makes fools of their betters. That's the way it is, ain't it? Ain't she arst you to stay and be 'er little boy?"

"?" said Dickie.

"Ah, I thought she 'ad," said the maid triumphantly; "and you'll stay. But if I'm expected to call you Master Whatever-your-silly-name-is, I gives a month's warning, so I tell you straight."

"I don't want to stay," said Dickie—"at least—"

"Oh, tell me another," said the girl impatiently, and left him, without having made the slightest use of the duster.

Dickie was taken for a drive in a little carriage drawn by a cream-colored pony with a long tail—a perfect dream of a pony, and the lady allowed him to hold the reins. But even amid this delight he remembered to ask whether she had put the police on to father yet, and was relieved to hear that she had not.

It was Markham who was told to wash Dickie's hands when the drive was over, and Markham was the enemy with the clever brothers and sisters.

"Wash 'em yourself," she said among the soap and silver and marble and sponges. "It ain't my work."

"You'd better," said Dickie, "or the lady'll know the difference. It ain't my work neither, and I ain't so used to washing as what you are, and that's the truth."

So she washed him, not very gently.

"It's no use your getting your knife into me," he said as the towel was piled. "I didn't arst to come ere, did I?"

"No, you little thief!"

"Stow that!" said Dickie, and after a quick glance at his set lips she said, "Well, next door to, anyhow. I should be ashamed to show my face 'ere, if I was you, after last night. There, you're dry now. Cut along down to the dining room. The servants' hall's good enough for honest people as don't break into houses."

All through that day of wonder, which included real roses that you could pick and smell and real gooseberries that you could gather and eat, as well as picture-books, a clockwork bear, a musical box, and a doll's house almost as big as a small villa, an idea kept on hammering at the other side of a locked door in Dickie's mind, and when he was in bed it got the door open and came out and looked at him. And he recognized it at once as a really useful idea.

"Markham will bring you some warm milk. Drink it up and sleep well, darling," said the lady; and with the idea very near and plain he put his arms round her neck and hugged her.

"Goodbye," he said; "you are good. I do love you." The lady went away very pleased.

When Markham came with the milk Dickie said, "You want me gone, don't you?"

Markham said she didn't care.

"Well, but how am I to get away—with my crutch?"

"Mean to say you'd cut and run if you was the same as me—about the legs, I mean?"

"Yes," said Dickie.

"And not nick anything?"

"Not a bloomin' thing," said he.

"Well," said Markham, "you've got a spirit, I will say that."

"You see," said Dickie, "I wants to get back to farver."

"Bless the child," said Markham, quite affected by this.

"Why don't you help me get out? Once I was outside the park I'd do all right."

"Much as my place is worth," said Markham; "don't you say another word getting me into trouble."

But Dickie said a good many other words, and fell asleep quite satisfied with the last words that had fallen from Markham. These words were: "We'll see."

It was only just daylight when Markham woke him. She dressed him hurriedly, and carried him and his crutch down the back stairs and into that very butler's pantry through whose window he had crept at the bidding of he red-haired man. No one else seemed to be about.

"Now," she said, "the gardener he has got a few hampers ready—fruit and flowers and the like—and he drives 'em to the station 'fore anyone's up. They'd only go to waste if 'e wasn't to sell 'em. See? An' he's a particular friend of mine; and he won't mind an extry hamper more or less. So out with you. Joe," she whispered, "you there?"

Joe, outside, whispered that he was. And Markham lifted Dickie to the window. As she did so she kissed him.

"Cheer-oh, old chap!" she said. "I'm sorry I was so short. An' you do want to get out of it, don't you?"

"No error," said Dickie; "An' I'll never split about him selling the vegetables and things."

"You're too sharp to live," Markham declared; and next moment he was through the window, and Joe was laying him in a long hamper half-filled with straw that stood waiting.

"I'll put you in the van along with the other hampers," whispered Joe as he shut the lid. "Then when you're in the train you just cut the string with this 'ere little knife I'll make you a present of and out you gets. I'll make it all right with the guard. He knows me. And he'll put you down at whatever station you say."

"Here, don't forget 'is breakfast," said Markham, reaching her arm through the window. It was a wonderful breakfast. Five cold rissoles, a lot of bread and butter, two slices of cake, and a bottle of milk. And it was fun eating agreeable and unusual things, lying down in the roomy hamper among the smooth straw. The jolting of the cart did not worry Dickie at all. He was used to the perambulator; and he ate as much as he wanted to eat, and when that was done he put the rest in his pocket and curled up comfortably in the straw, for there was still quite a lot left of what ordinary people consider night, and also there was quite a lot left of the sleepiness with which he had gone to bed at the end of the wonderful day. It was not only just body-sleepiness: the kind you get after a long walk or a long-play day. It was mind-sleepiness—Dickie had gone through so much in the last thirty-six hours that his poor little brain felt quite worn out. He fell asleep among the straw, fingering the clasp-knife in his pocket, and thinking how smartly he would cut the string when the time came.

And he slept for a very long time. Such a long time that when he did wake up there was no longer any need to cut the string of the hamper. Someone else had done that, and the lid of the basket was open, and three or four faces looked down at Dickie, and a girl's voice said—

"Why, it's a little boy! And a crutch—oh dear!" Dickie sat up. The little crutch, which was lying corner-wise above him in the hamper, jerked out and rattled on the floor.

"Well, I never did—never!" said another voice. "Come out, dearie; don't be frightened."

"How kind people are!" Dickie thought, and reached his hands to slender white hands that were held out to him. A lady in black—her figure was as slender as her hands—drew him up, put her arms round him, and lifted him on to a black bentwood chair.

THREE OR FOUR FACES LOOKED DOWN AT DICKIE.

His eyes, turning swiftly here and there, showed him that he was in a shop—a shop full of flowers and fruit.

"Mr. Rosenberg," said the slender lady—"oh, do come here, please! This extra hamper—"

A dark, handsome, big-nosed man came towards them.

"It's a dear little boy," said the slender lady, who had a pale, kind face, dark eyes, and very red lips.

"It's a practical joke, I shuppothe," said the dark man. "Our gardening friend wanth a liththon: and I'll thee he getth it."

"It wasn't his fault," said Dickie, wriggling earnestly in his high chair; "it was my fault. I fell asleep."

The girls crowded round him with questions and caresses.

"I ought to have cut the string in the train and told the guard—he's a friend of the gardener's," he said, "but I was asleep. I don't know as ever I slep' so sound afore. Like as if I'd had sleepy-stuff—you know. Like they give me at the orspittle."

I should not like to think that Markham had gone so far as to put "sleepy-stuff" in that bottle of milk; but I am afraid she was not very particular, and she may have thought it best to send Dickie to sleep so that he could not betray her or her gardener friend until he was very far away from both of them.

"But why," asked the long-nosed gentleman—"Why put boyth in bathketth? Upthetting everybody like thith," he added crossly.

"It was," said Dickie slowly, "a sort of joke. I don't want to go upsetting of people. If you'll lift me down and give me me crutch I'll 'ook it."

But the young ladies would not hear of his hooking it.

"We may keep him, mayn't we, Mr. Rosenberg?" they said; and he judged that Mr. Rosenberg was a kind man or they would not have dared to speak so to him; "let's keep him till closing-time, and then one of us will see him home. He lives in London. He says so."

Dickie had indeed murmured "words to this effect," as policemen call it when they are not quite sure what people really *have* said.

"Ath you like," said Mr. Rosenberg, "only you muthn't let him interfere with bithneth; thath all."

They took him away to the back of the shop. They were dear girls, and they were very nice to Dickie. They gave him grapes, and a banana, and some Marie biscuits, and they folded sacks for him to lie on.

And Dickie liked them and was grateful to them—and watched his opportunity. Because, however kind people were, there was one thing he had to do—to get back to the Gravesend lodging-house, as his "father" had told him to do.

The opportunity did not come till late in the afternoon, when one of the girls was boiling a kettle on a spirit-lamp, and one had gone out to get cakes in Dickie's honor, which made him uncomfortable, but duty is duty, and over the Gravesend lodging-house the star of duty shone and beckoned. The third young lady and Mr. Rosenberg were engaged in animated explanations with a fair young gentleman about a basket of roses that had been ordered, and had not been sent.

"Cath," Mr. Rosenberg was saying—"cath down enthureth thpeedy delivery."

And the young lady was saying,"I am extremely sorry, sir; it was a misunderstanding."

And to the music of their two voices Dickie edged along close to the grapes and melons, holding on to the shelf on which they lay so as not to attract attention by the tap-tapping of his crutch.

He passed silently and slowly between the rose-filled window and the heap of bananas that adorned the other side of the doorway, turned the corner, threw his arm over his crutch, and legged away for dear life down a sort of covered Areade; turned its corner and found himself in a wilderness of baskets, over fallen cabbage-leaves, under horses' noses, found a quiet street, a still quieter archway, pulled out the knife—however his adventure ended he was that knife to the good—and prepared to cut the money out of the belt Mr. Beale had buckled round him.

And the belt was not there! Had he dropped it somewhere? Or had he and Markham, in the hurry of that twilight dressing, forgotten to put it on? He did not know. All he knew was that the belt was not on him, and that he was alone in London, without money, and that at Gravesend his father was waiting for him—waiting, waiting. Dickie knew what it meant to wait.

He went out into the street, and asked the first good-natured-looking loafer he saw the way to Gravesend.

"Way to your grandmother," said the loafer; "don't you come saucing of me."

"But which *is* the way?" said Dickie.

The man looked hard at him and then pointed with a grimy thumb over his shoulder.

"It's thirty mile if it's a yard," he said. "Got any chink?"

"I lost it," said Dickie. "My farver's there awaitin' for me."

"Garn!" said the man; "you don't kid me so easy."

"I ain't arstin' you for anything except the way," said Dickie.

"More you ain't," said the man, hesitated, and pulled his hand out of his pocket. "Ain't kiddin'? Sure? Father at Gravesend? Take your Bible?"

"Yuss," said Dickie.

"Then you take the first to the right and the first to the left, and you'll get a blue 'bus as'll take you to the Elephant.' That's a bit of the way. Then you arst again. And 'ere—this'll pay for the 'bus." He held out coppers.

This practical kindness went to Dickie's heart more than all the kisses of the young ladies in the flower-shop. The tears came into his eyes.

"Well, you *are* a pal, and no error," he said. "Do the same for you some day," he added.

The lounging man laughed.

"I'll hold you to that, matey," he said; "when you're a ridin' in yer carriage an' pair p'raps you'll take me on ter be yer footman."

"When I am, I will," said Dickie, quite seriously. And then they both laughed.

The "Elephant and Castle" marks but a very short stage of the weary way between London and Gravesend. When he got out of the tram Dickie asked the way again, this time of a woman who was selling matches in the gutter. She pointed with the blue box she held in her hand.

"It's a long way," she said, in a tired voice; "nigh on thirty mile."

"Thank you, missis," said Dickie, and set out, quite simply, to walk those miles—nearly thirty. The way lay down the Old Kent Road, and presently Dickie was in familiar surroundings. For the Old Kent Road leads into the New Cross Road, and that runs right through the yellow brick wilderness where Dickie's aunt lived. He dared not follow the road through those well-known scenes. At any moment he might meet his aunt. And if he met his aunt... he preferred not to think of it.

Outside the "Marquis of Granby" stood a van, and the horses' heads were turned away from London. If one could get a lift? Dickie looked anxiously to right and left, in front and behind. There were wooden boxes in the van, a lot of them, and on the canvas of the tilt was painted in fat, white letters—

> ## FRY'S TONIC
>
> THE ONLY CURE

There would be room on the top of the boxes—they did not reach within two feet of the tilt.

Should he ask for a lift, when the carter came out of the "Marquis"? Or should he, if he could, climb up and hide on the boxes and take his chance of discovery on the lift? He laid a hand on the tailboard.

"Hi, Dickie!" said a voice surprisingly in his ear; "that you?"

Dickie owned that it was, with the feeling of a trapped wild animal, and turned and faced a boy of his own age, a school-fellow—the one, in fact, who had christened him "Dot-and-go-one."

"Oh, what a turn you give me!" he said; "thought you was my aunt. Don't you let on you seen me."

"Where you been?" asked the boy curiously.

"Oh, all about," Dickie answered vaguely. "Don't you tell me aunt."

"Yer aunt? Don't you know?" The boy was quite contemptuous with him for not knowing.

"Know? No. Know what?"

"She shot the moon—old Hurle moved her; says he don't remember where to. She give him a pint to forget's what I say."

"Who's livin' there now?" Dickie asked, interest in his aunt's address swallowed up in a sudden desperate anxiety.

"No one don't live there. It's shut up to let apply Roberts 796 Broadway," said the boy. "I say, what'll you do?"

"I don't know," said Dickie, turning away from the van, which had abruptly become unimportant. "Which way you goin'?"

"Down home—go past your old shop. Coming?"

"No," said Dickie. "So long—see you again some day. I got to go this way." And he went it.

All the same the twilight saw him creeping down the old road to the house whose back-yard had held the rabbit-hutch, the garden where he had sowed the parrot food, and where the moonflowers had come up so white and beautiful. What a long time ago! It was only a month really, but all the same, what a long time!

The news of his aunt's departure had changed everything. The steadfast desire to get to Gravesend, to find his father, had given way, at any rate for the moment, to a burning anxiety about Tinkler and the white stone. Had his aunt found them and taken them away? If she hadn't and they were still there, would it not be wise to get them at once? Because of course someone else might take the house and find the treasures. Yes, it would certainly be wise to go to-night, to get in by the front window—the catch had always been broken—to find his treasures, or at any rate to make quite sure whether he had lost them or not.

No one noticed him as he came down the street, very close to the railings. There are so many boys in the streets in that part of the world. And the front window went up easily. He climbed in, dragging his crutch after him.

He got upstairs very quickly, on hands and knees, went straight to the loose board, dislodged it, felt in the hollow below. Oh, joy! His hands found the soft bundle of rags that he knew held Tinkler and the seal. He put them inside the front of his shirt and shuffled down. It was not too late to do a mile or two of the Gravesend road. But the moonflower—he would like to have one more look at that.

He got out into the garden—there stood the stalk of the flower very tall in the deepening dusk. He touched the stalk. It was dry and hard—three or four little dry things fell from above and rattled on his head.

"Seeds, o' course," said Dickie, who knew more about seeds now than he had done when he saved the parrot seeds. One does not tramp the country for a month, at Dickie's age, without learning something about seeds.

He got out the knife that should have cut the string of the basket in the train, opened it and cut the stalk of the moonflower, very carefully so that none of the seeds should be, and only a few were, lost. He crept into the house holding the stalk upright and steady as an acolyte carries a processional cross.

The house was quite dark now, but a street lamp threw its light into the front room, bare, empty, and dusty. There was a torn newspaper on the floor. He spread a sheet of it out, kneeled by it and shook the moonflower head over it. The seeds came rattling out—dozens and dozens of them. They were bigger than sunflower seeds and flatter and rounder, and they shone like silver, or like the pods of the plant we call honesty.

"Oh, beautiful, beautiful!" said Dickie, letting the smooth shapes slide through his fingers. Have you ever played with mother-of-pearl card counters? The seeds of the moonflower were like those.

He pulled out Tinkler and the seal and laid them on the heap of seeds. And then knew quite suddenly that he was too tired to travel any further that night.

"I'll doss here," he said; "there's plenty papers"—he knew by experience that, as bed-clothes, newspapers are warm, if noisy—"and get on in the morning afore people's up."

He collected all the paper and straw—there was a good deal littered about in the house—and made a heap in the corner, out of the way of the window. He did not feel afraid of sleeping in an empty house, only very lordly and magnificent because he had a whole house to himself. The food still left in his pockets served for supper, and you could drink quite well at the wash-house tap by putting your head under and turning it on very slowly.

And for a final enjoyment he laid out his treasures on the newspaper—Tinkler and the seal in the middle and the pearly counters arranged in patterns round them, circles and squares and oblongs. The seeds lay very flat and fitted close together. They were excellent for making patterns with. And presently

HE MADE, WITH TRIPPLE LINES OF SILVERY SEEDS,
A SIX-POINTED STAR.

he made, with triple lines of silvery seeds, a six-pointed star, something like this—

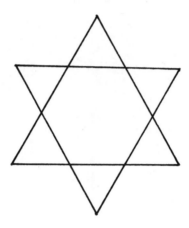

with the rattle and the seal in the middle, and the light from the street lamp shone brightly on it all.

"That's the prettiest of the lot," said Dickie Harding, alone in the empty house.

And then the magic began.

Which Was the Dream?

T he two crossed triangles of white seeds, in the midst
Tinkler and the white seal, lay on the floor of the little
empty house, grew dim and faint before Dickie's eyes, and his
eyes suddenly smarted and felt tired so that he was very glad
to shut them. He had an absurd fancy that he could see,
through his closed eyelids, something moving in the middle of
the star that the two triangles made. But he knew that this
must be nonsense, because, of course, you cannot see through
your eyelids. His eyelids felt so heavy that he could not take
the trouble to lift them even when a voice spoke quite near
him. He had no doubt but that it was the policeman come to
"take him up" for being in a house that was not his.

"Let him," said Dickie to himself. He was too sleepy to be
afraid.

But for a policeman, who is usually of quite a large
pattern, the voice was unusually soft and small. It said
briskly—

"Now, then, where do you want to go to?"

"I ain't particular," said Dickie, who supposed himself to
be listening to an offer of a choice of police-stations.

There were whispers—two small and soft voices. They
made a sleepy music.

"He's more yours than mine," said one.

"You're more his than I am," said the other.

"You're older than I am," said the first.

"You're stronger than I am," said the second.

"Let's spin for it," said the first voice, and there was a humming sound ending in a little tinkling fall.

"That settles it," said the second voice—"here?"

"And when?"

"Three's a good number."

Then everything was very quiet, and sleep wrapped Dickie like a soft cloak. When he awoke his eyelids no longer felt heavy, so he opened them. "That was a rum dream," he told himself, as he blinked in broad daylight.

He lay in bed—a big, strange bed—in a room that he had never seen before. The windows were low and long, with small panes, and the light was broken by upright stone divisions. The floor was of dark wood, strewn strangely with flowers and green herbs, and the bed was a four-post bed like the one he had slept in at Talbot House; and in the green curtains was woven a white pattern, very like the thing that was engraved on Tinkler and on the white seal. On the coverlet lavender and other herbs were laid. And the wall was hung with pictures done in needlework—tapestry, in fact, though Dickie did not know that this was its name. All the furniture was heavily built of wood heavily carved. An enormous dark cupboard or wardrobe loomed against one wall. High-backed chairs with tapestry seats were ranged in a row against another. The third wall was almost all window, and in the fourth wall the fireplace was set with a high-hooded chimney and wide, open hearth.

Near the bed stood a stool, or table, with cups and bottles on it, and on the necks of the bottles parchment labels were tied that stuck out stiffly. A stout woman in very full skirts sat in a large armchair at the foot of the bed. She wore a queer white cap, the like of which Dickie had never seen, and round her neck was a ruff which reminded him of the cut-paper frills in the ham and beef shop in the New Cross Road.

"What a curious dream!" said Dickie.

The woman looked at him.

"So thou'st found thy tongue," she said; "folk must look to have curious dreams who fall sick of the fever. But thou'st found thy tongue at last—thine own tongue, not the wandering tongue that has wagged so fast these last days."

"But I thought I was in the front room at—" Dickie began.

"Thou'rt here," said she; "the other is the dream. Forget it. And do not talk of it. To talk of such dreams brings misfortune. And 'tis time for thy posset."

She took a pipkin from the hearth, where a small fire burned, though it was summer weather, as Dickie could see by the green tree-tops that swayed and moved outside in the sun, poured some gruel out of it into a silver basin. It had wrought roses on it and "Drink me and drink again" in queer letters round the rim; but this Dickie only noticed later. She poured white wine into the gruel, and, having stirred it with a silver spoon, fed Dickie as one feeds a baby, blowing on each spoonful to cool it. The gruel was very sweet and pleasant. Dickie stretched in the downy bed, felt extremely comfortable, and fell asleep again.

Next time he awoke it was with many questions. "How'd I come 'ere? 'Ave I bin run over again? Is it a hospital? Who are you?"

"Now don't you begin to wander again," said the woman in the cap. "You're here at home in the best bed in your father's house at Deptford. And you've had the plague-fever. And you're better. Or ought to be. But if you don't know your own old nurse—"

"I never 'ad no nurse," said Dickie, "old nor new. So there. You're a takin' me for some other chap, that's what it is. Where did you get hold of me? I never bin here before."

"Don't wander, I tell you," repeated the nurse briskly. "You lie still and think, and you'll see you'll remember me very well. Forget your old nurse—why, you will tell me next that you've forgotten your own name."

"No, I haven't," said Dickie.

"What is it, then?" the nurse asked, laughing a fat, comfortable laugh.

Dickie's reply was naturally "Dickie Harding."

"Why," said the Nurse, opening wide eyes at him under grey bows, "you have forgotten it. They do say that the fever hurts the memory, but this beats all. Dost mean to tell me the fever has mazed thy poor brains till thou don't know that thy name's Richard —." And Dickie heard her name a name that did not sound to him at all like Harding.

"Is that my name?" he asked.

"It is indeed," she answered.

Dickie felt an odd sensation of fixedness. He had expected when he went to sleep that the dream would, in sleep, end, and that he would wake to find himself alone in the empty house at New Cross. But he had wakened to the same dream once more, and now he began to wonder whether he really belonged here, and whether this were the real life, and the other—the old, sordid, dirty New Cross life—merely a horrid dream, the consequences of his fever. He lay and thought, and looked at the rich, pleasant room, the kind, clear face of the nurse, the green, green branches of the trees, the tapestry and the rushes. At last he spoke.

"Nurse," said he.

"Ah! I thought you'd come to yourself," she said. "What is it, my dearie?"

"If I am really the name you said, I've forgotten it. Tell me all about myself, will you, Nurse?"

"I thought as much," she muttered, and then began to tell him wonderful things.

She told him how his father was Sir Richard—the King had made him a knight only last year—and how this place where they now were was his father's country house. "It lies," said the nurse, "among the pleasant fields and orchards of Deptford." And how he, Dickie, had been very sick of the pestilential fever, but was now, thanks to the blessing and to the ministrations of good Dr. Carey, on the high-road to health.

"And when you are strong enough," said she, "and the house purged of he contagion, your cousins from Sussex shall come and stay awhile here with you, and afterwards you shall go with them to their town house, and see the sights of London. And now," she added, looking out of the window, "I spy the good doctor a-coming. Make the best of thyself, dear heart, lest he bleed thee and drench thee yet again, which I know in my heart thou'rt too weak for it. But what do these doctors know of babes? Their medicines are for strong men."

The idea of bleeding was not pleasant to Dickie, though he did not all know what it meant. He sat up in bed, and was surprised to find that he was not nearly so tired as he thought. The excitement of all these happenings had brought a pink flush to his face, and when the doctor, in a full black robe and black stockings and a pointed hat, stood by his bedside and felt his pulse, the doctor had to own that Dickie was almost well.

"We have wrought a cure, Goody," he said; "thou and I, we have wrought a cure. Now kitchen physic it is that he needs—good broth and gruel and panada, and wine, the Rhenish and the French, and the juice of the orange and the lemon, or, failing those, fresh apple-juice squeezed from the fruit when you shall have brayed it in a mortar. Ha, my cure pleases thee? Well, smell to it, then. 'Tis many a day since thou hadst the heart to."

He reached the gold nob of his cane to Dickie's nose, and Dickie was surprised to find that it smelt sweet and strong, something like grocers' shops and something like a chemist's. There were little holes in the gold knob, such as you see in the tops of pepper castors, and the scent seemed to come through them.

"What is it?" Dickie asked.

"He has forgotten everything," said the nurse quickly; "'tis the good doctor's pomander, with spices and perfumes in it to avert contagion."

"As it warms in the hand the perfumes give forth," said the doctor. "Now the fever is past there must be a fumigatory. Make a good brew, Goody, make a good brew—amber and nitre and wormwood—vinegar and quinces and myrrh—with wormwood, camphor, and the fresh flowers of the camomile. And musk—forget not musk—a strong thing against contagion. Let the vapor of it pass to and fro through the chamber, burn the herbs form the floor and all sweepings on this hearth; strew fresh herbs and flowers, and set all clean and in order, and give thanks that you are not setting all in order for a burying."

With which agreeable words the black-gowned doctor nodded and smiled at the little patient, and went out.

And now Dickie literally did not know where he was. It was all so difficult. Was he Dickie Harding who had lived at New Cross, and sown the Artistic Parrot Seed, and taken the open road with Mr. Beale? Or was he that boy with the other name whose father was a knight, and who lived in a house in Deptford that had green trees outside the windows? He could not remember any house in Deptford that had green trees in its garden. And the nurse had said something about the pleasant fields and orchards. Those, at any rate, were not in the Deptford he knew. Perhaps there were two Deptfords. He knew there were two Bromptons and two Richmonds (one in Yorkshire). There was something about the way things happened at this place that reminded him of that nice Lady Talbot who had wanted him to stay and be her little boy.

Perhaps this new boy whose place he seemed to have taken had a real mother of his own, as nice as that nice lady.

The nurse had dropped all sorts of things into an iron pot with three legs, and had set it to boil in the hot ashes. Now it had boiled, and two maids were carrying it to and fro in the room, as the doctor had said. Puffs of sweet, strong, spicy steam rose out of it as they jerked it this way and that.

"Nurse," Dickie called; and she came quickly. "Nurse, have I got a mother?"

She hugged him. "Indeed thou hast," she said, "but she lies sick at your father's other house. And you have a baby brother, Richard."

"Then," said Dickie, "I think I will stay here, and try to remember who I am—I mean who you say I am—and not try to dream any more about New Cross and Mr. Beale. If this is a dream, it's a better dream than the other. I want to stay here, Nurse. Let me stay here and see my mother and my little brother."

"And shalt, my lamb—and shalt," the nurse said.

And after that there was more food, and more sleep, and nights, and days, and talks, and silences, and very gradually, yet very quickly, Dickie learned about this new boy who was, and wasn't, himself. He told the nurse quite plainly that he remembered nothing about himself, and after he had told her she would sit by his side by the hour and tell him of things that had happened in the short life of the boy whose place he filled, the boy whose name was *not* Dickie Harding. And as soon as she had told him a thing he found he remembered it—not as one remembers a tale that is told, but as one remembers a real thing that has happened.

And days went on, and he became surer and surer that he was really this other Richard, and that he had only dreamed all that old life in New Cross with his aunt and in the pleasant country roads with Mr. Beale. And he wondered how he could ever have dreamed such things.

Quite soon came the day when the nurse dressed him in clothes strange, but strangely comfortable and fine, and carried him to the window, from which, as he sat in a big oak chair, he could see the green fields that sloped down to the river, and the rigging and the masts of the ships that went up and down. The rigging looked familiar, but the shape of the ships was quite different. They were shorter and broader than the ships that Dickie Harding had been used to see, and they, most of them, rose up much higher out of the water.

"I should like to go and look at them closer," he told the nurse.

"Once thou'rt healed," she said, "thou'lt be forever running down to the dockyard. Thy old way—I know thee, hearing the master mariners' tales, and setting thy purpose for a galleon of thine own and the golden South Americas."

"What's a galleon?" said Dickie. And was told. The nurse was very patient with his forgettings.

He was very happy. There seemed somehow to be more room in this new life than in the old one, and more time. No one was in a hurry, and there was not another house within a quarter of a mile. All green fields. Also he was a person of consequence. The servants called him "Master Richard," and he felt, as he heard them, that being called Master Richard meant not only that the servants respected him as their master's son, but that he was somebody from whom great things were expected. That he had duties of kindness and protection to the servants; that he was expected to grow up brave and noble and generous and unselfish, to care for those who called him master. He felt now very fully, what he had felt vaguely and dimly at Talbot Court, that he was not the sort of person who ought to do anything mean and dishonorable, such as being a burglar, and climbing in at pantry windows; that when he grew up he would be expected to look after his servants and laborers, and all the men and women whom he would have under him—that their happiness and well-being would be his charge. And the thought swelled his heart, and it seemed that he was born to a great destiny. He—little lame Dickie Harding of Deptford—he would hold these people's lives in his hand. Well, he knew what poor people wanted; he had been poor—or he had dreamed that he was poor—it was all the same. Dreams and real life were so very much alike.

So Dickie changed, every hour of every day and every moment of every hour, from the little boy who lived at New Cross among the yellow houses and the ugliness, who tramped the white roads, and slept at the Inn of the Silver Moon, to Richard of the other name who lived well and slept softly, and knew himself called to a destiny of power and helpful kindness. For his nurse had told him that his father was a rich man; and that father's riches would be his one day, to deal with for the good of the men under him, for their happiness and the glory of God. It was a great and beautiful thought, and Dickie loved it.

He loved, indeed, everything in this new life—the shapes and colors of furniture and hangings, the kind old nurse, the friendly laughing maids, the old doctor with his long speeches and short smiles, his bed, his room, the ships, the river, the trees, the gardens—the very sky seemed cleaner and brighter than the sky that had been over the Deptford that Dickie Harding had known.

And then came the day when the nurse, having dressed him, bade him walk to the window, instead of being carried, as, so far, he had been.

"Where..." he asked, hesitatingly, "where's my...? Where have you put the crutch?"

Then the old nurse laughed.

"Crutch?" she said. "Come out of thy dreams. Thou silly boy! Thou wants no crutch with two fine, straight, strong legs like thou's got. Come, use them and walk."

Dickie looked down at his feet. In the old New Cross days he had not liked to look at his feet. He had not looked at them in these new days. Now he looked. Hesitated.

"Come," said the nurse encouragingly.

He slid from the high bed. One might as well try. Nurse seemed to think ... He touched the ground with both feet, felt the floor firm and even under them—as firm and even under the one foot as under the other. He stood up straight, moved the foot that he had been used to move—then the other, the one that he had never moved. He took two steps, three, four—and then he turned suddenly and flung himself against the side of the bed and hid his face in his arms.

"What, weeping, my lamb?" the nurse said, and came to him.

"Oh, Nurse," he cried, clinging to her with all his might. "I dreamed that I was lame! And I thought it was true. And it isn't!— it isn't!—it isn't!"

*   *   *   *   *

Quite soon Dickie was able to walk downstairs and out into the garden along the grassy walks and long alleys where fruit trees trained over trellises made such pleasant green shade, and even to try to learn to play at bowls on the long bowling-green behind the house. The house was by far the finest house Dickie had ever been in, and the garden was more beautiful even than the garden at Talbot Court. But it was not only the beauty of the house and garden that made Dickie's life a new and full delight. To limp along the leafy ways, to crawl up and down the carved staircase would have been a pleasure greater than any Dickie had ever known; but he could leap up and down the stairs three at a time, he could run in the arched alleys—run and jump as he had seen other children do, and as he had never thought to do himself. Imagine what you would feel if you had lived wingless all your life among people who could fly. That is how lame people feel among us who can walk and run. And now Dickie was lame no more.

His feet seemed not only to be strong and active, but clever on their own account. They carried him quite without mistake to the blacksmith's at the village on the hill—to the center of the maze of clipped hedges that was the center of the garden, and best of all they carried him to the dockyard.

Girls like dolls and tea-parties and picture-books, but boys like to see things made and done; else how is it that any boy worth his salt will leave the newest any brightest toys to follow a carpenter or a plumber round the house, fiddle with his tools, ask him a thousand questions, and watch him ply his trade? Dickie at New Cross had spent many an hour watching those interesting men who open square trapdoors in the pavement and drag out from them yards and yards of wire. I do not know why the men do this, but every London boy who reads this will know.

And when he got to the dockyard his obliging feet carried him to a man in a great leather apron, busy with great beams of wood and tools that Dickie had never seen. And the man greeted him as an old friend, kissed him on both cheeks—which he didn't expect, and felt much too old for—and spread a sack for him that he might sit in the sun on a big balk of timber.

"Thou'rt a sight for sore eyes, Master Richard," he said; "it's many a long day since thou was here to pester me with thy questions. And now I'll teach thee to make a galleon, like as I promised."

"Will you, indeed?" said Dickie, trembling with joy and pride.

"That will I," said the man, and threw up his pointed beard in a jolly laugh. "And see what I've made thee while thou'st been lazying in bed—a real English ship of war."

He laid down the auger he held and went into a low, rough shed, and next moment came out with a little ship in his hand—a perfect model of the strange high-built ships Dickie could see on the river.

"'Tis the picture," said he, proudly, "of my old ship, *The Golden Venture*, that I sailed in with Master Raleigh, and help to sink the accursed Armada, and clip the King of Spain his wings, and singe his beard."

"The Armada!" said Dickie, with a new and quite strange feeling, rather like going down unexpectedly in a lift. "The *Spanish* Armada?"

"What other?" asked the ship-builder. "Thou'st heard the story a thousand times."

"I want to hear it again," Dickie said. And heard the story of England's great danger and her escapes. It was just he same story as the one you read in your history book—and yet how different, when it was told by a man who had been there, who had felt the danger, known the escape. Dickie held his breath.

"And so," the story ended, "the breath of the Lord went forth and the storm blew, and fell on the fleet of Spain, and scattered them; and they went down in our very waters, they and their arms and their treasure, their guns and their gunners, their mariners and their men-of-war. And the remnant was scattered and driven northward, and some were wrecked on the rocks, and some our ships met and dealt with, and some poor few made shift to get back across the sea, trailing home like wounded mallards, to tell the King their master what the Lord had done for England."

"How long ago was it, all this?" Dickie asked. If his memory served it was hundreds of years ago—three, five—he could not remember how many, but hundreds. Could this man, whose hair was only just touched with grey, be hundreds of years old?

"How long?—a matter of twenty years or thereabouts," said the ship-builder. "See, the pretty little ship; and thy very own, for I made it for thee."

" 'Tis the picture," said he proudly, "of my old ship,
The Golden Venture."

It was indeed a pretty little ship, being a perfect model of an Elizabethan ship, built up high at bow and stern, "for," as Sebastian explained, "majesty and terror of the enemy, and with deck and orlop, waist and poop, hold and masts—all complete with forecastle and cabin, masts and spars, portholes and guns, sails, anchor, and carved figure-head. The woodwork wa painted in white and green and red, and at bow and stern was richly carved and gilded.

"For me," Dickie said—"really for me? And you made it yourself."

"Truth to tell. I began it long since in the long winter evenings," said his friend, "and now 'tis done and 'tis thine. See, I shall put an apron on thee and thou shalt be my 'prentice and learn to build another quaint ship like her—to be her consort; and we will sail them together in the pond in thy father's garden."

Dickie, still devouring the little *Golden Venture* with his eyes, submitted to he leather apron, and felt in his hand the smooth handle of the tool Sebastian put there.

"But," he said, "I don't understand. You remember the Armada—twenty years ago. I thought it was hundreds and hundreds."

"Twenty years ago—or nearer eighteen," said Sebastian; "thou'lt have to learn to reckon better than that if thou'st to be my 'prentice. 'Twas in the year of grace 1588, and we are now in the year 1606. This makes it eighteen years, to my reckoning."

"It was 1906 in my dream," said Dickie—"I mean in my fever.

"In fever," Sebastian said, "folk travel far. Now, hold the wood so, and the knife thus."

Then every day Dickie went down to the dockyard when lessons were done. For there were lessons now, with a sour-faced tutor in a black gown, whom Dickie disliked extremely. The tutor did not seem to like Dickie either. "The child hath forgot in his fever all that ever he learned of me," he complained to the old nurse, who nodded wisely and said he would soon learn all afresh. And he did, very quickly, learn a great deal, and always it was more like remembering than learning. And a second tutor, very smart in red velvet and gold, with breeches like balloons and a short cloak and a ruff, who was an extremely jolly fellow, came in the mornings to teach him to fence, to dance, and to run and to leap and to play bowls, and promised in due time to teach him wrestling, catching, archery, pall-mall, rackets, riding, tennis, and all sports and games proper for a youth of gentle blood.

And weeks went by, and still his father and mother had not come, and he had learned a little Greek and more Latin, could carve a box with the arms of his house on the lid, and make that lid fit; could bow like a courtier and speak like a gentleman, and play a simple air on the viol that hung in the parlor for guests to amuse themselves with while they waited to see the master or mistress.

And then came the day when old nurse dressed him in his best—a suit of cut velvet, purple slashed with gold-color, and a belt with a little sword to it, and a flat cap—and Master Henry, the games-master, took him in a little boat to a gilded galley full of gentlemen and ladies all finely dressed, who kissed him and made much of him and said how he was grown since the fever. And one gentleman, very fine indeed, appeared to be his uncle, and a most charming lady in blue and silver seemed to be his aunt, and a very jolly little boy and girl who sat by him and talked merrily all the while were his little cousins. Cups of wine and silver dishes of fruit and cakes were handed round; the galley was decked with fresh flowers, and from another boat quite near came the sound of music. The sun shone overhead and the clear river sparkled and more and more boats, all gilded and glower-wreathed, appeared on the water. Then there was a sound of shouting, the river suddenly grew alive with the glitter of drawn swords, the butterfly glitter of ladies waved scarves and handkerchiefs, and a great gilded barge came slowly down-stream, followed by a procession of smaller craft. Everyone in the galley stood up: the gentlemen saluted with their drawn swords, the ladies fluttered their scarves.

"His Majesty and the Queen," the little cousins whispered as the State Barge went by.

Then all the galleys fell into place behind the King's barge, and the long, beautiful procession went slowly on down the river.

Dickie was very happy. The little cousins were so friendly and jolly, the grown-up people so kind—everything so beautiful and so clean. It was a perfect day.

The river was very beautiful; it ran between backs of willows and alders where loosestrife and meadowsweet and willow-herb and yarrow grew tall and thick. There were water-lilies in shady back-waters, and beautiful gardens sloping down to the water.

At last the boats came to a pretty little town among trees.

"This is where we disembark," said the little girl cousin. "The King lies here tonight at Sir Thomas Bradbury's. And we lie at our grandfather's house. And tomorrow it is the Masque in Sir Thomas's Park. And we are to see it. I shouldn't have liked it half so well if thou hadn't been here," she said, smiling. And of course that was a very nice thing to have said to one.

"And then we go home to Deptford with thee," said the boy cousin. "We are to stay a month. And we'll see thy galleon, and get old Sebastian to make me one too..."

"Yes," said Dickie, as the boat came against the quay. "What is this place?"

"Gravesend, thou knowest that," said the little cousins, "or hadst thou forgotten that, too, in thy fever?"

"Gravesend?" Dickie repeated, in quite a changed voice.

"Come, children," said the aunt—oh, what a different aunt to the one who had slapped Dickie in Deptford, sold the

THE GALLEY WAS DECKED WITH FRESH FLOWERS.

rabbit-hutch, and shot the moon!—"you boys remember how I showed you to carry my train. And my girl will not forget how to fling the flowers from the gilt basket as the King and Queen come down the steps."

The grandfather's house and garden—the stately, white-haired grandfather, whom they called My Lord, and who was, it seemed, the aunt's father—the banquet, the picture-gallery, the gardens lit up by little colored oil lamps hung in festoons from tree to tree, the blazing torches, the music, the Masque —a sort of play without words in which everyone wore the most wonderful and beautiful dresses, and the Queen herself took a part dressed all in gauze and jewels and white swan's feathers—all these things were like a dream to Dickie, and through it all the words kept on saying themselves to him very gently, very quietly, and quite without stopping—

"Gravesend. That's where the lodging-house is where Beale is waiting for you—the man you called father. You promised to go there as soon as you could. Why haven't you gone? Gravesend. That's where the lodging-house is where Beale—" And so on, over and over again.

And how can anyone enjoy anything when this sort of thing keeps on saying itself under and over and through and between everything he sees and hears and feels and thinks? And the worst of it was that now, for the first time since he had found that he was not lame, he felt—more than felt, he knew—that the old New Cross life had not been a fever dream, and that Beale, who had been kind to him and taken him through the pleasant country and slept with him in the bed with the green curtains, was really waiting for him at Gravesend.

"And this is all a dream," said Dickie, "and I *must* wake up."

But he couldn't wake up.

And the trees and grass and lights and beautiful things, the kindly great people with their splendid dresses, the King and Queen, the aunts and uncles and the little cousins—all these things refused to fade away and jumble themselves up as things do in dreams. They remained solid and real. He knew that this must be a dream, and that Beale and Gravesend and New Cross and the old lame life were the real thing, and yet he could not wake up. All the same the light had gone out of everything, and it is small wonder that when he got home at last, very tired indeed, to his father's house at Deptford he burst into tears as nurse was undressing him.

"What ails my lamb?" she asked.

"I can't explain; you wouldn't understand," said Dickie.

"Try," said she, very earnestly.

He looked round the room at the tapestries and the heavy furniture.

"I can't," he said.

"Try," she said again.

"It's ... don't laugh, Nurse. There's a dream that feels real—about a dreadful place—oh, so different from this. But there's a man waiting there for me that was good to me when I was—when I wasn't . . . that was good to me; he's waiting in the dream and I want to get back to him. And I can't."

"Thou'rt better here than in that dreadful place," said the nurse, stroking his hair.

"Yes—but Beale. I know he's waiting there. I wish I could bring him here."

"Not yet," said the nurse surprisingly; "'tis not easy to bring those we love from one dream to another."

"One dream to another?"

"Didst never hear that all life is a dream?" she asked him. "But thou shalt go. Heaven forbid that one of thy race should fail a friend. Look! there are fresh sheets on thy bed. Lie still and think of him that was good to thee."

He lay there, very still. He had decided to wake up—to wake up to the old, hard, cruel life—to poverty, dulness, lameness. There was no other thing to be done. He *must* wake up and keep his promise to Beale. But it was hard—hard—hard. The beautiful house, the beautiful garden, the games, the boat-building, the soft clothes, the kind people, the uplifting sense that he was Somebody... yet he must go. Yes, if he could he would.

The nurse had taken burning wood from the hearth and set it on a silver plate. Now she strewed something on the glowing embers.

"Lie straight and still," she said, "and wish thyself where thou wast when thou leftest that dream."

He did so. A thick, sweet smoke rose from the little fire in the silver plate, and the nurse was chanting something in a very low voice.

> "Men die,
>> Man dies not.
> Times fly,
>> Time flies not."

That was all he heard, though he heard confusedly that were was more.

He seemed to sink deep into a soft sea of sleep, to be rocked on its tide, and then to be flung by its waves, roughly, suddenly, on some hard shore of awakening. He opened his eyes. He was in the little bare front room in New Cross. Tinkler and the white seal lay on the floor among white moonflower seeds confusedly scattered, and the gas lamp from the street shone through the dirty panes on the newspapers and sacking.

"What a dream!" said Dickie, shivering, and very sleepy. "Oh, what a dream!" He put Tinkler and the seal in one pocket, gathered up the moon-seeds and put them in the other, drew the old newspapers over him and went to sleep.

*　　*　　*　　*　　*

The morning sun woke him.

"How odd," said he, "to dream all that—weeks and weeks, in just a little bit of one little night! If it had only been true!"

He jumped up, eager to start for Gravesend. Since he had wakened out of that wonderful dream on purpose to go to Gravesend, he might as well start at once. But his jump ended in a sickening sideways fall, and his head knocked against the wainscot.

"I had forgotten," he said slowly. "I shouldn't have thought any dream could have made me forget about my foot."

For he had indeed forgotten it, had leaped up, eagerly, confidently, as a sound child leaps, and the lame foot had betrayed him, thrown him down.

He crawled across to where the crutch lay—the old broom, cut down, that Lady Talbot had covered with black velvet for him.

"And now," he said, "I must get to Gravesend." He looked out of the window at he dismal, sordid street. "I wonder," he said, "if Deptford was ever really like it was in my dream—the gardens and the clean river and the fields?"

He got out of the house when no one was looking, and went off down the street.

"Clickety-clack" went the crutch on the dusty pavement.

His back ached; his lame foot hurt; his "good" leg was tired and stiff, and his heart, too, was very tired. About this time, in the dream he had chosen to awaken from, for the sake of Beale, a bowl of porridge would be smoking at the end of a long oak table, and a great carved chair be set for a little boy who was not there.

Dickie strode on manfully, but the pain in his back made him feel sick.

"I don't know as I can do it," he said.

Then he saw the three gold balls above the door of the friendly pawnbroker.

He looked, hesitated, shrugged his shoulders, and went in.

"Hullo!" said the pawnbroker, "here we are again. Want to pawn the rattle, eh?"

"No," said Dickie, "but what'll you give me on the seal you gave me?"

The pawnbroker stared, frowned, and burst out laughing.

"If you don't beat all!" he said. "I give you a present, and you come to pledge it with me! You should have been one of our people! So you want to pledge the seal. Well, well!"

"I'd much rather not," said Dickie seriously, "because I love it very much. But I must have my fare to Gravesend. My father's there, waiting for me. And I don't want to leave Tinkler behind."

He showed the rattle.

"What's the fare to Gravesend?"

"Don't know. I thought you'd know. Will you give me the fare for the seal?"

The pawnbroker hesitated and looked hard at him. "No," he said, "no. The seal's not worth it. Not but what it's a very good seal," he added, "very good indeed."

"See here," said Dickie suddenly, "I know what honor is now, and the word of a gentleman. You will not let me pledge the seal with you. Then let me pledge my word—my word of honor. Lend me the money to take me to Gravesend, and by the honor of a gentleman I will repay you within a month."

The voice was firm; the accent, though strange, was not the accent of Deptford street boys. It was the accent of the boy who had had two tutors and a big garden, a place in the King's water-party, and a knowledge of what it means to belong to a noble house.

The pawnbroker looked at him. With the unerring instinct of his race, he knew that this was not play-acting, that there was something behind it—something real. The sense of romance, of great things all about them transcending the ordinary things of life—this in the Jews has survived centuries of torment, shame, cruelty, and oppression. This inherited sense of romance in the pawnbroker now leapt to answer Dickie's appeal. (And I do hope I am not confusing you; stick to it; read it again if you don't understand. What I mean is that the Jews always see the big beautiful things; they don't just see that grey is made of black and white; they see how incredibly black black can be, and that there may be a whiteness transcending all the whitest dreams in the world.)

"You're a rum little chap," was what the pawnbroker said, "but I like your pluck. Every man's got to make a fool of himself one time or the other," he added, apologizing to the spirit of business.

"You mean you will?" said Dickie eagerly.

"More fool me," said the man, feeling in his pocket.

"You won't be sorry; not in the end you won't," said Dickie, as the pawnbroker laid certain monies before him on the mahogany counter. "You'll lend me this? You'll trust me?"

"Looks like it," said the pawnbroker.

"Then some day I shall do something for you. I don't know what, but something for you. I don't know what, but something. We never forget, we—" He stopped. He remembered that he was poor little lame Dickie Harding, with no right to that other name which had been his in the dream.

He picked up the coins, put them in his pocket—felt the moon-seeds.

"I cannot repay your kindness," he said, "though some day I will repay your silver. But these seeds—the moon-seeds," he pulled out a handful. "You like the flowers?" He handed a generous score across the red-brown polished wood.

"Thank you, my lad," said the pawnbroker. "I'll raise them in gentle heat."

"I think they grow best by moonlight," said Dickie.

*   *   *   *   *

So he came to Gravesend and the common lodging-house, and a weary, sad, and very anxious man rose up from his place by the fire when the clickety-clack of the crutch sounded on the threshold.

"It's the nipper!" he said; and came very quickly to the door and got his arm round Dickie's shoulders. "The little nipper, so it ain't! I thought you'd got pinched. No, I didn't, I knew your clever ways—I knew you was bound to turn up."

"Yes," said Dickie, looking round the tramps' kitchen, and remembering the long, clean tapestry-hung dining-hall of his dream. "Yes, I was bound to turn up. You wanted me to, didn't you?" he added.

"Wanted you to?" Beale answered, holding him close, and looking at him as men look at some rare treasure gained with much cost and after long seeking. "Wanted you? Not 'arf! I *don't* think," and drew him in and shut the door.

"Then I'm glad I came," said Dickie. But in his heart he was not glad. In his heart he longed for that pleasant house where he was the young master, and was not lame any more. But in his soul he was glad, because the soul is greater than the heart, and knows greater things. And now Dickie loved Beale more than ever, because for him he had sacrificed his dream. So he had gained something. Because loving people is the best thing in the world—better even than being loved. Just think this out, will you, and see if I am not right.

There were herrings for tea. And in the hard bed, with his clothes and his boots under the pillows, Dickie slept soundly.

But he did not dream.

Yet when he woke in the morning, remembering many things, he said to himself—

"Is this the dream? Or was the other the dream?"

And it seemed a foolish question—with the feel of the coarse sheets and the smell of the close room, and Mr. Beale's voice saying, "Rouse up, nipper! there's sossingers for breakfast."

"To Get Your Own Living"

N o," said Mr. Beale, "we ain't agoin' to crack no more cribs. It's low—that's what it is. I quite grant you it's low. So I s'pose we'll 'ave to take the road again."

Dickie and he were sitting in the sunshine on a sloping field. They had been sitting there all the morning, and Dickie had told Mr. Beale all his earthly adventures from the moment the red-headed man had lifted him up to the window of Talbot Court to the time when he had come in by the open door of the common lodging-house.

"What a nipper it is, though!" said Mr. Beale regretfully. "For the burgling, I mean—sharp—clever—no one to touch him. But I don't cotton to it myself," he added quickly, "not the burgling, I don't. You're always liable to get yourself into trouble over it, one way or the other—that's the worst of it. I don't know how it is," he ended pensively, "but somehow it *always* leads to trouble."

Dickie picked up seven straws from among the stubble and idly plaited them together; the nurse had taught him this in the dream when he was still weak from the fever.

"That's very flash, that what you're doing," said Beale; "who learned you that?"

"I dreamed I 'ad a fever—and—I'll tell you if you like: it's a good yarn—good as Here Ward, very near."

Beale lay back on the stubble, his pipe between his teeth.

"Fire away," he said, and Dickie fired away.

When the long tale ended, the sun was beginning to go down towards its bed in the west. There was a pause.

"You'd make a tidy bit on the 'alls," said Beale, quite awestruck. "The things you think of! When did you make all that up?"

"I dreamed it, I tell you," said Dickie.

"You always could stick it on," said Mr. Beale admiringly.

"I ain't goin' to stick it on never no more," said Dickie. "They called it lying and cheating, where I was—in my dream, I mean."

"Once let a nipper out of yer sight," said Mr. Beale sadly, "and see what comes of it! 'No. 2' a-goin' to stick it on no more! Then how's us to get a honest living? Answer me that, young chap."

"I don't know," said Dickie, "but we got to do it som'ow."

"It ain't to be done—not with all the unemployed there is about," said Mr. Beale. "Besides, you've got a regular gift for sticking it on—a talent I call it. And now you want to throw it away. But you can't. We *got* to live."

"In the dream," said Dickie, "there didn't seem to be no unemployed. Every one was 'prenticed to a trade. I wish it was like that here."

"Well, it ain't," said Mr. Beale shortly. "I wasn't never 'prenticed to no trade, no more'n what you'll be."

"Worse luck," said Dickie. "But I started learning a lot of things—games mostly, in the dream, I did—and I started making a boat—a galleon they called it. All the names is different there. And I carved a little box—a fair treat it was—with my father's arms on it."

"Yer father's *what?*"

"Coat of arms. Gentlemen there all has different things—patterns like; they calls 'em coats of arms, and they put it on their silver and on their carriages and their furniture."

"Put *what?*" Beale asked again.

"The blazon. All gentlepeople have it."

"Don't you come the blazing toff over me," said Beale with sudden fierceness, "cause I won't 'ave it. See? It's them bloomin' Talbots put all this rot into your head."

"The Talbots?" said Dickie. "Oh! the Talbots ain't been gentry more than a couple of hundred years. Our family's as old as King Alfred."

"Stow it, I say!" said Beale, more fiercely still. "I see what you're after; you want us to part company, that's what you want. Well, go. Go back to yer old Talbots and be the nice lady's little boy with velvet kicksies and a clean anky once a week. That's what you do."

Dickie looked forlornly out over the river.

"I can't 'elp what I dreams, can I?" he said. "In the dream I'd got lots of things. Uncles and aunts an' a little brother. I never seen him though. An a farver and muvver an' all. It's different 'ere. I ain't got nobody but you'ere—farver."

"Well, then," said Beale more gently, "what do you go settin of yourself up again me for?"

"I ain't," said Dickie. "I thought you liked me to tell you everything."

Silence. Dickie could not help noticing the dirty shirt, the dirty face, the three days' beard, the filthy clothes of his friend, and he thought of his other friend, Sebastian of the Docks. He saw the pale blue reproachful eyes of Beale looking out of that dirty face, and he spoke aloud, quite without meaning to.

"All that don't make no difference," he said.

"Eh?" said Beale with miserable, angry eyes.

"Look 'ere," said Dickie desperately. "I'm a-goin' to show you. This 'ere's my Tinkler, what I told you about, what pawns for a bob. I wouldn't show it to no one but you, swelp me, I wouldn't."

He held the rattle out.

Beale took it. "it's a fancy bit, I will say," he owned.

"Look 'ere," said Dickie, "what I mean to say—"

He stopped. What was the use of telling Beale that he had come back out of the dream just for *his* sake? Beale who did not believe in the dream—did not understand it—hated it?

"Don't you go turning again me," he said; "whether I dream or not, you and me'll stand together. I'm not goin' to do things wot's wrong—low, dirty tricks—so I ain't. But I knows we can get on without that. What would you *like* to do for your living if you could choose?"

"I warn't never put to no trade," said Beale, "'cept being 'andy with a 'orse. I was a wagoner's mate when I was a boy. I likes a 'orse. Or a dawg," he added. "I ain't no good wiv me 'ands—not at working, you know—not to say working."

Dickie suppressed a wild notion he had had of forgetting into that dream again, learning some useful trade there, waking up and teaching it to Mr. Beale.

"Ain't there *nothing* else you'd like to do?" he asked.

"I don't know as there is," said Mr. Beale drearily; "without it was pigeons."

Then Dickie wondered whether things that you learned in dreams would "*stay* learnt." Things you learned to do with your hands. The Greek and the Latin "stayed learned" right enough and sang in his brain encouragingly.

"Don't you get shirty if I talks about that dream," he said. "You dunno what a dream it was. I wasn't kidding you. I did dream it, honor bright. I dreamed I could carve wood—make boxes and things. I wish I 'ad a bit of fine-grained wood. I'd like to try. I've got the knife they give me to cut the string of the basket in the train. It's jolly sharp."

"What sort o' wood?" Beale asked.

"It was mahogany I dreamed I made my box with," said Dickie. "I would like to try."

"Off 'is poor chump," Beale murmured with bitter self-reproach; "my doin' too—puttin' 'im on to a job like Talbot Court, the nipper is."

He stretched himself and got up.

"I'll get yer a bit of mahogany from somewheres," he said very gently. "I didn't mean nothing, old chap. You keep all on about yer dreams. I don't mind. I likes it. Let's get a brace o' kippers and make a night of it."

So they went back to the Gravesend lodging-house.

Next day Mr. Beale produced the lonely leg of a sofa—mahogany, a fat round turned leg, old and seasoned.

"This what you want?" he asked.

Dickie took it eagerly. "I do wonder if I can," he said. "I feel just exactly like as if I could. I say, farver, let's get out in the woods somewheres quiet and take our grub along. Somewheres where nobody can't say, 'What you up to?' and make a mock of me."

They found a place such as Dickie desired, a warm, sunny nest in the heart of a green wood, and all through the long, warm hours of the autumn day Mr. Beale lay lazy in the sunshine while Dickie, very pale and determined, sliced, chipped, and picked at the sofa leg with the knife the gardener had given him.

It was hard to make him lay the work down even for dinner, which was of delicious and extravagant kind—new bread, German sausage, and beer in a flat bottle. For from the moment when the knife touched the wood Dickie knew that he had not forgotten, and that what he had done in the Deptford dockyard under the eyes of Sebastian, the shipwright who had helped to sink the Armada, he could do now alone in the woods beyond Gravesend.

It was after dinner that Mr. Beale began to be interested.

"Swelp me!" he said; "but you've got the hang of it somehow. A box, ain't it?"

"A box," said Dickie, smoothing a rough corner; "a box with a lid that fits. And I'll carve our arms on the top—see, I've left that bit stickin' up a purpose."

It was the hardest day's work Dickie had ever done. He stuck to it and stuck to it and stuck to it till there was hardly light left to see it by. But before the light was wholly gone the box had wholly come—with the carved coat-of-arms and the lid that fitted.

"Well," said Mr. Beale, striking a match to look at it; "if that ain't a fair treat! There's many a swell bloke 'ud give 'arf a dollar for that to put 'is baccy in. You've got a trade, my son, that's sure. Why didn't you let on before as you could? Blow the beastly match! It's burnt me finger."

The match went out and Beale and Dickie went back to supper in the crowded, gas-lit room. When supper was over—it was tripe and onions and fried potatoes, very luxurious—Beale got up and stood before the fire.

"I'm a goin' to 'ave a hauction, I am," he said to the company at large. "Here's a thing and a very pretty thing, a baccy-box, or a snuff-box, or a box to shut yer gold money in, or yer diamonds. What offers?"

"'And it round," said a black-browed woman, with a basket covered in American cloth no blacker than her eyes.

"That I will," said Beale readily. "I'll 'and it round *in* me 'and. And I'll do the 'andin' meself."

He took it round from one to another, showed the neat corners, the neat carving, the neat fit of the square lid.

"Where'd yer nick that?" asked a man with a red handkerchief.

"The nipper made it."

"Pinched it more likely," someone said.

"I see 'im make it," said Beale, frowning a little.

"Let me' ave a squint," said a dingy grey old man sitting apart. For some reason of his own Beale let the old man take the box into his hand. But he kept very close to him and he kept his eyes on the box.

"All outer one piece," said the old man. "I dunno oo made it an' I don't care, but that was made by a workman as know'd his trade. I was a cabinetmaker once, though you wouldn't think it to look at me. There ain't nobody here to pay what that little hobjec's worth. Hoil it up with a drop of cold linseed and leave it all night, and then in the morning you rub it on yer trowser leg to shine it, and then rub it in the mud to dirty it, and then hoil it again and dirty it again, and you'll get 'arf a thick un for it as a genuwine hold antique. That's wot you do."

"Thankee, daddy," said Beale, "an' so I will."

He slipped the box in his pocket. When Dickie next saw the box it looked as old as any box need look.

"Now we'll look out for a shop where they sells these 'ere hold antics," said Beale. They were on the road and their faces were set towards London. Dickie's face looked pinched and white. Beale noticed it.

"You don't look up to much," he said; "warn't your bed to your liking?"

"The bed was all right," said Dickie, thinking of the bed in the dream. "I diden sleep much, though."

"Any more dreams?" Beale asked kindly enough.

"No," said Dickie. "I think p'raps it was me wanting so to dream it again kep' me awake."

"I dessey," said Beale, picking up a straw to chew.

Dickie limped along in the dust, the world seemed very big and hard. It was a long way to London and he had not been able to dream that dream again. Perhaps he would never be able to dream it. He stumbled on a big stone and would have fallen but that Beale caught him by the arm, and as he swung round by that arm Beale saw that the boy's eyes were thick with tears.

"Ain't 'urt yerself, 'ave yer?" he said—for in all their wanderings these were the first tears Dickie had shed.

"No," said Dickie, and hid his face against Beale's coat sleeve. "It's only—"

What is it, then?" said Beale, in the accents of long-discussed tenderness; "tell your old farver, then—"

"It's silly," sobbed Dickie.

"Never you mind whether it's silly or not," said Beale. "You out with it."

"In that dream," said Dickie, "I wasn't lame."

"Think of that now," said Beale admiringly. "You best dream that every night. Then you won't mind so much of a daytime."

"But I mind more," said Dickie, sniffing hard; "much, much more."

Beale, without more words, made room for him in the crowded perambulator, and they went on. Dickie's sniffs subsided. Silence. Presently—

"I say, farver, I'm sorry I acted so silly. You never see me blub afore and you won't again," he said; and Beale said awkwardly, "That's all right, mate."

"You pretty flush?" the boy asked later on.

"Not so dusty," said the man.

"'Cause I wanter give that there little box to a chap I know wot lent me the money for the train to come to you at Gravesend."

"Pay 'im some other day when we're flusher."

"I'd rather pay 'im now," said Dickie. "I could make another box. The's a bit of the sofer leg left, ain't there?"

There was, and Dickie worked away at it in the odd moments that cluster round meal times, the half-hours before bed and before the morning start. Mr. Beale begged of all likely foot-passengers, but he noted that the "nipper" no longer "stuck it on." For the most part he was quite silent. Only when

Beale appealed to him he would say, "Farver's very good to me. I don't know what I should do without farver."

And so at last they came to New Cross again, and Mr,. Beale stepped in for half a pint at the Railway hotel, while Dickie went clickety-clack along the pavement to his friend the pawnbroker.

"Here we are again," said the tradesmen; "come to pawn the rattle?"

Dickie laughed. Pawning the rattle seemed suddenly to have become a very old and good joke between them.

"Look 'ere, mister," he said; "that chink wot you lent me to get to Gravesend with." He paused, and added in his other voice, "It was very good of you, sir."

"I'm not going to lend you any more, if that's what you're after," said the pawnbroker, who had already reproached himself for his confiding generosity.

"It's not that I'm after," said Dickie, with dignity. "I wish to repay you."

"Got the money?" said the man, laughing not unkindly.

"No," said Dickie; "but I've got this." He handed the little box across the counter.

"Where'd you get it?"

"I made it."

The pawnbroker laughed again. "Well, well, I'll ask no questions and you'll tell me no lies, eh?"

"I shall certainly tell you no lies," said Dickie, with the dignity of the dream boy who was not a cripple and was heir to a great and gentle name; "will you take it instead of the money?"

The pawnbroker turned the box over in his hands, while kindness and honesty struggled fiercely within him against the habits of a business life. Dickie eyed the china vases and concertinas and teaspoons tied together in fan shape, and waited silently.

"It's worth more than what I lent you," the man said at last with an effort; "and it isn't everyone who would own that, mind you."

"I know it isn't, said Dickie; "Will you please take it to pay my debt to you, and if it is worth more, accept it as a grateful gift from one who is still gratefully your debtor."

"You'd make your fortune on the halls," said the man, as Beale had said; "the way you talk beats everything. All serene. I'll take the box in full discharge of your debt. But you might as well tell me where you got it."

"I made it," said Dickie, and put his lips together very tightly.

"You did—did you? Then I'll tell you what. I'll give you four bob for every one of them you make and bring to me. You might do different coats of arms—see?"

"I was only taught to do one," said Dickie.

Just then a customer came in—a woman with her Sunday dress and a pair of sheets to pawn because her man was out of work and the children were hungry.

"Run along, now," said the man, "I've nothing more for you today." Dickie flushed and went.

Three days later the crutch clattered in at the pawnbroker's door, and Dickie laid two more little boxes on the counter.

"Here you are," he said. The pawnbroker looked and exclaimed and questioned and wondered, and Dickie went away with eight silver shillings in his pocket, the first coins he had ever carried in his life. They seemed to have been coined in some fairy mint; they were so different from any other money he had ever handled.

Mr. Beale, waiting for him by New Cross Station, put his empty pipe in his pocket and strolled down to meet him. Dickie drew him down a side street and held out the silver. "Two days' work," he said. "We ain't no call to take the road 'cept for a pleasure trip. I got a trade, I 'ave. 'Ow much a week's four bob a day? Twenty-four bob I make it."

"Lor!" said Mr. Beale, with his mouth open.

"Now I tell you what, you get 'old of some more old sofy legs and a stone and a strap to sharpen my knife with. And there we are. Twenty-four shillings a week for a chap an' 'is nipper ain't so dusty, farver, is it? I've thought it all up and settled it all out. So long as the weather holds we'll sleep in the bed with the green curtains, and I'll 'ave a greenwood for my workshop, and when the nights get cold we'll rent a room of our very own and live like toffs, won't us?"

The child's eyes were shining with excitement.

"'Pon my sam, I believe you *like* work," said Mr. Beale in tones of intense astonishment.

"I like it better'n cadgin'," said Dickie.

They did as Dickie had said, and for two days Mr. Beale was content to eat and doze and wake and watch Dickie's busy fingers and eat and doze again. But on the third day he announced that he was getting the fidgets in his legs.

"I must do a prowl," he said; "I'll be back afore sundown. Don't you forget to eat your dinner when the sun comes level the top of that high tree. So long, matey."

Mr. Beale slouched off in the sunshine in his filthy old clothes, and Dickie was left to work alone in the green and golden wood. It was very still. Dickie hardly moved at all, and the chips that fell from his work fell more softly than the twigs and acorns that dropped now and then from some high bough. A goldfinch swung on a swaying hazel branch and looked at him with bright eyes, unafraid; a grass snake slid swiftly by—it was out of particular business of its own, so it was not afraid of Dickie nor her of it. A wood-pigeon swept rustling wings across the glade where he sat, and once a squirrel ran right along a bough to look down at him and chatter, thickening its tail as a cat does hers when she is angry.

It was a long and very beautiful day, the first that Dickie had ever spent alone. He worked harder than ever, and when by the lessening light it was impossible to work any longer, he lay back against a tree root to rest his tired back and to gloat over the thought that he had made two boxes in one day—eight shillings—in one single day, eight splendid shillings.

The sun was quite down before Mr. Beale returned. He looked unnaturally fat, and as he sat down on the moss something inside the front of his jacket moved and whined.

"Oh! what is it?" Dickie asked, sitting up, alert in a moment; "not a dawg? Oh! farver, you don't know how I've always want a dawg."

"Well, you've a-got yer want now, three times over, you 'ave," said Beale, and, unbuttoning his jacket, took out a double handful of soft, fluffy sprawling arms and legs and heads and tails—three little fat, white puppies.

"Oh, the jolly little beasts!" said Dickie; "Ain't they fine? where did you get them?"

"They was give me," said Mr. Beale, reknotting his handkerchief, "by a lady in the country."

He fixed his eyes on the soft blue of the darkening sky.

"Try another," said Dickie calmly.

"Ah! it ain't no use trying to deceive the nipper—that sharp he is," said Beale, with a mixture of pride and confusion. "Well, then, not to deceive you, mate, I bought 'em."

"What with?" said Dickie, lightning quick.

"With—with money, mate—with money, of course."

"How'd you get it?"

No answer.

"You didn't pinch it?"

"No—on my sacred sam, I didn't," said Beale eagerly; "pinching leads to trouble. I've 'ad my lesson."

"You cadged it, then?" said Dickie.

"Well," said Beale sheepishly, "what if I did?"

"You've spoiled everything," said Dickie, furious, and he flung the two newly finished boxes violently to the ground, and sat frowning with eyes downcast.

Beale, on all fours, retrieved the boxes.

"Two," he said, in awestruck tones; "there never was such a nipper!"

"It doesn't matter," said Dickie in a heart-broken voice, "you've spoiled everything, and you lie to me, too. It's all spoilt. I wish I'd never come back outer the dream, so I do."

"Now lookee here," said Beale sternly, "Don't you come this over us, 'cause I won't stand it, d'y 'ear? Am I the master or is it you? D'ye think I'm going to put up with being bullied and druv by a little nipper like as I could lay out with one 'and as easy as what I could one of them pups?" He moved his foot among the soft, strong little thing that were uttering baby-growls and biting at his broken boot with their little white teeth.

"Do," said Dickie bittelry, "lay me out if you want to. I don't care."

"Now, now, matey"—Beale's tone changed suddenly to affectionate remonstrance—"I was only kiddin'. Don't take it like that. You know I wouldn't 'urt a 'air of yer 'ed, so I wouldn't"

"I wanted us to live honest by our work—we was doing it. And you've lowered us to the cadgin' again. That's what I can't stick," said Dickie.

"It wasn't. I didn't have to do a single bit of patter for it anyhow. It was a wedding, and I stopped to 'ave a squint, and there'd been a water-cart as 'ad stopped to 'ave a squint too, and made a puddle as big as a tea-tray, and all the path wet. An' the lady in her white, she looks at the path and the gent 'e looks at 'er white boots—an' I off's with me coat like that there Rally gent you yarned me about, and flops it down in the middle of the puddle, right in front of the gal. And she tips me a smile like a hangel and 'olds out 'er hand—in 'er white glove and all—and yer know what my 'ands is like, matey."

"Yes," said Dickie, "go on."

"And she just touched me 'and walks across me coat. And the people laughed and clapped-silly apes! And the gent 'e tipped me a thick un, and I spotted the pups a month ago, and I knew I could have 'em for five bob, so I got 'em. And I'll sell 'em for thrible the money, you see if I don't. An' I thought you'd be as pleased as pleased—me actin' so silly, like as if I was one of them yarns o' yourn an' all. And then first minute I gets 'ere, you sets onto me. But that's always the way."

"Please, please forgive me, father," said Dickie, very much ashamed of himself; "I am so sorry, And I *was* nice to you and I am pleased—and I do love the pups—and we won't sell all three, will us? I would so like to have one. I'd call it 'True.' One of the dogs in my dream was called that. You do forgive me, don't you, father?"

"Oh! that's all right," said Beale.

Next day again a little boy worked alone in a wood, and yet not alone, for a small pup sprawled and yapped and scrapped and grunted round him as he worked. Now squirrels or birds came that day to lighten Dickie's solitude, but True was more to him than many birds or squirrels. A woman they had overtaken on the road had given him a bit of blue ribbon for the puppy's neck, in return for the lift which Mr. Beale had given her basket on the perambulator. She was selling ribbons and cottons and needles from door to door, and made a poor thing of it, she told them. "An' my grandfather 'e farmed 'is own land in Sussex," she told them, looking with bleared eyes across the fields.

Dickie only made a box and a part of a box that day. And while he sat making it, far away in London a respectable-looking man was walking up and down Regent Street among

"AN' I OFF'S WITH ME COAT, AND FLOPS IT DOWN IN THE MIDDLE OF
THE PUDDLE, RIGHT IN FRONT OF THE GAL."

the shoppers and the motors and carriages, with a fluffy little white dog under each arm. And he sold both the dogs.

"One was a lady in a carriage," he told Dickie later on. "Arst 'er two thick uns, I did. Never turned a hair, no more I didn't. She didn't care what its price was, bless you. Said it was a dinky darling and she wanted it. Gent said he'd get her plenty better. No—she wanted that. An' she got it too. A fool and his money's soon parted's what I say. And t'other one I let 'im go cheap, for fourteen bob, to a black clergyman —black as your hat he was, from foreign parts. So now we're bloomin' toffs, an' I'll get a pair of reach-me-downs this very bloomin' night. And what price that room you was talkin' about?"

It was the beginning of a new life. Dickie wrote out their accounts on a large flagstone near the horse trough by the "Chequers," with a bit of billiard chalk that a man gave him. It was like this:—

Got	Box	4
	Box	4
	Box	4
	Box	4
	Dog	40
	Dog	14
		70

Spent	Dogs	4
	Grub	19
	Tram	4
	Leg	2
		29

and he made out before he rubbed the chalk off the stone that the difference between twenty-nine shillings and seventy was about two pounds—and that was more than Dickie had ever had, or Beale either, for many a long year.

Then Beale came, wiping his mouth, and they walked idly up the road. Lodgings. Or rather *a* lodging. A room. But when you have had what is called the key of the street for years enough, you hardly know where to look for the key of a room.

"Where'd you like to be?" Beale asked anxiously. "You like country best, don't yer?"

"Yes," said Dickie.

"But in the winter-time?" Beale urged.

"Well, town then," said Dickie, who was trying to invent a box of a new and different shape to be carved next day.

"I could keep a look-out for likely pups," said Beale; "there's a plenty here and there all about—and you with your boxes. We might go to three bob a week for the room."

"I'd like a 'ouse with a garden" said Dickie.

"Go back to yer Talbots," said Beale.

"No—but look 'ere," said Dickie, "if we was to take a 'ouse—just a little 'ouse, and let half of it."

"We ain't got no sticks to put in it."

"Ain't there some way you get furniture without payin' for it?"

"'Ire systim. But that's for toffs on three quid a week, reg'lar wages. They wouldn't look at us."

"We'll get three quid right enough afore we fone," said Dickie firmly; "and if you want London, I'd like our old house because of the seed I sowed in the garden; I lay they'll keep on a coming up, forever and ever. That's what annuals means. The chap next door told me. It means flowers as comes up fresh every year. Let's tramp up, and I'll show it to you—where we used to live."

And when they had tramped up and Dickie had shown Mr. Beale the sad-faced little house, Mr. Beale owned that it would do 'em a fair treat.

"But we must 'ave some bits of sticks or else nobody won't let us have no 'ouses."

They flattened their noses against the front window. The newspapers and dirty sackings still lay scatered on the floor as they had fallen from Dickie when he had got up in the morning after the night when he had had The Dream.

The sight pulled at Dickie's heart strings. He felt as a man might feel who beheld once more the seaport from which in old and beautiful days he had set sail for the shores of romance, the golden splendor of The Fortunate Islands.

"I could doss 'ere again," he said wistfully; "it 'ud save fourpence. Both 'ouses both sides is empty. Nobody wouldn't know."

"We don't need to look to our fourpences so sharp's all that," said Beale.

"I'd like to."

"Wonder you ain't afeared."

"I'm used to it," said Dickie; "it was our own 'ouse, you see."

"You come along to yer supper," said Beale; "don't be so flash with yer own 'ouses."

They had supper at a coffee-shop in the Broadway.

"Two mugs, four billiard balls, and 'arf a dozen doorsteps," was Mr. Beale's order. You or I, more polite if less picturesque, would perhaps have said, "Two cups of tea, four eggs, and some thick bread and butter." It was a pleasant meal. Only just at the end it turned into something quite different. The shop was one of those old-fashioned ones, divided by partitions like the stalls in a stable, and over the top of this partition there suddenly appeared a head.

Dickie's mug paused in air half-way to his mouth, which remained open.

"What's up?" Beale asked, trying to turn on the narrow seat and look up, which he couldn't do.

"It's 'im," whispered Dickie, setting down the mug. "That red-'eaded chap wot I never see."

And then the red-headed man came round the partition and sat down beside Beale and talked to him, and Dickie wished he wouldn't. He heard little of the conversation; only "better luck next time" from the red-headed man, and "I don't know as I'm taking any" from Beale, and at the parting the red-headed man saying, "I'll doss same shop as wot you do," and Beale giving the name of the lodging-house where, on the way to the coffee-shop, Beale had left the perambulator and engaged their beds.

"Tell you all about it in the morning" were the last words of the red-headed one as he slouched out, and Dickie and Beale were left to finish doorsteps and drink the cold tea that had slopped into their saucers.

When they went out Dickie said—

"What did he want, farver—that red-headed chap?"

Beale did not at once answer.

"I woudn't if I was you," said Dickie, looking straight in front of him as they walked.

"Wouldn't what?"

"Whatever he wants to."

"Why, I ain't told you yet what he *does* want."

"'E ain't up to no good—I know that."

"'E's full of notions, that's wot 'e is," said Beale. "If some of 'is notions come out right 'e'll be a-ridin' in 'is own cart and 'orse afor we know where we are—and us a-tramping in 'is dust."

"Ridin' in Black Maria, more like," said Dickie.

"Well, I ain't askin' *you* to do anything, am I?" said Beale.

"No!—you ain't. But whatever you're in, I'm a-goin' to be in, that's all."

"Don't you take on," said Beale comfortably; "I ain't said I'll be in anything yet, 'ave I? let's 'ear what 'e says in the morning. If 'is lay ain't a safe lay old Beale won't be in it—you may lay to that."

"Don't let's," said Dickie earnestly. "Look 'ere, father, let us go, both two of us, and sleep in that there old 'ouse of ours. I don't want that red-'eaded chap. He'll spoil everything—I know 'e will, just as we're a-gettin' along so straight and gay. Don't let's go to that there doss; let's lay in the old 'ouse."

"Ain't I never to 'ave never a word with nobody without it's you?" said Beale, but not angrily.

"Not with 'im; 'e ain't no class," said Dickie firmly; "and oh! farver, I do so wanter sleep in that 'ouse, that was where I 'ad The Dream, you know."

"Oh, well—come on, then," said Beale; "lucky we've got our thick coats on."

It was quite easy for Dickie to get into the house, just as he had done before, and to go along the passage and open the front door for Mr. Beale, who walked in as bold as brass. They made themselves comfortable with the sacking and old papers—but one at least of the two missed the luxury of clean air and soft moss and a bed canopy strewn with stars. Mr. Beale was soon asleep and Dickie lay still, his heart beating to the tune of the hope that now at last, in this place where it had once come, his dream would come again. But it did not come—even sleep, plain, restful, dreamless sleep, would not come to him. At last he could lie still no longer. He slipped from under the paper, whose rustling did not disturb Mr. Beale's slumbers, and moved into the square of light thrown through the window by the street lamp. He felt in his pockets, pulled out Tinkler and the white seal, set them on the floor, and, moved by memories of the great night when his dream had come to him, arranged the moon-seeds round them in the same pattern that they had lain in on that night of nights. And the moment that he had lain the last seed, completing the crossed triangles, the magic began again. All was as it had been before. The tired eyes that must close, the feeling that through his closed eyelids he could yet see something moving in the center of the star that the two triangles made.

"Where do you want to go to?" said the same soft small voice that had spoken before. But this time Dickie did not reply that he was "not particular." instead, he said, "Oh, *there!* I want to go there!" feeling quite sure that whoever owned that voice would know as well as he, or even better, where "there" was, and how to get to it.

And as on that other night everything grew very quiet, and sleep wrapped Dickie round like a soft garment. When he awoke he lay in the big four-post bed with the green and white curtains; about him were the tapestry walls and the heavy furniture of The Dream.

"Oh!" he cried aloud, "I've found it again!—I've found it!—I've found it!"

And then the old nurse with the hooped petticoats and the queer cap and the white ruff was bending over him; her wrinkled face was alight with love and tenderness.

"So thou'rt awake at last," she said. "Did'st thou find thy friend in thy dreams?"

Dickie hugged her.

"I've found the way back," he said; "I don't know which is the dream and which is real—but *you* know."

"Yes," said the old nurse, "I know. The one is as real as the other."

He sprang out of bed and went leaping round the room, jumping on to chairs and off them, running and dancing.

"What ails the child?" the nurse grumbled; "get thy hose on, for shame, taking a chill as like as not. What ails thee to act so?"

"It's the not being lame," Dickie explained, coming to a standstill by the window that looked out on the good green garden. "You don't know how wonderful it seems, just at first, you know, *not* to be lame."

Buried Treasure

And then, as he stood there in the sunshine, he suddenly knew.

Having succeeded in dreaming once again the dream which he had so longed to dream, Dickie Harding looked out of the window of the dream-house in Deptford into the dream-garden with its cut yew-trees and box avenues and bowling-greens, and perceived without doubt that this was no dream, but real—as real as the other Deptford where he had sown Artistic Bird Seed and gathered moon flowers and reaped the silver seeds of magic, for it *was* magic. Dickie was sure of it now. He had not lived in the time of the First James, he sure, without hearing magic talked of. And it seemed quite plain to him that if this that had happened to him was not magic, then there never was and never would be any magic to happen to anyone. He turned from the window and looked at the tapestry-hung room—the big bed, the pleasant, wrinkled face of the nurse—and he knew that all this was as real as anything that had happened to him in that other life where he was a little lame boy who took the road with a dirty tramp for father, and lay in the bed with green curtains.

"Was thy friend well, in thy dream?" the nurse asked.

"Yes, oh, yes," said Dickie, "and I carved boxes in my dream, and sold them, and did want to learn a lot more things, so that when I go back again—I mean when I dream again—I shall be able to earn more money."

"'Tis shame that one of thy name should have to work for money," said the nurse.

"It *isn't* my name there," said Dickie; "and old Sebastian told me everyone ought to do some duty to his country, or he wasn't worth his meat and ale. And you don't know how good it is having money that you've *earned yourself*."

"I ought to," she said; "I've earned mine long enough. Now haste and dress—and then breakfast and thy fencing lesson."

When the fencing lesson was over, Dickie hesitated. He wanted, of course, to hurry off to Sebastian and to go on learning how to make a galleon. But also he wanted to learn some trade that he could teach Beale at Deptford, and he knew, quite as surely as any master craftsman could have known it, that nothing which required delicate handling, such as wood-carving or the making of toy boats, could ever be mastered by Beale. But Beale was certainly fond of dogs. Dickie remembered how little True had cuddled up to him and nestled inside his coat when he lay down to sleep under the newspapers and the bits of sacking in Lavender Terrace, Rosemary Lane.

So Dickie went his way to the kennels to talk to the kennelman. He had been there before with Master Roger Fry, his fencing master, but he had never spoken to the kennelman. And when he got to the kennels he knocked on the door of the kennelman's house and called out, "What ho! within there!" just as people do in old plays. And the door was thrown open by a man in a complete suit of leather, and when Dickie looked in that man's face he saw that it was the face of the man who had lived next door in Lavender Terrace, Rosemary Lane—the man who dug up the garden for the parrot seed.

"Why," said Dickie, "it's you!"

"Who would it be but me, little master?" the man asked with a respectful salute, and Dickie perceived that though this man had the face of the Man Next Door, he had not the Man Next Door's memories.

"Do you live here?" he asked cautiously—"always, I mean."

"Where else should I live?" the man asked, "that have served my lord, your father, all my time, boy and man, and know every hair of every dog my lord owns."

Dickie thought that was a good deal to know—and so it was.

He stayed an hour at the kennels and came away knowing very much more about dogs than he did before, though some of the things he learned would surprise a modern veterinary surgeon very much indeed. But the dogs seemed well and happy, though they were doctored with herb tea instead of stuff from the chemist's, and the charms that were said over them to make them swift and strong certainly did not make them any the less strong and swift.

When Dickie had learned as much about dogs as he felt he could bear for that day, he felt free to go down to the dockyard and go on learning how ships were built. Sebastian looked up at the voice and ceased the blows with which his axe was smoothing a great tree trunk that was to be a mast, and smiled in answer to his smile.

"Oh, what a long time since I have seem thee!" Dickie cried.

And Sebastian, gently mocking him, answered, "A great while indeed—two whole long days. And those thou'st spent merrymaking in the King's water pageant. Two days—a great while, a great, great while."

"I want you to teach me everything you know," said Dickie, picking up an awl and feeling its point.

"Have patience with me," laughed Sebastian; "I will teach thee all thou canst learn, but not all in one while. Little by little, slow and sure."

"OH, WHAT A LONG TIME SINCE I HAVE SEEN THEE!" DICKIE CRIED.

"You must not think," said Dickie, "that it 's only play, and that I do not need to learn because I am my father's son."

"Should I think so?" Sebastian asked; "I that have sailed with Captain Drake and Captain Raleigh, and seen how a gentleman venturer needs to turn his hand to every guess craft? If thou's so pleased to learn as Sebastian is to teach, then he'll be as quick to teach as thou to learn. And so to work!"

He fetched out from the shed the ribs of the little galleon that he and Dickie had begun to put together, and the two set to work on it. It was a happy day. And one happiness was to all the other happiness of that day as the sun is to little stars—and that happiness was the happiness of being once more a little boy who did not need to use a crutch.

And now the beautiful spacious life opened once more for Dickie, and he learned many things and found the days all good and happy and all the nights white and peaceful, in the big house and the beautiful garden on the slopes above Deptford. And the nights had no dreams in them, and in the days Dickie lived gaily and worthily, the life of the son of a great and noble house, and now he had no prickings of conscience about Beale, left alone in the little house in Deptford. Because one day he said to his nurse—

"How long did it take me to dream that dream about making the boxes and earning the money in the ugly place I told you of?"

"Dreams about that place," she answered him, "take none of *our* time here. And dreams about this place take none of what is time in that other place."

"But my dream endured all night," objected Dickie.

"Not so," said the nurse, smiling between her white cap frills. "It was *after* the dream that sleep came—a whole good nightful of it."

So Dickie felt that for Beale no time at all had passed, and that when he went back—which he meant to do—he would get back to Deptford at the same instant as he left it. Which is the essence of this particular kind of white magic. And thus it happened that when he did go back to Mr. Beale he went because his heart called him, and not for any other reason at all.

Days and weeks and months went by and it was autumn, and the apples were ripe on the trees, and the grapes ripe on the garden walls and trellises. And then came a day when all the servants seemed suddenly to go mad—a great rushing madness of mops and brooms and dusters and pails and everything in the house already perfectly clean was cleaned anew, and everything that was already polished was polished freshly, and when Dickie had been turned out to three rooms one after the other, had tumbled over a pail and had a dishcloth pined to his doublet by an angry cook, he sought out the nurse, very busy in the linen-room, and asked her what all the fuss was about.

"It can't be a spring-cleaning," he said, "because it's the wrong time of the year."

"Never say I did not tell thee," she answered, unfolding a great embroidered cupboard cloth and holding it up critically. "Tomorrow thy father and mother come home, and thy baby brother, and today sennight they little cousins come to visit thee."

"How perfectly glorious!" said Dickie. "But you *didn't* tell me."

"If I didn't 'twas because you never asked."

"I—I didn't dare to," he said dreamily; "I was so afraid. You see, I've seen them."

"Afraid?" she said, laying away the folded cloth and taking out another from the deep press, oaken, with smooth-worn, brown iron hinges and lock; "never seen thy father and mother, forsooth!"

"Perhaps it was the fever," said Dickie, feeling rather deceitful. "You said it made me forget things. I don't remember them. Not at all, I don't."

"Do not say that to them," the nurse said, looking at him very gravely.

"I won't. Unless they ask me," he added. "Oh, nurse, let me do something too. What can I do to help?"

"Thou canst gather such flowers as are left in the garden to make a nosegay for thy mother's room; and set them in order in fair water. And bid thy tutor teach thee a welcome song to say to them when they come in."

Gathering the flowers and arranging them was pleasant and easy. Asking so intimate a favor from the sour-faced tutor whom he so much disliked was neither easy nor pleasant. But Dickie did it. And the tutor was delighted to set him to learn a particularly hard and uninteresting piece of poetry, beginning—

> "Happy is he
>   Who, to sweet home retired,
>   Shuns glory so admired
> And to himself lives free;
> While he who strives with pride to climb the skies
> Falls down with foul disgrace before he dies."

Dickie could not help thinking that the father and mother who were to be his in this beautiful world might have preferred something simple and more affectionate from their little boy than this difficult piece whose last verse was the only one which seemed to Dickie to mean nothing in particular. In this verse Dickie was made to remark that he hoped people would say of him, "He died a good old man," which he did *not* hope, and indeed had never so much as thought of. The poetry, he decided, would have been nicer if it had been more about his father and mother and less about fame and trees and burdens. He felt this so much that he tried to write a poem himself, and got as far as—

"They say there is no other
Can take the place of mother.
I say there is no one I'd rather
See than my father."

But he could not think of any more to say, and besides, he had a haunting idea that the first two lines—which were quite the best—were not his own make-up. So he abandoned the writing of poetry, deciding that it was not his line, and painfully learned the dismal verses appointed by his tutor.

But he never got them said. When the bustle of arrival had calmed a little, Dickie, his heart beating very fast indeed, found himself led by his tutor into the presence of the finest gentleman and the dearest lady he had ever beheld. The tutor gave him a little push so that he had to go forward two steps and to stand alone on the best carpet, which had been spread in their honor, and hissed in a savage whisper—

"Recite your song of welcome."

"'Happy the man,'" began Dickie, in tone of gloom, and tremblingly pronounced the first lines of that unpleasing poem.

But he had not got to "strive with pride" before the dear lady caught him in her arms, exclaiming, "Bless my dear son! how he has grown!" and the fine gentleman thumped him on the back, and bade him "bear himself like a gentleman's son, and not like a queasy squaretoes." And they both laughed, and he cried a little, and the tutor seemed to be blotted out, and there they were, all three as jolly as if they had known each other all their lives. And a stout young nurse brought the baby, and Dickie loved it and felt certain it loved him, though it only said "Goo ga goo," exactly as your baby brother does now, and got hold of Dickie's hair and pulled it and would not let go.

There was a glorious dinner, and Dickie waited on this new father of his, changed his plate, and poured wine out of a silver jug into the silver cup that my lord drank from. And after dinner the dear lady-mother must go all over the house to see everything, because she had been so long away, and Dickie walked in the garden among the ripe apples and grapes with his father's hand on his shoulder, the happiest, proudest boy in all Deptford—or in all Kent either.

His father asked what he had learned, and Dickie told, dwelling, perhaps, more on the riding, and the fencing, and the bowls, and the music than on the sour-faced tutor's side of the business.

"But I've learned a lot of Greek and Latin, too," he added in a hurry, "and poetry and things like that."

"I fear," said the father, "thou dost not love thy book."

"I do, sir; yet I love my sports better," said Dickie, and looked up to meet the fond, proud look of eyes as blue as his own.

"Thou'rt a good, modest lad," said his father when they began their third round of the garden, "not once to ask for what I promised thee."

Dickie could not stand this, "I might have asked," he said presently, "but I have forgot what the promise was—the fever—"

"Ay, ay, poor lad! And of a high truth, too! Owned he had forgot! Come, jog that poor peaked remembrance."

Dickie could hardly believe the beautiful hope that whispered in his ear.

"I almost think I remember," he said. "Father—did you promise—?"

"I promised, if thou wast a good lad and biddable and constant at thy book and thy manly exercises, to give thee, so soon as thou should'st have learned to ride him—"

"A little horse?" said Dickie breathlessly; "oh, father, not a little horse?" It was good to hear one's father laugh that big, jolly laugh—to feel one's fathers's arm laid like that across one's shoulders.

The little horse turned round to look at them from his stall in the big stables. It was really rather a big horse.

What colored horse would you choose—if a horse were to be yours for the choosing? Dickie would have chosen a grey, and a grey it was.

"What is his name?" Dickie asked, when he had admired the grey's every point, had had him saddled, and had ridden him proudly round the pasture in his father's sight.

"We call him Rosinante," said his father, "because he is so fat," and he laughed, but Dickie did not understand the joke. He had not read "Don Quixote," as you, no doubt, have.

"I should like," said Dickie, sitting square on the grey, "to call him Crutch. May I?"

"*Crutch?*" the father repeated.

"Because his paces are so easy," Dickie explained. He got off the horse very quickly and came to his father. "I mean even a lame boy could ride him. Oh! father, I am so happy!" he said, and burrowed his nose in a velvet doublet, and perhaps snivelled a little. "I am so glad I am not lame."

"Fancy-full as ever," said his father; "come, come! Thou'rt weak yet from the fever. Be a man. Remember of what blood thou art. And thy mother—she also hath a gift for thee—from thy grandfather. Hast thou forgotten that? It hangs to the book learning. A reward—and thou hast earned it."

"I've forgotten that, too," said Dickie. "You aren't vexed because I forget? I can't help it, father."

"That I'll warrant thou cannot. Come, now, to thy mother. My little son! The Earl of Scilly chid me but this summer for sparing the rod and spoiling the child. But thy growth in all this bears out in what I answered him. I said: 'The boys of our house, my lord, take that pride in it that they learn of their own free will what many an earl's son must be driven to with rods.' He took me. His own son is little better than an idiot, and naught but the rod to blame for it, I verily believe."

They found the lady-mother and her babe by a little fire in a wide hearth.

"Our son comes to claim the guerdon of learning," the father said. And the lady stood up with the babe in her arms.

"Call the nurse to take him," she said. But Dickie held out his arms.

"Oh, mother," he said, and it was the first time in all his life that he had spoken that word to any one. "Mother, do let me hold him."

A warm, stiff bundle was put into his careful arms, and his little brother instantly caught at his hair. It hurt, but Dickie liked it.

The lady went to one of the carved cabinets and with a bright key from a very bright bunch unlocked once of the heavy panelled doors. She drew out of the darkness within a dull-colored leather bag embroidered in gold thread and crimson silk.

"He has forgot," said Sir Richard in an undertone, "what it was that the grandfather promised him. Though he has well earned the same. 'Tis the fever."

The mother put the bag in Dickie's hands.

"Count it out," she said, taking her babe from him; and Dickie untied the leathern string, and poured out on to the polished long table what the bag held. Twenty gold pieces.

"And all with the image of our late dear Queen," said the mother; "the image of that incomparable virgin Majesty whose example is a beacon for all time to all virtuous ladies."

"Ah, yes, indeed," said the father; "put them up in the bag, boy. They are thine own to thee, to spend as thou wilt."

"Not unwisely," said the mother gently.

"As he wills," the father firmly said; "wisely or unwisely. As he wills. And none," he added, "shall ask how they be spent."

The lady frowned; she was a careful housewife, and twenty gold pieces were a large sum.

IT HURT, BUT DICKIE LIKED IT.

"I will not waste it," said Dickie. "Mother, you may trust me not to waste it."

It was the happiest moment of his life to Dickie. The little horse—the gold pieces. . . . Yes, but much more, the sudden, good, safe feeling of father and mother and little brother; of a place where he belonged, where he loved and was loved. And by his equals. For he felt that, as far as a child can be the equal of grown people, he was the equal of these. And Beale was not his equal, either in the graces of the body or in the inner treasures of mind and heart. And hitherto he had loved only Beale; had only, so far as he could remember, been loved by Beale and by that shadowy father, his "Daddy," who had died in hospital, and dying, had given him the rattle, his Tinkler, that was Harding's Luck. And in the very heart of that happiest moment came, like a sharp dagger prick, the thought of Beale. What wonders could be done for Beale with those twenty gold sovereigns? For Dickie thought of them just as sovereigns—and so they were.

And as these people who loved him, who were his own, drew nearer and nearer to his heart, his heart, quickened by love of them, felt itself drawn more and more to Mr. Beale. Mr. Beale, the tramp, who had been kind to him when no one else was. Mr. Beale, the tramp and housebreaker.

So when the nurse took him, tired with new happinesses, to that beautiful tapestried room of his, he roused himself from his good soft sleepiness to say—

"Nurse, you know a lot of things, don't you?"

"I know what I know," she answered, undoing buttons with speed and authority.

"You know that other dream of mine—that dream of mine, I mean, the dream of a dreadful place?"

"And then?"

"Could I take anything out of this dream—I mean out of this time into the other one?"

"You could, but you must bring it back when you come again. And you could bring things thence. Certain things: your rattle, your moon-seeds, your seal."

He stared at her.

"You *do* know things," he said; "but I want to take things there and leave them there."

She knitted thoughtful brows.

"There's three hundred thick years between now and then," she said. "Oh, yes, I know. And if you held it in your hand, you'd lose it like as not in some of the years you go through. Money's mortal heavy and travels slow. Slower than the soul of you, my lamb. Someone would have time to see it and snatch it and hold to it."

"Isn't there any way?" Dickie asked, insisting to himself that he wasn't sleepy.

"There's the way of everything—the earth," she said; "bury it, and lie down on the spot where it's buried, and then, when you get back into the other dream, the kind, thick earth will have hid your secret, and you can dig it up again. It will be there . . . unless other hands have dug there in the three hundred years. You must take your chance of that."

"Will you help me?" Dickie asked. "I shall need to dig it very deep if I am to cheat three hundred years. And suppose," he added, struck by a sudden and unpleasing thought, "there's a house built on the place. I should be mixed up with the house. Two things can't be in the same place at the same time. My tutor told me that. And the house would be so much stronger than me—it would get the best of it, and where should I be then?"

"I'll ask where thou'd be," was the very surprising answer. "I'll ask someone who knows. But it'll take time—put thy money in the great press, and I'll keep the key. And next Friday as ever is, come your little cousins."

They came. It was more difficult with them than it was with the grown-ups to conceal the fact that he had not always been the Dickie he was now; but it was not so difficult as you might suppose. It was no harder than not talking about the dreams you had last night.

And now he had indeed a full life: headwork, bodily exercises, work, home life, and joyous hours of play with two children who understood play as the poor little, dirty Deptford children do not and cannot understand it.

He lived and learned, and felt more and more that this was the life to which he really belonged. And days and weeks and months went by and nothing happened, and that is the happiest thing than can happen to anyone who is already happy.

Then one night the nurse said—

"I have asked. You are to bury your treasure down under the window of the solar parlor, and lie down and sleep on it. You'll take no harm, and when you're asleep I will say the right words, and you'll wake under the same skies and not under a built house, like as your feared."

She wrapped him in a warm cloth mantle of her own, when she took him from his bed that night after all the family were asleep, and put on his shoes and led him to the hole she had secretly dug below the window. They had put his embroidered leather bag of gold in a little wrought-iron coffer that tightly fastened the join of lid and box with wax and resin. The box was wrapped in a silk scarf, and the whole packet put into a big earthenware jar with a lid, and the join of lid and jar was smeared with resin and covered with clay. The nurse had shown him how to do all this.

"Against the earth spirits and the three hundred years," she said.

Now she lifted the jar into the hole, and together they filled the hole with earth, treading it in with their feet.

"And when you would return," said the nurse, "you know the way."

"Do I?"

"You lay the rattle, the seal, and the moonseeds as before, and listen to the voices."

And then Dickie lay down in the cloth cloak, and the nurse sat by him and held his hand till he fell asleep. It was June now, and the scent of the roses was very sweet, and the nightingales kept him awake awhile. But the sky overhead was an old friend of his, and as he lay he could see the shining of the dew among the grass blades of the lawn. It was pleasant to lie again in the bed with the green curtains.

When he awoke there was his old friend the starry sky, and for a moment he wondered. Then he remembered. He raised himself on his elbow. There were houses all about—little houses with lights in some of the windows. A broken paling was quite close to him. There was no grass near, only rough trample earth; the smell all about him was not of roses, but of dust-bins, and there were no nightingales—but far away he could hear that restless roar that is the voice of London, and near at hand the foolish song and unsteady footfall of a man going home from the "Cat and Whistle." He scratched across on the hard ground with a broken bit of a plate to mark the spot, got up and crept on hands and knees to the house, climbed in and found the room where Beale lay asleep.

$$*\quad*\quad*\quad*\quad*$$

"Father," said Dickie, next morning, as Mr. Beale stretched and grunted and rubbed sleepy eyes with his unwashed fists in the cold daylight that filled the front room of 15, Lavender Terrace, Rosemary Lane. "You got to take this house—that's what you got to do: you remember."

"Can't say I do," said Beale, scratching his head; "but if the nipper says so, it *is* so. Let's go and get a mug and a doorstep, and then we'll see."

"You get it—if you're hungry," said Dickie. "I'd rather wait here in case anybody else was to take the house. You go and see 'im now. "E'll think you're a man in reglar work by your being up so early."

"P'raps," said Beale thoughtfully, running his hand over the rustling stubble of his two-days' beard—"p'raps I'd best get a wash and brush-up first, eh? It might be worth it in the end. I'll 'ave to go to the doss to get our pram and things, any'ow."

The landlord of the desired house really thought Mr. Beale a quite respectable working man, and Mr. Beale accounted for their lack of furniture by saying, quite truthfully, that he and his nipper had come up from Gravesend, doing a bit of work on the way.

"I could," he added, quite untruthfully, "give you the gentleman I worked with for me reference—Talbott, 'is name is—a bald man with a squint and red ears—but p'raps this'll do as well." He pulled out of one pocket all their money—two pounds eighteen shillings—except six pennies which he had put in the other pocket to rattle. He rattled them now, "I'm anxious," he said, confidentially, "to get settled on account of the nipper. I don't deceive you; we 'oofed it up, not to waste our little bit, and he's a hoppy chap."

"That's odd," said the landlord; "there was a lame boy lived there along of the last party that had it. It's a cripple's home by rights, I should think."

Beale had not foreseen this difficulty, and had no story ready. So he tried the truth.

"It's the same lad, mister," he said; "that's why I'm rather set on the 'ouse. You see, it's 'ome to 'im like," he added sentimentally.

"You 'is father?" said the landlord sharply. And again Beale was inspired to truthfulness—quite a lot of it.

"No," he said cautiously, "wish I was. The fact is, the little chap's aunt wasn't much class. An' I found 'im wandering. An' not 'avin' none of my own, I sort of adopted 'im."

"Like Wandering Hares at the theater," said the landlord, who had been told by Dickie's aunt that the ungrateful little varmint had run away. "I see."

"And 'e's a jolly little chap," said Beale, warming to his subject and forgetting his caution, "as knowing as a dog-ferret; and his patter—enough to make a cat laugh, 'e is sometimes. And I'll pay a week down if you like, mister—and we'll get our bits of sticks in today."

"Well," said the landlord, taking a key from a nail on the wall, "let's go down and have a look at the 'ouse. Where's the kid?"

"'E's there awaitin' for me," said Beale; "couldn't get 'im away."

Dickie was very polite to the landlord, at whom in unhappier days he had sometimes made faces, and when the landlord went he had six of their shillings and they had the key.

"So now we've got a 'ome of our own," said Beale, rubbing his hands when they had gone through the house together; "an Englishman's 'ome is 'is castle—and what with the boxes you'll cut out and the dogs what I'll pick up, Buckingham Palace'll look small alongside of us—eh, matey?"

They locked up the house and went to breakfast, Beale gay as a lark and Dickie rather silent. He was thinking over a new difficulty. It was all very well to bury twenty sovereigns and to know exactly where they were. And they were his own beyond a doubt. But if anyone saw those sovereigns dug up, those sovereigns would be taken away from him. No one would believe that they were his own. And the earthenware pot was so big. And so many windows looked out on the garden. No one could hope to dig up a big thing like that from his back garden without attracting some attention. Besides, he doubted whether he were strong enough to dig it up, even if he could do so unobserved. He had not thought of this when he had put the gold there in that other life. He was so much stronger then. He sighed.

"Got the 'ump, mate?" asked Beale, with his mouth full.

"No, I was just a-thinkin'."

"We'd best buy the sticks first thing," said Beale; "it's a cruel world. No sticks, no trust is the landlord's motto."

Do you want to know what sticks they bought? I will tell you. They bought a rusty old bedstead, very big, with laths that hung loose like a hammock, and all its knobs gone and only bare screws sticking up spikily. Also a flock mattress and pillows of a dull dust color to go on the bed, and some blankets and sheets, all matching the mattress to a shade. They bought a table and two chairs, and a kitchen fender with a round steel moon—only it was very rusty—and a hand-bowl for the sink, and a small zinc bath, "to wash your shirt in," said Mr. Beale. Four plates, two cups and saucers, two each of knives, forks, and spoons, a tin teapot, a quart jug, a pail, a bit of Kidder-mister carpet, half a pound of yellow soap, a kettle, a saucepan and a baking-dish, and a pint of paraffin. Also there was a tin lamp to hang on the wall with a dazzling crinkled tin reflector. This was the only thing that was new, and it cost tenpence halfpenny. all the rest of the things together cost twenty-six shillings and sevenpence halfpenny, and I think they were cheap.

But they seemed very poor and very little of them when they were dumped down in the front room. The bed especially looked far from its best—a mere heap of loose iron.

"And we ain't got our droring-room suit, neither," said Mr. Beale. "Lady's and gent's easy-chairs, four hoccasionals, pianner, and foomed oak booreau."

"Curtains," said Dickie—"white curtains for the parlor and short blinds everywhere else. I'll go and get 'em while you clean the winders. That old shirt of mine. It won't hang through another washing. Clean 'em with that."

"You don't give your orders, neither," said Beale contentedly.

The curtains and a penn'orth of tacks, an hammer borrowed from a neighbor, and an hour's cheerful work completed the fortification of the Englishman's house against the inquisitiveness of passers-by. But the landlord frowned anxiously as he went past the house.

"Don't like all that white curtain," he told himself; "not much be'ind it, if you ask me. People don't go to that extreme in Nottingham lace without there's something to hide—a house full of emptiness, most likely."

Inside Dickie was telling a very astonished Mr. Beale that there was money buried in the garden.

"It was give me," said he, "for learning of something—and we've got to get it up so as no one sees us. I can't think of nothing but build a chicken-house and then dig inside of it. I wish I was cleverer. Here Ward would have thought of something first go off."

"Don't you worry," said Beale; "you're clever enough for this poor world. *You're* all right. Come on out and show us where you put it. Just peg with yer foot on the spot, looking up careless at the sky."

They went out. And Dickie put his foot on the cross he had scratched with the broken bit of plate. It was close to the withered stalk of the moonflower.

"This 'ere garden's in a poor state," said Beale in a loud voice; "wants turning over's what *I* think—against the winter. I'll get a spade and 'ave a turn at it this very day, so I will. This 'ere old artichook's got some roots, I lay."

The digging began at the fence and reached the moonflower, whose roots were indeed deep. Quite a hole Mr. Beale dug before the tall stalk sloped and fell with slow dignity, like a forest tree before the axe. Then the man and the child went in and brought out the kitchen table and chairs, and laid blankets over them to air in the autumn sunlight. Dickie played at houses under the table—it was not the sort of game he usually played, but the neighbors could not know that. The table happened to be set down just over the hole that had held the roots of the moonflower. Dickie dug a little with a trowel in the blanket house.

After dark they carried the blankets and things in. Then one of the blankets was nailed up over the top-floor window, and on the iron bedstead's dingy mattress the resin was melted from the lid of the pot that Mr. Beale had brought in with the other things from the garden. Also it was melted from the crack of the iron casket. Mr. Beale's eyes, always rather prominent, almost resembled the eyes of the lobster or the snail as their gaze fell on the embroidered leather bag. And when Dickie opened this and showered the twenty gold coins into a hollow of the drab ticking, he closed his eyes and sighed, and opened them again and said—

"*Give* you? They give you that. I don't believe you."

"You got to believe me," said Dickie firmly. "I never told you a lie, did I?"

"Come to think of it, I don't know as you ever did," Beale admitted.

"Well," said Dickie, "they was give me—see?"

"We'll never change 'em, though," said Beale despondently. "We'd get lagged for a cert. They'd say we pinched 'em."

"No, they won't. 'Cause I've got a friend as'll change 'em for me, and then we'll 'ave new clobber and some more furniture, and a carpet and a crockery basin to wash our hands and faces in 'stead of that old tin thing. And a bath we'll 'ave. And you shall buy some more pups. And I'll get some proper carving tools. And our fortune's made. See?"

"You nipper," said Beale, slowly and fondly, "the best day's work ever I done was when I took up with you. You're straight, you are—one of the best. Many's the boy would 'ave done a bunk and took the sinners along with him. But you stuck to old Beale, and he'll stick to you."

"That's all right," said Dickie, beginning to put the bright coins back into the bag.

"But it ain't all right," Beale insisted stubbornly; "it ain't no good. I must 'ave it all out, or bust. I didn't never take you along of me 'cause I fancied you like what I said. I was just a-looking out for a nipper to shove through windows—see?—along of that red-headed chap what you never see eyes on."

"I've known that a long time," said Dickie, gravely watching the candle flicker on the bare mantelshelf.

"I didn't mean no good to you, not at first I didn't," said Beale, "when you wrote on the sole of my boot. I'd bought that bit of paper and pencil a-purpose. There!"

"You ain't done me no 'arm, anyway," said Dickie.

"No—I know I ain't. 'Cause why? 'Cause I took to you the very first day. I allus been kind to you—you can't say I ain't." Mr Beale was confused by the two desires which make it difficult to confess anything truthfully—the desire to tell the worst of oneself and the desire to do full justice to oneself at the same time. It is so very hard not to blacken the blackness, or whiten the whiteness, when one comes to trying to tell the truth about oneself. "But I been a beast all the same," said Mr. Beale helplessly.

"Oh, stow it!" Dickie said; "now you've told me, it's all square."

"You won't keep a down on me for it?"

"Now, should I?" said Dickie, exasperated and very sleepy. "Now all is open as the day and we can pursue our career as honorable men and comrades in all high emprise. I mean," he explained, noticing Mr. Beale's open mouth and eyes more lobster-like than ever—"I mean that's all right, farver, and you see it don't make any difference to me. I knows you're straight now, even if it didn't begin just like that. Let's get to be, shan't us?"

Mr. Beale dreamed that he was trying to drown Dickie in a pond full of stewed eels. Dickie didn't dream at all.

*   *   *   *   *

You may wonder why, since going to the beautiful other world took no time and was so easy, Dickie did not do it every night, or even at odd times during the day.

Well, the fact was he dared not. He loved the other life so much that he feared that, once again there, he might not have the courage to return to Mr. Beale and Deptford and the feel of dirty clothes and the smell of dust-bins. It was no light thing to come back from that to this. And now he made a resolution—that he would not set out the charm to Tinkler and seal and moon-seeds until he had established Mr. Beale in an honorable calling and made a life for him in which he could be happy. A great undertaking for a child? Yes. But then Dickie was not an ordinary child, or none of these adventures would ever have happened to him.

The pawnbroker, always a good friend to Dickie, had the wit to see that the child was not lying when he said that the box and the bag and the gold pieces had been given to him.

He changed the gold pieces stamped with the image of Queen Elizabeth for others stamped with the image of Queen Victoria. And he gave five pounds for the wrought-iron box, and owned that he should make a little—a very little—out of it. "And if your grand society friends give you any more treasures, you know the house to come to—the fairest house in the trade, though I say it."

"Thank you very much," said Dickie; "you've been a good friend to me. I hope some day I shall do you a better turn than the little you make out of my boxes and things."

The pawnbroker sold the wrought-iron box that very week for twenty guineas.

And Dickie and Mr Beale now possessed twenty-seven pounds. New clothes were bought — more furniture. Twenty-two pounds of the money was put in the savings bank. Dickie bought carving tools and went to the Goldsmiths' Institute to learn to use them. The front bedroom was fitted with a bench for Dickie. The back sitting-room was a kennel for the dogs which Mr. Beale instantly began to collect. The front room was a parlor—a real parlor. A decent young woman—Amelia by name—was engaged to come in every day and "do for" them. The clothes they wore were clean; the food they ate was good. Dickie's knowledge of an ordered life in a great house helped him to order life in a house that was little. And day by day they earned their living. The new life was fairly started. And now Dickie felt that he might dare to go back through the three hundred years to all that wa waiting for him there.

"But I will only stay a month," he told himself, "a month here and a month there, that will keep things even. Because if I were longer there than I am here I should not be growing up so fast here as I should there. And everything would be crooked. And how silly if I were a grown man in that life and had to come back and be a little boy in this!"

I do not pretend that the idea did not occur to Dickie, "Now that Beale is fairly started he could do very well without me." But Dickie knew better. He dismissed the idea. Besides, Beale had been good to him and he loved him.

The white curtains had now no sordid secrets to keep—and when the landlord called for the rent Mr. Beale was able to ask him to step in—into a comfortable room with a horsehair sofa and a big, worn easy-chair, a carpet, four old mahogany chairs, and a table with a clean blue-and-red checked cloth on it. There was a bright clock on the mantelpiece, and vases with chrysanthemums in them, and there were red woollen curtains as well as the white lace ones.

"You're as snug as snug in here," said the landlord.

"Not so dusty," said Beale, shining from soap; "'ave a look at my dawgs?"

He succeeded in selling the landlord a pup for ten shillings and came back to Dickie sitting by the pleasant firelight.

"It's all very smart," he said, "but don't you never feel the fidgits in your legs? I've kep' steady, and keep steady I will. But in the spring—when the weather gets a bit open—what d'you say to shutting up the little 'ouse and taking the road for a bit? Gentlemen do it even," he added wistfully. "Walking towers they call 'em."

"I'd like it," said Dickie, "but what about the dogs?"

"Oh! Amelia'd do for them a fair treat, all but Fan and Fly, as 'ud go along of us. I dunno what it is," he said, "makes me 'anker so after the road. I was always like it from a boy. Couldn't get me to school, so they couldn't —allus after birds' nests or rabbits or the like. Not but what I like it well enough were I was bred. I didn't tell you, did I, we passed close longside our old 'ome that time we slep' among the furze bushes? I don't s'pose my father's alive now. But 'e was a game old chap—shouldn't wonder but what he'd stuck it out."

"Let's go and see him some day," said Dickie.

"I dunno," said Beale: "you see, I was allus a great hanxiety to 'im. And besides, I shouldn't like to find 'im gone. Best not know nothing. That's what I say."

But he sighed as he said it, and he filled his pipe in a thoughtful silence.

Dickie Learns Many Things

That night Dickie could not sleep. And as he lay awake a great resolve grew strong within him. He would try once more the magic of the moon-seeds and the rattle and the white seal, and try to get back into that other world. So he crept down into the parlor where a little layer of clear, red fire still burned.

And now the moon-seeds and the voices and the magic were over and Dickie awoke, thrilled to feel how cleverly he had managed everything, moved his legs in the bed, rejoicing that he was no longer lame. Then he opened his eyes to feast them on the big, light tapestried room. But the room was not tapestried. It was panelled. And it was rather dark. And it was so small as not to be much better than a cupboard.

This surprised Dickie more than anything else that had ever happened to him, and it frightened him a little too. If the spell of the moon-seeds and the rattle and the white seal was not certain to take him where he wished to be, nothing in the world was certain. He might be anywhere where he didn't wish to be—he might be anyone whom he did not wish to be.

"I'll never try it again," he said: "if I get out of this I'll stick to the wood-carving, and not go venturing about any more among dreams and things."

He got up and looked out of a narrow window. From it he saw a garden, but it was not a garden he had ever seen before. It had marble seats, balustrades, and the damp dews of autumn hung chill about its almost unleafed trees.

"It might have been worse; it might have been a prison yard," he told himself. "Come, keep your heart up. Wherever I've come to it's an adventure."

He turned back to the room and looked for his clothes. There were no clothes there. But the shirt he had on was like the shirt he had slept in at the beautiful house.

He turned to open the door, and there was no door. All was dark, even panelling. He was not shut in a room but in a box. Nonsense, boxes did not have beds in them and windows.

And then suddenly he was no longer the clever person who had managed everything so admirably—who was living two lives with such credit in both, who was managing a grown man for that grown man's good; but just a little boy rather badly frightened.

The little shirt was the only thing that helped, and that only gave him the desperate courage to beat on the panels and shout, "Nurse! Nurse! Nurse—!"

A crack of light split and opened between two panels, they slid back and between them the nurse came to him—the nurse with the ruff and the frilled cap and the kind, wrinkled face.

He got his arms round her big, comfortable waist.

"There, there, my lamb!" she said, petting him. His clothes hung over her arm, his doublet and little fat breeches, his stockings and the shoes with rosettes.

"Oh, I am here—oh, I *am* so glad. I thought I'd got to somewhere different."

She sat down on the bed and began to dress him, soothing him back to confidence with gentle touches and pet names.

"Listen," she said, when it came to the silver sugar-loaf buttons of the doublet. "You must listen carefully. It is a month since you went away."

"But I thought time didn't move—I thought . . ."

"It was the money upset everything," she said; "it always does upset everything. I ought to have known. Now attend carefully. No one knows you have been away. You've seemed to be here, learning and playing and doing everything like you used. And you're on a visit now to your cousins at your uncles' town house. And you all have lessons together—thy tutor gives them. And thy cousins love him no better than thou dost. All thou hast to do is to forget thy dream, and take up thy life here—and be slow to speak, for a day or two, till thou hast grown used to thine own place. Thou'lt have lessons alone today. One of the cousins goes with his mother to be her page and bear her train at the King's revels at Whitehall, and the other must sit and sew her sampler. Her mother says she hath run wild too long."

So Dickie had lessons alone with his detested tutor, and his relief from the panic fear of the morning raised his spirits to a degree that unfortunately found vent in what was, for him, extreme naughtiness. He drew a comic picture of his tutor—it really was rather like—with a scroll coming out of his mouth, and on the scroll the words, "Because I am ugly I need not be hateful!" His tutor, who had a nasty way of creeping up behind people, came up behind him at the wrong moment. Dickie was caned on both hands and kept in. Also his dinner was of bread and water, and he had to write out two hundred times, "I am a bad boy, and I ask the pardon of my good tutor. The fifth day of November, 1608." So he did not see his aunt and cousin in their Whitehall finery—and it was quite late in the afternoon before he even saw his other cousin, who had been sampler-sewing. He would not have written out the lines, he felt sure he would not, only he thought of his cousin and wanted to see her again. For she was the only little girl friend he had.

When the last was done he rushed into the room where she was—he was astonished to find that he knew his way about the house quite well, though he could not remember ever having been there before—and cried out—

"Thy task done? Mine is, too. Old Parrot-nose kept me hard at it, but I thought of thee, and for this once I did all his biddings. So now we are free. Come play ball in the garden!"

His cousin looked up from her sampler, set the frame down and jumped up.

"I am so glad," she said. "I do hate this horrid sampler!"

And as she said it Dickie had a most odd feeling, rather as if a clock had struck, or had stopped striking—a feeling of sudden change. But he could not wait to wonder about it or to question what it was that he really felt. His cousin was waiting.

"Come, Elfrida," he said, and held out his hand. They went together into the garden.

Now if you have read a book called "The House of Arden" you will already know that Dickie's cousins were called Edred and Elfrida, and that their father, Lord Arden, had a beautiful castle by the sea, as well as a house in London, and that he and his wife were great favorites at the court of King James the First. If you have not read that book, and didn't already know these things—well, you know them now. And Arden was Dickie's own name too, in this old life, and his father was Sir Richard Arden, of Deptford and Aylesbury. And his tutor was Mr. Parados, called Parrot-nose "for short" by his disrespectful pupils.

Dickie and Elfrida played ball, and they played hide-and-seek, and they ran races. He preferred play to talk just then; he did not want to let out the fact that he remembered nothing whatever of the doings of the last month. Elfrida did not seem very anxious to talk, either. The garden was most interesting, and the only blot on the scene was the black figure of the tutor walking up and down with a sour face and his thumbs in one of his dull-looking books.

The children sat down on the step of one of the stone seats, and Dickie was wondering why he had felt that queer clock-stopping feeling, when he was roused from his wonderings by hearing Elfrida say—

"Please to remember
The Fifth of november,
The gunpowder treason and plot.
I see no reason
Why gunpowder treason
Should ever be forgot."

"How odd!" he thought. "I didn't know that was so old as all this." And he remembered hearing his father, Sir Richard Arden, say, "Treason's a dangerous word to let lie on your lips these days." So he said—

"'Tis not a merry song, cousin, nor a safe one. 'Tis best not to sing of treason."

"But it didn't come off, you know, and he's always burnt in the end."

So already Guy Fawkes burnings went on. Dickie wondered whether there would be a bonfire tonight. It *was* the Fifth of November. He had had to write the date two hundred times so he was fairly certain of it. He was afraid of saying too much or too little. And for the life of him he could not remember the date of the Gunpowder Plot. Still he must say something, so he said—

"Are there more verses?"

"No," said Elfrida.

"I wonder," he said, trying to feel his way, "what treason the ballad deals with?"

He felt it had been the wrong thing to say, when Elfrida answered in surprised tones—

"Don't you know? *I* know. And I know some of the names of the conspirators and who they wanted to kill and everything."

"Tell me" seemed the wisest thing to say, and he said it as carelessly as he could.

"The King hadn't been fair to the Catholics, you know," said Elfrida, who evidently knew all about the matter, "so a lot of them decided to kill him and the House of Parliament. They made a plot—there were a whole lot of them in it."

The clock-stopping feeling came on again. Elfrida was different somehow. The Elfrida who had gone on the barge to Gravesend and played with him at the Deptford house had never used such expressions as "a whole lot of them in it." He looked at her and she went on—

"They said Lord Arden was in it, but he wasn't, and some of them were to pretend to be hunting and to seize the Princess Elizabeth and proclaim her Queen, and the rest were to blow the Houses of Parliament up when the King went to open them."

"I never heard this tale from my tutor," said Dickie. And without knowing why he felt uneasy, and because he felt uneasy, and because he felt uneasy he laughed. Then he said, "Proceed, cousin."

Elfrida went on telling him about the Gunpowder Plot, but he hardly listened. The stopped-clock feeling was growing so strong. But he heard her say, "Mr. Tresham wrote to his relation, Lord Monteagle, that they were going to blow up the King," and he found himself saying, "What King?" though he knew the answer perfectly well.

"Why, King James the First," said Elfrida, and suddenly the horrible tutor pounced and got Elfrida by the wrist. Then all in a moment everything grew confused. Mr. Parados was asking questions and little Elfrida was trying to answer them, and Dickie understood that the Gunpowder Plot *had not happened yet*, and that Elfrida had given the whole show away. How did she know? And the verse?

"Tell me all—every name, every particular," the loathsome tutor was saying, "or it will be the worse for thee and thy father."

Elfrida was positively green with terror, and looked appealingly at Dickie.

"Come, sir," he said, in as manly a voice as he could manage, "you frighten my cousin. It is but a tale she told. She is always merry and full of many inventions."

But the tutor would not be silenced.

"And it's in history," he heard Elfrida say.

What followed was a mist of horrible things. When the mist cleared Dickie found himself alone in the house with Mr. Parados, the nurse, and the servants, for the Earl and Countess of Arden, Edred and Elfrida were lodged in the Tower of London on a charge of high treason.

For this was, it seemed, the Fifth of November, the day on which the Gunpowder Plot should have been carried out; and Elfrida it was, and not Mr. Tresham, Lord Monteagle's cousin, who had given away the whole business.

But how had Elfrida know? Could it be that she had dreams like his, and in those dreams visited later times when all this was matter of history? Dickie's brain felt fat—swollen—as though it would burst, and he was glad to go to bed—even in that cupboardy place with the panels. But he begged the nurse to leave the panel open.

And when he woke next day it was all true. His aunt and uncle and his two cousins were in the Tower and gloom hung over Arden House in Soho like a black thunder-cloud over a mountain. And the days went on, and lessons with Mr. Parados were a sort of Inquisition torture to Dickie. For the tutor never let a day pass without trying to find out whether Dickie had shared in any way that guilty knowledge of Elfrida's which had, so Mr. Parados insisted, overthrown the fell plot of the Papists and preserved to a loyal people His Most Gracious Majesty James the First.

And then one day, quite as though it were the most natural thing in the world, his cousin Edred and Lady Arden his aunt were set free from the tower and came home. The King had suddenly decided that they at least had had nothing to do with the plot. Lady Arden cried all the time, and, as Dickie owned to himself, "There was enough to make her." But Edred was full of half thought-out plans and schemes for being revenged on old Parrot-nose. And at last he really did arrange a scheme for getting Elfrida out of the Tower—a perfectly workable scheme. And what is more, it worked. If you want to know how it was done, ask some grown-up to tell you how Lady Nithsdale got her husband out of the Tower when he was a prisoner there, and in danger of having his head cut off, and you will readily understand the kind of scheme it was. A necessary part of it was the dressing up of Elfrida in boy's clothes, and her coming out of the Tower, pretending to be Edred, who, with Richard, had come in to visit Lord Arden. Then the guard at the Tower gateway was changed, and another Edred came out, and they all got into a coach, and there was Elfrida under the coach seat among the straw and other people's feet, and they all hugged each other in the dark coach as it jolted through the snowy streets to Arden House in Soho.

Dickie, feeling very small and bewildered among all these dangerous happenings, found himself suddenly caught by the arm. The nurse's hand it was.

"Now," she said, "master Richard will go take off his fine suit, and —" He did not hear the end, for he was pushed out of the room. Very discontentedly he found his way to his panelled bed-closet, and took off the smart velvet and fur which he had worn in his visit to the Tower, and put on his everyday things. You may be sure he made every possible haste to get back to his cousins. He wanted to talk over the whole wonderful adventure with them. He found them whispering in a corner.

"What is it?" he asked.

"We're going to be even with old Parrot-nose," said Edred, "but you mustn't be in it, because we're going away, and you've got to stay here, and whatever we decide to do you'll get the blame of it."

"I don't see," said Richard, "why I shouldn't have a hand in what I've wanted to do these four years." He had not known that he had known the tutor for four years, but as he said the words he felt that they were true.

"There is a reason," said Edred. "You go to bed, Richard."

"Not me," said Dickie of Deptford firmly.

"If we tell you," said Elfrida, explaining affectionately, "you won't believe us."

"You might at least," said Richard Arden, catching desperately at the grand manner that seemed to suit these times of ruff and sword and cloak and conspiracy—"you might at least make the trial."

"Very well, I will," said Elfrida abruptly. "No, Edred, he has a right to hear. He's one of us. He won't give us away. Will you, Dickie dear."

"You know I won't," Dickie assured her.

"Well, then," said Elfrida slowly, "we are . . . You listen hard and believe with both hands and with all your might, or you won't be able to believe at all. We are not what we seem, Edred and I. We don't really belong here at all. I don't know what's become of the *real* Elfrida and Edred who belong to this time. Haven't we seemed odd to you at all? Different, I mean, from the Edred and Elfrida you've been used to?"

The remembrance of the stopped-clock feeling came strongly on Dickie and he nodded.

"Well, that's because we're *not* them. We don't belong here. We belong three hundred years later in history. Only we've got a charm—because in our time Edred is Lord Arden, and there's a white mole who helps us, and we can go anywhere in history we like."

"Not quite," said Edred.

"No; but there are chests of different clothes, and whatever clothes we put on we come to that time in history. I know it sounds like silly untruths," she added rather sadly, "and I knew you wouldn't believe it, but it *is* true. And now we're going back to our times—Queen Alexandra, you know, and King Edward the Seventh and electric light and motors and 1908. Don't try to believe it if it hurts you, Dickie dear. I know it's most awfully rum—but it's the real true truth."

Richard said nothing. Had never thought it possible but that he was the only one to whom things like this happened.

"You don't believe it," said Edred complacently. "I knew you wouldn't."

Dickie felt a swimming sensation. It was impossible that this wonderful change should happen to anyone besides himself. This just meant that the whole thing was a dream. And he said nothing.

"Never mind," said Elfrida in comforting tones; "don't try to believe it. I know you can't. Forget it. Or pretend we were just kidding you."

"Well, it doesn't matter," Edred said. "What can we do to pay out old Parrot-nose?"

Then Richard found a voice and words.

"I don't understand a word you're saying," said Edred; and, darting to a corner, produced a photographic camera, of the kind called "Brownie."

"Look here," he said, "you've never seen anything like *this* before. This comes from the times we belong to."

Richard knew it well. A boy at school had had one. And he had borrowed it once. And the assistant master had had a larger one of the same kind. It was horrible to him, this intrusion of the scientific attainments of the ugly times in which he was born into the beautiful times that he had grown to love.

"Oh, stow it!" he said. "I know now it's all a silly dream. But it's not worth while to pretend I don't know a Kodak when I see it. That's a Brownie."

"If you've dreamed about our time," said Elfrida. . . . "Did you ever dream of fire carriages and fire-boats, and—"

Richard explained that he was not a baby, that he knew all about railways and steamboats and the triumphs of civilization. And added that Kent made 615 against Derbyshire last Thursday. Edred and Elfrida began to ask questions. Dickie was much too full of his own questionings to answer theirs.

"I shan't tell you anything more," he said. "But I'll help you to get even with old Parrot-nose." And suggested shoveling the snow off the roof into the room of that dismal tyrant through the skylight conveniently lighting it.

But Edred wanted that written down—about Kent and Derbyshire—so that they might see, when they got back to their own times, whether it was true. And Dickie found he had a bit of paper in his doublet on which to write it. It was a bill—he had had it in his hand when he made the magic moon-seed pattern, and it had unaccountably come with him. It was a bill for three ship's guns and compasses and six flags, which Mr. Beale had bought for him in London for the fitting out of a little ship he had made to order for the small son of the amiable pawnbroker. He scribbled on the back of this bill, gave it to Edred, and then they all went out on the roof and shovelled snow in on to Mr. Parados, and when he came out on the roof very soon and angry, they slipped round the chimney-stacks and through the trapdoor, and left him up on the roof in the snow, and shut the trapdoor and hasped it.

And then the nurse caught them and Richard was sent to bed. But he did not go. There was no sleep in that house that night. Sleepiness filled it like a thick fog. Dickie put out his rushlight and stayed quiet for a little while, but presently it was impossible to stay quiet another moment, so very softly and carefully he crept out and hid behind a tall press at the end of the passage. He felt that strange things were happening in the house and that he must know what they were. Presently there were voices below, voices coming up the stairs—the nurse's voice, his cousins', and another voice. Where had he heard that other voice? The stopped-clock feeling was thick about him as he realized that this was one of the voices he had heard on that night of the first magic—the voice that had said, "He is more yours than mine."

The light the nurse carried gleamed and disappeared up the second flight of stairs. Dickie followed. He had to follow. He could not be left out of this, the most mysterious of all the happenings that had so wonderfully come to him.

He saw, when he reached the upper landing, that the others were by the window, and that the window was open. A keen wind rushed through it, and by the blown candle's light he could see snowflakes whirled into the house through the window's dark, star-studded square. There was whispering going on. He heard her words, "Here. So! Jump."

And then a little figure—Edred it must be; no, Elfrida—climbed up on to the window-ledge. And jumped out. Out of the third-floor window undoubtedly jumped. Another followed it—that was Edred.

"It *is* a dream," said Dickie to himself, "but if they've been made to jump out, to punish them for getting even with old Parrot-nose or anything, I'll jump too."

He rushed past the nurse, past her voice and the other voice that was talking with hers, made one bound to the window, set his knee on it, stood up and jumped; and he heard, as his knee touched the icy window-sill, the strange voice say, "Another," and then he was in the air falling, falling.

"I shall wake when I reach the ground," Dickie told himself, "and then I shall know it's all only a dream, a silly dream."

But he never reached the ground. He had not fallen a couple of yards before he was caught by something soft as heaped feathers or drifted snow; it moved and shifted under him, took shape; it was a chair—no, a carriage. And there were reins in his hand—white reins. And a horse? No—a swan with wide, white wings. He grasped the reins and guided the strange steed to a low swoop that should bring side the great front door. And as the swan laid its long neck low in downward flight he saw his cousins in a carriage like his own rise into the sky and sail away towards the south. Quite without meaning to do it he pulled on the reins; the swan rose. He pulled again and the carriage stopped at the landing window.

Hands dragged him in. The old nurse's hands. The swan glided away between snow and stars, and on the landing inside the open window the nurse held him fast in her arms.

"My lamb!" she said; "my dear, foolish, brave lamb!"

Dickie was pulling himself together.

"If it's a dream," he said slowly, "I've had enough. I want to wake up. If it's real—real, with magic in it—you've got to explain it all to me—every bit. I can't go on like this. It's not fair."

"Oh, tell him and have done," said the voice that had begun all the magic, and it seemed to him that something small and white slid along the wainscot of the corridor and vanished quite suddenly, just as a candle flame does when you blow the candle out.

"I will," said the nurse. "Come, love, I *will* tell you everything." She took him down into a warm curtained room, blew to flame the grey ashes on the open hearth, gave him elder wine to drink, hot and spiced, and kneeling before him, rubbing his cold, bare feet, she told him.

"There are certain children born now and then—it does not often happen, but now and then it does—children who are not bound by time as other people are. And if the right bit of magic comes their way, those children have the power to go back and forth in time just as other children go back and forth in space—the space of a room, a playing-field, or a garden alley. Often children lose their power when they are quite young. Sometimes it comes to them gradually so that they hardly know when it begins, and leaves them as gradually, like a dream when you wake and stretch yourself. Sometimes it comes by the saying of a charm. That is how Edred and Elfrida found it. They came from the time that you were born in, and they have been living in this time with you, and now they have gone back to their own time. Didn't you notice any difference in them? From what they were at Deptford?"

"I should think I did," said Dickie—"at least, it wasn't that I *noticed* any difference so much as that I *felt* something queer. I couldn't understand it—it felt stuffy—as if something was going to burst."

"That was because they were not the cousins you knew at Deptford."

"But where have the real cousins I knew at Deptford been then—all this time—while those other kids were here pretending to be them?" Dickie asked.

"Oh, they were somewhere else—in Julius Caesar's time, to be exact—but they don't know it, and never will know it. They haven't the charm. To them it will be like a dream that they have forgotten."

"But the swans and the carriages and the voice—and jumping out of the window . . . ." Dickie urged.

"The swans were white magic—the white Mouldiwarp of Arden did all that."

Then she told him all about the white Mouldiwarp of Arden, and how it was the badge of Arden's house—its picture being engraved on Tinkler, and how it had done all sorts of magic for Edred and Elfrida, and would do still more.

Dickie and the nurse sat most of the night talking by the replenished fire, for the tale seemed endless. Dickie learned that the Edred and Elfrida who belonged to his own times had a father who was supposed to be dead. "I am forbidden to tell them," said the nurse, "but *thou* canst help them, and shalt."

"I should like that," said Dickie—"but can't *I* see the white Mouldiwarp?"

"I dare not—even *I* dare not call it again tonight," the nurse owned. "But maybe I will teach thee a little spell to bring it on another day. It is an angry little beast at times, but kindly, and hard-working."

Then Dickie told her about the beginnings of the magic, and how he had heard *two* voices, one of them the Mouldiwarp's.

"There are three white Mouldiwarps friends to thy house," she told him—"the Mouldiwarp who is the badge, and the Mouldiwarp who is the crest, and the Great Mouldiwarp who sits on the green and white checkered field of the Ardens' shield of arms. It was the first two who talked of thee."

"And how can I find my cousins and help them to find their father?"

"Lay out the moon-seeds and the other charms, and wish to be where they are going. Then thou canst speak with them. Wish to be there a week before they come, that thou mayst know the place and the folk."

"Now?" Dickie asked, but not eagerly, for he as very tired.

"Not now, my lamb," she said; and so at last Dickie went to bed, his weary brain full of new things more dreamlike than any dreams he had ever had.

After this he talked with the nurse every day, and learned more and more wonders, of which there is no time now for me to tell you. But they are all written in the book of "The House of Arden." In that book, too, it is written how Dickie went back from the First James's time to the time of the Eighth Henry, and took part in the merry country life of those days, and there found the old nurse herself, Edred and Elfrida, and helped them to recover their father from a far country. There also you may read of the marvels of the white clock, and the cliff that none could climb, and the children who were white cats, and the Mouldiwarp who became as big as a polar bear, with other wonders. And when all this was over, Elfrida and Edred wanted Dickie to come back with them to their own time. But he would not. He went back instead to the time he loved, when James the First was King. And when he woke in the little panelled room it seemed to him that all this was only dreams and fancies.

In the course of this adventure he met the white Mouldiwarp, and it was just a white mole, very funny and rather self-important. The second Mouldiwarp he had not yet met. I have told you all these things very shortly, because they were so dream-like to Dickie, and not at all real like the double life he had been leading.

"That always happens," said the nurse; "if you stumble into someone else's magic it never feels real. But if you bring them into yours it's quite another pair of sleeves. Those children can't get any more magic of their own now, but you could take them into yours. Only for that you'd have to meet them in your own time that you were born in, and you'll have to wait till it's summer, because that's where they are now. They're seven months ahead of you in your own time."

"But," said Dickie, very much bewildered, as I am myself, and as I am afraid you too must be, "if they're seven months ahead, won't they always be seven months ahead?"

"Odds bodkins," said the nurse impatiently, "how often am I to tell you that there's no such thing as time? But there's seasons, and the season they came out of was summer, and the season you'll go back to 'tis autumn—so you *must* live the seven months in their time, and then it'll be summer and you'll meet them."

"And what about Lord Arden in the Tower? Will he be beheaded for treason?" Dickie asked.

"Oh, *that's* part of their magic. It isn't in your magic at all. Lord Arden will be safe enough. And now, my lamb, I've more to tell thee. But come into thy panelled chamber where thy tutor cannot eavesdrop and betray us, and have thee given over to him wholly, and me burned for a witch."

These terrible words kept Dickie silent till he and the nurse were safe in his room, and then he said, "Come with me to my time, nurse—they don't burn people for witches there."

"No," said the nurse, "but they let them live such lives in their ugly towns that my life here with all its risks is far better worth living. Thou knowest how folk live in Deptford in thy time—how all the green trees are gone, and good work is gone, and people do bad work for just so much as will keep together their worn bodies and desolate souls. And sometimes they starve to death. And they won't burn me if thou'lt only keep a still tongue. Now listen." She sat down on the edge of the bed, and Dickie cuddled up against her stiff bodice.

"Edred and Elfrida first went into the past to look for treasure. It is a treasure buried in Arden Castle by the sea, which is their home. They want the treasure to restore the splendor of the old Castle, which in your time is fallen into ruin and decay, and to mend the houses of the tenants, and to do good to the poor and needy. But you know that now they have used their magic to get back their father, and can no longer use it to look for treasure. But your magic will hold. And if you lay out your moon-seeds round *them*, in the old shape, and stand with them in the midst, holding your Tinkler and your white seal, you will all go whithersoever you choose."

"I shall choose to go straight to the treasure, of course," said practical Dickie, swinging his feet in their rosetted shoes.

"That thou canst not. Thou canst only choose some year in the past—any year—go into it and then seek for the treasure there and then,"

"I'll do it," Dickie said, "and then I may come back to you, mayn't I?"

"If thou'rt not needed elsewhere. The Ardens stay where duty binds them, and go where duty calls."

"But I'm not an Arden *there*," said Dickie sadly.

"Thou'rt Richard Arden there as here," she said; "thy grandfather's name got changed, by breathing on it, from Arden to Harden, and that again to Harding. Thus names are

changed ever and again. And Dickie of Deptford has the honor
of the house of Arden to uphold there as here, then as now."

"I shall call myself Arden when I go back," said Dickie
proudly.

"Not yet," she said; "wait."

"If you say so," said Dickie rather discontentedly.

"The time is not ripe for thee to take up all thine honors
there," she said. "And now, dear lamb, since thy tutor is
imagining unkind things in his heart for thee, go quickly. Set
out thy moon-seeds and, when thou hearest the voices, say, 'I
would see both Mouldiwarps,' and thou shalt see them both."

"Thank you," said Dickie. "I do want to see them both."

See them he did, in a blue-grey mist in which he could feel
nothing solid, not even the ground under his feet or the touch
of his clenched fingers against his palms.

They were very white, the Mouldiwarps, outlined distinctly
against the grey blueness, and the Mouldiwarp he had seen in
that wonderful adventure in the far country smiled, as well as
a mole can, and said—

"Thou'rt a fair sprig of de old tree, Muster Dickie, so 'e
be," in the thick speech of the peasant people round about
Talbot house where Dickie had once been a little burglar.

"He is indeed a worthy scion of the great house we serve,"
said the other Mouldiwarp with precise and gentle utterance.
"As Mouldierwarp to the Ardens I can but own that I am
proud of him."

The Mouldierwarp had, as well as a gentle voice, a finer
nose than the Mouldiwarp, his fur was more even and his
claws sharper.

"Eh, you be a gentleman, you be," said the Mouldiwarp,
"so's 'e—so there's two of ye sure enough."

It was very odd to see and hear these white moles talking
like real people and looking like figures on a magic-lantern
screen. But Dickie did not enjoy it as much as perhaps you or

I would have done. it was not his pet kind of magic. He liked the good, straight-forward, old-fashioned kind of magic that he was accustomed to—the kind that just took you out of one life into another life, and made both lives as real one as the other. Still one must always be polite. So he said—

"I am very glad to see you both."

"There's purty manners," the Mouldiwarp said.

"The pleasure is ours," said the Mouldierwarp instantly. Dickie could not help seeing that both these old creatures were extremely pleased with him.

"When shall I see the other Mouldiwarp?" he asked, to keep up the conversation—"the one on our shield of arms?"

"You mean the Mouldiestwarp?" said the Mouldier, as I will now call him for short; "you will not see him till the end of the magic. He is very great. I work the magic of space, my brother here works the magic of time, and the Great Mouldiestwarp controls us, and many things beside. You must only call on him when you wish to end our magics and to work a magic greater than ours."

"What could be greater?" Dickie asked, and both the creatures looked very pleased.

"He is a worthier Arden than those little black and white chits of thine," the Mouldier said to the Mouldy (which is what, to save time, we will now call the Mouldiwarp).

"An' so should be—an' so should be," said the Mouldy shortly. "All's for the best, and the end's to come. Where'd ye want to go, my lord?"

"I'm not 'my lord'; I'm only Richard Arden," said Dickie, "and I want to go back to Mr. Beale and stay with him for seven months, and then to find my cousins."

"Back thou goes then," said the Mouldy; "that part's easy."

"And for the second half of thy wish no magic is needed but the magic of steadfast heart and the patient purpose, and these thou hast without any helping or giving of ours," said the courtly Mouldierwarp.

They waved their white paws on the grey-blue curtain of mist, and behold they were not there anymore, and the blue-grey mist was only the night's darkness turning to dawn, and Dickie was able again to feel solid things—the floor under him, his hand on the sharp edge of the arm-chair, and the soft, breathing, comfortable weight of True, asleep against his knee. He moved, the dog awoke, and Dickie felt its oft nose nuzzled into his hand.

"And now for seven months' work, and not one good dream," said Dickie, got up, put Tinkler and the seal and the moon-seeds into a very safe place, and crept back to bed.

He felt rather heroic. He did not want the treasure. It was not for him. He was going to help Edred and Elfrida to get it. He did not want the life at Lavender Terrace. He was going to help Mr. Beale to live it. So let him feel a little bit of a hero, since that was what indeed he was, even though, of course, all right-minded children are modest and humble, and fully sensible of their own intense unimportance, no matter how heroically they may happen to be behaving.

Going Home

In Deptford the seven months had almost gone by; Dickie had worked much, learned much, and earned much. Mr. Beale, a figure of cleanly habit and increasing steadiness, seemed like a plant growing quickly towards the sun of respectability, or a lighthouse rising bright and important out of a swirling sea—of dogs.

For the dog-trade prospered exceedingly, and Mr. Beale had grown knowing in thorough-breeds and the prize bench, had learned all about distemper and doggy fist, and when you should give an ailing dog sal-volatile and when you should merely give it less to eat. And the money in the bank grew till it, so to speak, burst the bank-book, and had to be allowed to overflow into a vast sea called Consols.

The dogs also grew, in numbers as well as in size, and the neighbors, who had borne a good deal very patiently, began, as Mr. Beale said, to "pass remarks."

"It ain't so much the little uns they jib at," said Mr. Beale, taking his pipe out of his mouth and stretching his legs in the back-yard, "though to my mind they yaps for more aggravatin'. It's the cocker spannel and the Great Danes upsets them."

"The cocker spannel has got rather a persevering bark," said Dickie, looking up at the creeping-jenny in the window-boxes. No flowers would grow in the garden, now trampled hard by the indiarubber-soled feet of many dogs; but Dickie did his best with window-boxes, and every window was underlined by a bright dash of color—creeping-jenny, Brompton stocks, stone-crop, and late tulips, and all bought from the barrows in the High Street, made a brave show.

"I don't say as they're actin' unneighborly in talking about the pleece, so long as they don't do no *more* than talk," said Beale, with studded fairness and moderation. "What I do say is, I wish we 'ad more elbow-room for 'em. an' as for exercisin' of 'em all every day, like the books say—well, 'ow's one pair of 'ands to do it, let alone legs, and you in another line of business and not able to give yer time to 'em?"

"I wish we had a bigger place, too," said Dickie; "we could afford one now. Not but what I should be sorry to leave the old place, too. We've 'ad some good times here in our time, farver, ain't us?" He sighed with the air of an old man looking back on the long-ago days of youth.

"You lay to it we 'as," said Mr. Beale; "but this 'ere back-yard, it ain't a place where dogs can what you call exercise, not to *call* it exercise. Now is it?"

"Well, then," said Dickie, "let's get a move on us."

"Ah," said Mr. Beale, laying his pipe on his knee, "now you're talkin'. Get a move on us. That's what I 'oped you'd say. 'Member what I says to you in the winter-time that night Mr. Fuller looked in for his bit o' rent—about me gettin' of the fidgets in my legs? An' I says, "Why not take to the road a bit, now and again?' an' you says, 'We'll see about that, come summer.' And 'ere *is* come summer. What if we was to take the road a bit, mate—where there's room to stretch a chap's legs without kickin' a dog or knockin' the crockery over? There's the ole pram upstairs in the back room as lively as ever she was—only wants a little of paint to be fit for a dook, she does. An' 'ere's me, an' 'ere's you, an' 'ere's the pick of the dogs. Think of it, matey—the bed with the green curtains, and the good smell of the herrings you toasts yerself and the fire you makes outer sticks, and the little starses a comin' out and a-winkin' at you, and all so quiet, a-smokin' yer pipe till it falls outer yer mouth with sleepiness, and no fear o' settin' the counterpin a-fire. What you say, matey, eh?"

Dickie looked lovingly at the smart back of the little house—its crisp white muslin blinds, its glimpses of neat curtains, its flowers; and then another picture came to him—he saw the misty last light fainting beyond the great shoulders of the downs, and the "little starses" shining so bright and new through the branches of fir-trees that interlaced above, a sweet-scented bed of soft fallen brown pine-needles.

"What say, mate?" Mr. Beale repeated; and Dickie answered—

"Soon as ever you like's what I say. And what I say is, the sooner the better."

Having made up his mind to go, Mr. Beale at once found a dozen reasons why he could not leave home, and all the reasons were four-footed, and wagged loving tails at him. He was anxious, in fact, about the dogs. Could he really trust Amelia?

"Dunno oo you *can* trust then?" said Amelia, tossing a still handsome head. "Anybody 'ud think the dogs was babies, to hear you."

"So they are—to me—as precious as, anyway. Look here, you just come and live 'ere, 'Melia—see? An' we'll give yer five bob a week. An' the nipper 'e shall write it all down in lead-pencil on a bit o' paper for you, what they're to 'ave to eat an' about their physic and which of 'em's to have what."

This took some time to settle, and some more time to write down. And then, when the lick of paint was nearly dry on the perambulator and all their shirts and socks were washed and mended, and lying on the kitchen window-ledge ready for packing, what did Mr. Beale do but go out one morning and come back with a perfectly strange dachshund.

"An' I can't go and leave the little beast till he knows 'imself a bit in 'is noo place," said Mr. Beale, "an' 'ame 'im boltin' off gracious knows where, and being pinched or carted off to the Dogs' Home, or that. Can I, now?"

The new dog was very long, very brown, very friendly and charming. When it had had its supper it wagged its tail, turned a clear and gentle eye on Dickie, and without any warning stood on its head.

"Well," said Mr. Beale, "if there ain't money in that beast! A trick don 'e is. "E's wuth wot I give for 'im, so 'e is. Knows more tricks than that 'ere, I'll be bound."

He did. He was a singularly well-educated dog. Next morning Mr. Beale, coming downstairs, was just in time to bang the front door in the face of Amelia coming in, pail-laden, from "doing" the steps, and this to prevent the flight of the new dog. The door of one of the dog-rooms was open, and a fringe of inquisitive dogs ornamented the passage.

"What you open that door at all for?" Mr. Beale asked Amelia.

"I didn't," she said, and stuck to it.

That afternoon Beale, smoking in the garden, got up, as he often did, to look through the window at the dogs. He gazed a moment, muttered something, and made one jump to the back door. It was closed. Amelia was giving the scullery floor a "thorough scrub over," and had fastened the door to avoid having it opened with suddenness against her steaming pail or her crouching form.

But Mr. Beale got in at the back-door and out at the front just in time to see the dachshund disappearing at full speed, "like a bit of brown toffee-stick," as he said, round the end of the street. They never saw that dog again.

"Trained to it," Mr. Beale used to say sadly whenever he told the story; "trained to it from a pup, you may lay your life. I see 'im as plain as I see you. 'E listens an' he looks, and 'e doesn't 'ear nor see nobody. An' 'e ups on his 'ind legs and turns the 'andle with 'is little twisty front pawses, clever as a monkey, and hout 'e goes like a harrow in a bow. Trained to it, ye see. I bet his master wot taught 'im that's sold him time and again, makin' a good figure every time, for 'e was a 'andsome dawg as ever I see. Trained the dawg to open the door and bunk 'ome. See? Clever, I call it."

"It's a mean trick," said Dickie when Beale told him of the loss of the dog; "that's what I call it. I'm sorry you've lost the dog."

"I ain't exactly pleased myself," said Beale, "but no use crying over broken glass. It's the cleverness I think of most," he said admiringly. "Now I'd never a thought of a thing like that myself—not if I'd lived to a hundred, so I wouldn't. *You* might 'ave," he told Dickie flatteringly, "but I wouldn't myself."

"We don't need to," said Dickie hastily. "We earns our livings. We don't need to cheat to get our livings."

"No, no, dear boy," said Mr. Beale, more hastily still; "course we don't. That's just what I'm a-saying, ain't it? We shouldn't never 'ave thought o' that. No need to, as you say. The cleverness of it!"

This admiration of the cleverness by which he himself had been cheated set Dickie thinking. He said, very gently and quietly, after a little pause—

"This 'ere walking tower of ours. We pays our own way? No cadging?"

"I should 'ope you know me better than that," said Beale virtuously; "not a patter have I done since I done the Rally and started in the dog line."

"Nor yet no dealings with that red-headed chap what I never see?"

"Now, is it likely?" Beale asked reproachfully. "I should 'ope we're a cut above a low chap like wot 'e is. The pram's dry as a bone and shiny as yer 'at, and we'll start the first thing in the morning."

And in the early morning, which is fresh and sweet even in Deptford, they bade farewell to Amelia and the dogs and set out.

Amelia watched them down the street and waved a farewell as they turned the corner. "It'll be a bit lonesome," she said. "One thing, I shan't be burgled, with all them dogs in the house."

The voices of the dogs, as she went in and shut the door, seemed to assure her that she would not even be so very lonely.

And now they were really on the road. And they were going to Arden—to that place by the sea where Dickie's uncle, in the other life, had a castle, and where Dickie was to meet his cousins, after his seven months of waiting.

You may think that Dickie would be very excited by the thought of meeting, in this workaday, nowadays world, the children with whom he had had such wonderful adventures in the other world, the dream world—too excited, perhaps, to feel really interested in the little everyday happenings of "the road." But this was not so. The present was after all the real thing. The dreams could wait. The knowledge that they were there, waiting, made all the ordinary things more beautiful and more interesting. The feel of the soft dust underfoot, the bright, dewy grass and clover by the wayside, the lessening of houses and the growing wideness of field and pasture, all contented and delighted Dickie. He felt to the full all the joy that Mr. Beale felt, in "oofing it," and when as the sun was sinking they overtook a bent, slow-going figure, it was with a thrill of real pleasure that Dickie recognized the woman who had given him the blue ribbon for True.

True himself, now grown large and thick of coat, seemed to recognize a friend, gambolled round her dreadful boots, sniffed at her withered hand.

"Give her a lift with her basket, shall us?" Dickie whispered to Mr. Beale and climbed out of the perambulator. "I can make shift to do this last piece."

So the three went on together, in friendly silence. As they neared Orpington the woman said, "Our road parts here; and thank you kindly. A kindness is never wasted, so they say."

"That ain't nothing," said Beale; "besides, there's the blue ribbon."

"That the dog?" the woman asked.

"Same ole dawg," said Beale, with pride.

"A pretty beast," she said. "Well—so long."

She looked back to smile and nod to them when she had taken her basket and the turning to the right, and Dickie suddenly stiffened all over, as a pointer does when it sees a partridge.

"I say," he cried, "you're the nurse—"

"I've nursed a many in my time," she called back.

"But in the dream . . . you know."

"Dreams is queer things," said the woman. "And," she added, "least said is soonest mended."

"But . . ." said Dickie.

"Keep your eyes open and your mouth shut's a good motto," said she, nodded again, and turned resolutely away.

"Not very civil, I don't think," said Beale, "considerin'—"

"Oh, she's all right," said Dickie, wondering very much, and very anxious that Beale should not wonder. "May I ride in the pram, farver? My foot's a bit blistered, I think. We ain't done so much walkin' lately, 'ave us?"

"Ain't tired in yourself, are you?" Mr. Beale asked, "'cause there's a place called Chevering Park, pretty as a picture—I thought we might lay out there. I'm a bit 'to in the 'oof meself; but I can stick it if you can."

Dickie could; and when they made their evening camp in a deep gully soft with beech-leaves, and he looked out over the ridge—cautiously, because of keepers—at the smoothness of a mighty slope, green-grey in the dusk, where rabbits frisked and played, he was glad that he had not yielded to his tiredness and stopped to rest the night anywhere else. Chevering Park is a very beautiful place, I would have you to know. And the travellers were lucky. The dogs were good and quiet, and no keeper disturbed their rest or their masters. Dickie slept with True in his arms, and it was like a draught of soft magic elixir to lie once more in the still, cool night and look up at the stars through the trees.

"Can't think why they ever invented houses," he said, and then he fell asleep.

By short stages, enjoying every step of every day's journey, they went slowly and at their ease through the garden-land of Kent. Dickie loved every minute of it, every leaf in the hedge, every blade of grass by the roadside. And most of all he loved the quiet nights when he fell asleep under the stars with True in his arms.

It was all good, all. . . . And it was worth waiting and working for seven long months, to feel the thrill that Dickie felt when Beale, as they topped a ridge of the great South Downs, said suddenly, "There's the sea," and, a dozen yards further on, "There's Arden Castle."

There it lay, grey and green, with its old stones and ivy—the same Castle which Dickie had seen on the day when they lay among the furze bushes and waited to burgle Talbot court. There were red roofs at one side of the Castle where a house had been built among the ruins. As they drew nearer, and looked down at Arden Castle, Dickie saw two little figures in its green courtyard, and wondered whether they could possibly be Edred and Elfrida, the little cousins whom he had met in King James the First's time, and who, the nurse said, really belonged to the times of King Edward the Seventh, or Nowadays, just as he did himself. It seemed as though it could hardly be sure; but, if it were true, how splendid! What games he and they could have! And what a play-place it was that spread out before him—green and glorious, with the sea on one side and the downs on the other, and in the middle the ruins of Arden Castle.

But as they went on through the furze bushes Dickie perceived that Mr. Beale was growing more and more silent and uneasy.

"What's up?" Dickie asked at last. "Out with it, farver."

"It ain't nothing," said Mr. Beale.

"You ain't afraid those Talbots will know you again?"

"Not much I ain't. They never see my face; and I 'adn't a beard that time like what I've got now."

"Well, then?" said Dickie.

"Well, if you must 'ave it," said Beale, "we're a-gettin' very near my ole dad's place, and I can't make me mind up."

"I thought we was settled we'd go to see 'im."

"I dunno. If 'e's under the daisies I shan't like it—I tell you straight I shan't like it. But we're a long-lived stock—p'raps 'e's all right. I dunno."

"Shall I go up by myself to where he lives and see if he's all right?"

"Not much," said Mr. Beale; "if I goes I goes, and if I stays away I stays away. It's just the not being able to make me mind up."

"If he's there," said Dickie, "don't you think you *ought* to go, just on the chance of him being there and wanting you?"

"If you come to oughts," said Beale, "I oughter gone 'ome any time this twenty year. Only I ain't. See?"

"Well," said Dickie, "it's your look out. I know what I should do if it was me."

Remembrance showed him the father who had leaned on his shoulder as they walked about the winding walks of the pleasant garden in old Deptford—the father who had given him the little horse, and insisted that his twenty gold pieces should be spent as he chose.

"I dunno," said Beale. "What you think? Eh, matey?"

"I think *let's*," said Dickie. "I lay if he's alive it 'ud be as good as three Sundays in the week to him to see you. You was his little boy once, wasn't you?"

"Ay," said Beale; "he was wagoner's mate to one of Lord Arden's men. 'E used to ride me on the big cart-horses. 'E was a fine set-up chap."

To hear the name of Arden on Beale's lips gave Dickie a very odd, half-pleasant, half-frightened feeling. It seemed to bring certain things very near.

"Let's," he said again.

"All right," said Beale, "only if it all goes wrong it ain't my fault—an' there used to be a footpath a bit further on. You cut through the copse and cater across the eleven-acre medder, and bear along to the left by the hedge an' it brings you out under Arden Knoll, where my old man's place is."

So they cut and catered and bore along, and came out under Arden Knoll, and there was a cottage, with a very neat garden full of gay flowers, and a brick pathway leading from the wooden gate to the front door. And by the front door sat an old man in a Windsor chair, with a brown spaniel at his feet and a bird in a wicker cage above his head, and he was nodding, for it was a hot day, and he was an old man and tired.

"Swelp me, I can't do it!" whispered Beale. "I'll walk on a bit. You just arst for a drink, and sort of see 'ow the land lays. It might turn 'im up seeing me so sudden. Good old dad!"

He walked quickly on, and Dickie was left standing by the gate. Then the brown spaniel became aware of True, and barked, and the old man said, "Down, Trusty!" in his sleep, and then woke up.

His clear old eyes set in many wrinkles turned full on Dickie by the gate.

"May I have a drink of water?" Dickie asked.

"Come in," said the old man.

And Dickie lifted the latch of smooth, brown, sun-warmed iron, and went up a brick path, as the old man slowly turned himself about in the chair.

"Yonder's the well," he said; "draw up a bucket, if thy leg'll let thee, poor little chap!"

"I draws water with my arms, not my legs," said Dickie cheerfully.

"There's a blue mug in the wash-house window-ledge," said the old man. "Fetch me a drop when you've had your drink, my lad."

Of course, Dickie's manners were too good for him to drink first. He drew up the dripping oaken bucket from the cool darkness of the well, fetched the mug, and offered it brimming to the old man. Then he drank, and looked at the garden ablaze with flowers—blush-roses and damask roses, and sweet-williams and candytuft, white lilies and yellow lilies, pansies, larkspur, poppies, begamot, and sage.

It was just like a play at the Greenwich Theater, Dickie thought. He had seen a scene just like that, where the old man sat in the sun and the Prodigal returned.

Dickie would not have been surprised to see Beale run up the brick path and throw himself on his knees, exclaiming, "Father, it is I—your erring but repentant son! Can you forgive me? If a lifetime of repentance can atone..." and so on.

If Dickie had been Beale he would certainly have made the speech, beginning, "Father, it is I." But as he was only Dickie, he said—

"Your name's Beale, ain't it?"

"It might be," old Beale allowed.

"I seen your son in London. 'E told me about yer garden."

"I should a thought 'e'd a-forgot the garden same as 'e's forgot me," said the old man.

"'E ain't forgot you, not 'e," said Dickie; "'e's come to see you, an' 'e's waiting outside now to know if you'd like to see 'im."

"Then 'e oughter know better," said the old man, and shouted in a thin, high voice, "Jim, Jim, come along in this minute!"

Even then Beale didn't act a bit like the prodigal in the play. He just unlatched the gate without looking at it—his hand had not forgotten the way of it, for all it was so long since he had passed through that gate. And he walked slowly and heavily up the path and said, "Hullo, dad!—how goes it?"

And the old man looked at him with his eyes half shut and said, "Why, it *is* James—so it is," as if he had expected it to be some one quite different.

And they shook hands, and then Beale said, "The garden's looking well."

And the old man owned that the garden 'ud do all right if it wasn't for the snails.

That was all Dickie heard, for he thought it polite to go away. Of course, they could not be really affectionate with a stranger about. So he shouted from the gate something about "back presently," and went off along the cart track towards Arden Castle and looked at it quite closely. It was the most beautiful and interesting thing he had ever seen. But he did not see the children.

When he went back the old man was cooking steak over the kitchen fire, and Beale was at the sink straining summer cabbage in a colander, as though he had lived there all his life and never anywhere else. He was in his shirt-sleeves too, and his coat and hat hung behind the back-door.

So then they had dinner, when the old man had set down the frying-pan expressly to shake hands with Dickie, saying, "So this is the lad you told me about. Yes, yes." It was a very nice dinner, with cold gooseberry pastry as well as the steak and vegetables. The kitchen was pleasant and cozy though rather dark, on account of the white climbing rose that grew round the window. After dinner the men sat in the sun and smoked, and Dickie occupied himself in teaching the spaniel and True that neither of them was a dog who deserved to be growled at. Dickie had just thrown back his head in a laugh at True's sulky face and stiffly planted paws, when he felt the old man's dry, wrinkled hand under his chin.

"Let's 'ave a look at you," he said, and peered closely at the child. "Where'd you get that face, eh? What did you say your name was?"

"Harding's his name," said Beale. "Dickie Harding."

"Dickie *Arden*, I should a-said if you'd asked *me*," said the old man. "Seems to me it's a reg'lar Arden face he's got. But my eyes ain't so good as wot they was. What d'you say to stopping along of me a bit, my boy? There's room in the cottage for all five of us. My son James here tells me you've been's good as a son to him."

"I'd love it," said Dickie. So that was settled. There were two bedrooms for Beale and his father, and Dickie slept in a narrow, whitewashed slip of a room that had once been a larder. The brown spaniel and True slept on the rag hearth-rug in the kitchen. And everything was as cozy as cozy could be.

"We can send for any of the dawgs any minute if we feel we can't stick it without 'em," said Beale, smoking his pipe in the front garden.

"You mean to stay a long time, then," said Dickie.

"I dunno. You see, I was born and bred 'ere. The air tastes good, don't it? An' the water's good. Didn't you notice the tea tasted quite different from what it does anywhere else? That's the soft water, that is. An' the old chap . . . Yes—and there's one or two other things—yes—I reckon us'll stop on 'ere a bit."

And Dickie was very glad. For now he was near Arden Castle, and could see it any time that he chose to walk a couple of hundred yards and look down. And presently he would see Edred and Elfrida. Would they know him? That was the question. Would they remember that he and they had been cousins and friends when James the First was King?

Kidnapped

And now New Cross seemed to go backwards and very far away, its dirty streets, its sordid shifts, its crowds of anxious, unhappy people who never had quite enough of anything, and Dickie's home was in a pleasant cottage from whose windows you could see great green rolling downs, and the smooth silver and blue of the sea, and from whose door you stepped, not on to filthy pavements, but on to a neat brick path, leading between beds glowing with flowers.

Also, he was near Arden, the goal of seven months' effort. Now he would see Edred and Elfrida again, and help them to find the hidden treasure, as he had once helped them to find their father.

This joyful thought put the crown on his happiness.

But he presently perceived that though he was so close to Arden Castle he did not seem to be much nearer to the Arden children. It is not an easy thing to walk into the courtyard of a ruined castle and ring the bell of a strange house and ask for people whom you have only met in dreams, or as good as dreams. And I don't know how Dickie would have managed if Destiny had not kindly come to his help, and arranged that, turning a corner in the lane which leads to the village, he should come face to face with Edred and Elfrida Arden. And they looked exactly like the Edred and Elfrida Arden whom he had played with and quarrelled with in the dream. He halted, leaning on his crutch, for them to come up and speak to him. They came on, looking hard at him—the severe might have called it staring—looked, came up to him, and passed by without a word! But he saw them talking eagerly to each other.

Dickie was left in the lane looking after them. It was a miserable moment. But quite quickly he roused himself. They were talking to each other eagerly, and once Elfrida half looked round. Perhaps it was his shabby clothes that made them not so sure whether he was the Dickie they had known. If they did not know him it should not be his fault. He balanced himself on one foot, beat with his crutch on the ground, and shouted, "Hi!" and "Hullo!" as loud as he could. the other children turned, hesitated, and came back.

"What is it?" the little girl called out; "have you hurt yourself?" And she came up to him and looked at him with kind eyes.

"No," said Dickie; "but I wanted to ask you something."

The other two looked at him and at each other, and the boy said "Righto."

"You're from the Castle, aren't you?" he said. "I was wondering whether you'd let me go down and have a look at it?"

"Of course," said the girl. "Come on."

"Wait a minute," said Dickie, nerving himself to the test. If they didn't remember him they'd think he was mad, and never show him the Castle. Never mind! Now for it!

"Did you ever have a tutor called Mr. Parados?" he asked. And again the others looked at him and at each other. "Parrot-nose for short," Dickie hastened to add; "and did you ever shovel snow on to his head and then ride away in a carriage drawn by swans?"

"It *is* you!" cried Elfrida, and hugged him.

"Edred, it *is* Dickie! We were saying, *could* it be you? Oh! Dickie darling, how did you hurt your foot?"

Dickie flushed. "My foot's always been like that," he said, "in Nowadays time. When we met in the magic times I was like everybody else, wasn't I?"

Elfrida hugged him again, and said no more about the foot. Instead, she said, "Oh, how ripping it is to really and truly find you here! We thought you couldn't be real because we wrote a letter to you at the address it said on that bill you gave us. And the letter came back with 'not known' outside."

"What address was it?" Dickie asked.

"Laurie Grove, New Cross," Edred told him.

"Oh, that was just an address Mr. Beale made up to look grand with," said Dickie. "I remember his telling me about it. He's the man I live with; I call him father because he's been kind to me. But my own daddy's dead."

"Let's go up on the downs," said Elfrida, "and sit down, and you tell us all about everything from the very beginning."

So they went up and sat among the furze bushes, and Dickie told them all his story—just as much of it as I have told to you. And it took a long time. And then they reminded each other how they had met in the magic or dream world, and how Dickie had helped them to save their father—which he did do, only I have not had time to tell you about it; but it is all written in "The House of Arden."

"But our magic is all over now," said Edred sadly. "We had to give up ever having any more magic, so as to get father back. And now we shall never find the treasure or be able to buy back the old lands and restore the Castle and bring the water back to the moat, and build nice, dry, warm, cozy cottages for the tenants. But we've got father."

"Well, but look here," said Dickie. "We got *my* magic all right, and old nurse said I could work it for you, and that's really what I've come for, so that we can look for the treasure together."

"That's awfully jolly of you," said Elfrida.

"What is your magic?" Edred asked; and Dickie pulled out Tinkler and the white seal and the moon-seeds, and laid them on the turf and explained.

And in the middle of the explanation a shadow fell on the children and the Tinkler and the moon-seeds and the seal, and there was a big, handsome gentleman looking down at them and saying—

"Introduce your friend, Edred."

"Oh, Dickie, this is my father," cried Edred, scrambling up. And Dickie added very quickly, "My name's Dick Harding." It took longer for Dickie to get up because of the crutch, and Lord Arden reached his hand down to help him. He must have been a little surprised when the crippled child in the shabby clothes stood up, and instead of touching his forehead, as poor children are taught to do, held out his hand and said—

"How do you do, Lord Arden?"

"I am very well, I thank you," said Lord Arden. "And where did you spring from? You are not a native of these parts, I think?"

"No, but my adopted father is," said Dickie, "and I came from London with him, to see *his* father, who is old Mr. Beale, and we are staying at his cottage."

Lord Arden sat down beside them on the turf and asked Dickie a good many questions about where he was born, and who he had lived with, and what he had seen and done and been.

Dickie answered honestly and straightforwardly. Only of course he did not tell about the magic, or say that in that magic world he and Lord Arden's children were friends and cousins. And all the time they were talking Lord Arden's eyes were fixed on his face, except when they wandered to Tinkler and the white seal. Once he picked these up, and looked at the crest on them.

"Where did you get these?" he asked.

Dickie told. And then Lord Arden handed the seal and Tinkler to him and went on with his questions.

At last Elfrida put her arms round father's neck and whispered, "I know it's not manners, but Dickie won't mind," she said before the whispering began.

"Yes, certainly," said Lord Arden when the whispering was over; "it's tea-time. Dickie, you'll come home to tea with us, won't you?"

"I must tell Mr. Beale," said Dickie; "he'll be anxious if I don't."

"Shall I hurt you if I put you on my back?" Lord Arden asked, and next minute he was carrying Dickie down the slope towards Arden Castle, while Edred went back to Beale's cottage to say where Dickie was. When Edred got back to Arden Castle teas was ready in the parlor, and Dickie was resting in a comfortable chair.

"Isn't old Beale a funny man?" said Edred. "He said Arden Castle was the right place for Dickie, with a face like that. What could he have meant? What are you doing that for?" he added in injured tones, for Elfrida had kicked his hand under the table.

Before tea was over there was a sound of horses' hoofs and carriage wheels in the courtyard. And the maid-servant opened the parlor door and said, "Lady Talbot." Though he remembered well enough how kind she had been to him, Dickie wished he could creep under the table. It was too hard; she *must* recognize him. And now Edred and Elfrida, and Lord Arden, who was so kind and jolly, they would all know that he had once been a burglar, and that she had wanted to adopt him, and that he had been ungrateful and had run away. He trembled all over. It was too hard.

Lady Talbot shook hands with the others, and then turned to him. "And who is your little friend?" she asked Edred, and in the same breath cried out—"why, it's my little runaway!"

Dickie only said; "I wasn't ungrateful, I wasn't—I had to go." But his eyes implored.

And Lady Talbot—Dickie will always love her for that—understood. Not a word about burglars did she say, only—

"I wanted to adopt Dickie once, Lord Arden, but he would not stay."

"I had to get back to father," said Dickie.

"Well, at any rate it's pleasant to see each other again," she said. "I always hoped we should some day. No sugar, thank you, Elfrida"—and then sat down and had tea and was as jolly as possible. The only thing which made Dickie at all uncomfortable was when she turned suddenly to the master of the house and said, "Doesn't he remind you of anyone, Lord Arden?"

And Lord Arden said, "Perhaps he does," with that sort of look that people have when they mean "Not before the children! I'd rather talk about it afterwards if you don't mind."

Then the three were sent out to play, and Dickie was shown the Castle ruins, while Lord Arden and Lady Talbot walked up and down on the daisied grass, and talked for a long time. Dickie knew they were talking about him, but he did not mind. He had that feeling you sometimes have about grown-up people, that they really do understand, and are to be trusted.

"You'll be too fine presently to speak to the likes of us, you nipper," said Beale, when a smart little pony cart had brought Dickie back to the cottage. "You an' your grand friends. Lord Arden indeed—"

"They was as jolly as jolly," said Dickie; "nobody weren't never kinder to me nor what Lord Arden was an' Lady Talbot too—without it was you, farver."

"Ah," said Beale to the old man, "'e knows how to get round his old father, don't 'e?"

"What does he want to talk that way for?" the old man asked. "'E can talk like a little gentleman all right 'cause we 'eard 'im."

"Oh, that's the way we talks up London way," said Dickie. "I learnt to talk fine out o' books."

Mr. Beale said nothing, but that night he actually read for nearly ten minutes in a bound volume of the *Wesleyan Magazine*. And he was asleep over the same entertaining work when Lord Arden came the next afternoon.

You will be able to guess what he came about. And Dickie had a sort of feeling that perhaps Lord Arden might have seen by his face, as old Beale had, that he was an Arden. So neither he nor you will be much surprised. The person to be really surprised was Mr. Beale.

"You might a-knocked me down with a pick-axe," said Beale later, "so help me three men and a boy you might. It's a rum go. My lord 'e says there's some woman been writing letters to 'im this long time saying she'd got 'old of 'is long-lost nephew or cousin or something, and a-wanting to get money out of him—though what for, goodness knows. An' 'e says you're a Arden by rights, you nipper you, an' 'e wants to take you and bring you up along of his kids—so there's an end of you and me, Dickie, old boy. I didn't understand more than 'arf of wot 'e was saying. But I tumbled to that much. It's all up with you and me and Amelia and the dogs and the little 'ome. You're a-goin' to be a gentleman, you are—an' I'll have to take to the road by meself and be a poor beast of a cadger again. That's what I'll come to, I know."

"Don't you put yourself about," said Dickie calmly. "I ain't a-goin' to leave yer. Didn't Lady Talbot ask me to be her boy—and didn't I cut straight back to you? I'll play along o' them kids if Lord Arden'll let me. But I ain't a-goin' to leave you, not yet I ain't. So don't you go snivelling afore any one's 'urt yer, farver. See?"

But that was before Lord Arden had his second talk with Mr. Beale. After that it was—

"Look 'ere, you nipper, I ain't a-goin' to stand in your light. You're goin' up in the world, says you. Well, you ain't the only one. Lord Arden's bought father's cottage an' e's goin' to build on to it, and I'm to 'ave all the dawgs down 'ere, and sell 'em through the papers like. And you'll come an' 'ave a look at us sometimes."

"And what about Amelia?" said Dickie, "and the little ones?"

"Well, I did think," said Beale, rubbing his nose thoughtfully, "of asking 'Melia to come down 'ere along o' the dawgs. Seems a pity to separate 'em somehow. It was Lord Arden put it into my 'ed. 'You oughter be married you ought,' 'e says to me pleasant like, man to man; 'ain't there any young woman I could give a trifle to, to set you and her up in housekeeping?' So then I casts about, and I thinks of 'Melia. As well'er as anybody, and she's used to the dawgs. And the trifle's an hundred pounds. That's all. *That's all!* So I'm sending to her by this post, and it's an awful toss up getting married, but 'Melia ain't like a stranger, and it couldn't ever be the same with us two and nipper after all this set out. What you say?"

I don't know what Dickie said; what he felt was something like this:—

"I *have* tried to stick to Beale, and help him along, and I did come back from the other old long-ago world to help him, and I have been sticking to things I didn't like so as to help him and get him settled. He was my bit of work, and now someone else comes along and takes my work out of my hands, and finishes it. And here's Beale provided for and settled. And I meant to provide for him myself. And I don't like it!"

That was what he felt at first. But afterwards he had to own that it was "a jolly lucky thing for Beale." And for himself too. He found that to be at Arden Castle with Edred and Elfrida all day, at play and at lessons, was almost as good as being with them in the beautiful old dream-life. All the things that he had hated in this modern life, when he was Dickie of Deptford, ceased to trouble him now that he was Richard Arden. For the difference between being rich and poor is as great as the difference between being warm and cold.

After that first day a sort of shyness came over the three children, and they spoke no more of the strange adventures they had had together, but just played at all the ordinary everyday games, till they almost forgot that there was any magic, had ever been any. The fact was, the life they were leading was so happy in itself that they needed no magic to make them contented. It was not till after the wedding of 'Melia and Mr. Beale that Dickie remembered that to find the Arden Treasure for his cousins had been one of his reasons for coming back to this the Nowadays world.

I wish I had time to tell you about the wedding. I could write a whole book about it. How Amelia came down from London and was married in Arden Church. How she wore a wreath of orange blossoms, a filmy veil, and real kid gloves—all gifts of Miss Edith Arden, Lord Arden's sister. How Lord Arden presented an enormous wedding cake and a glorious wedding breakfast, and gave away the bride, and made a speech saying he owed a great debt to Mr Beale for his kindness to his nephew Richard Arden, and how surprised everyone was to hear Dickie's new name. How all the dogs wore white favors and had each a crumb of wedding cake; and how when the wedding feast was over and the guests gone, the bride tucked up her white dress under a big apron and set about arranging in the new rooms the "sticks" of furniture which Dickie and Beale had brought together from the little home in Deptford, and which had come in a van by road all the way to Arden.

The Ardens had gone back to the Castle, and Dickie with them, and old Beale was smoking in his usual chair by his front door—so there was no one to hear Beale's compliment to his bride. He came behind her and put his arm round her as she was dusting the mantel-piece. "Go on with you," said the new Mrs. Beale; "any one 'ud think we was courting."

"So we be," said Beale, and kissed 'Melia for the first time. "We got all our courtin' to do now. See? I might a-picked an' choosed," he added reflectively, "but there—I daresay I might a-done worse."

'Melia blushed with pleasure at the compliment, and went on with the dusting.

*   *   *   *   *

It was as the Ardens walked home over the short turf that Lord Arden said to his sister, "I wish all the cottages about here were like Beale's. It didn't cost so very much. If I could only buy back the rest of the land, I'd show some people what a model village is like. Only I can't buy it back. He wants far more than we can think of managing."

And Dickie heard what he said. That was why, when next he was alone with his cousins, he began—

"Look here—you aren't allowed to use your magic any more, to go and look for the treasure. But *I* am. And I vote we go and look for it. And then your father can buy back the old lands, and build the new cottages and mend up Arden Castle, and make it like it used to be."

"Oh, let's," said Elfrida, with enthusiasm. But Edred unexpectedly answered, "I don't know." The three children were sitting in the window of the gate-tower looking down on the green turf of the Castle yard.

"What do you mean you don't know?" Elfrida asked briskly.

"I *mean* I don't know," said Edred stolidly; "we're all right as we are, *I* think. I used to think I like magic and things. But if you come to think of it something horrid happened to us every single time we went into the past with our magic. We were always being chased or put in prison or bothered somehow or other. The only really nice thing was when we saw the treasure being hidden, because that looked like a picture and we hadn't to do anything. And we don't know where the treasure is, anyhow. And I don't like adventures nearly so much as I used to think I did. We're all right and jolly as we are. What I say is, 'Don't let's.'"

This cold water damped the spirit of the others only for a few minutes.

"You know," Elfrida explained to Dickie, "our magic took us to look for treasure in the past. And once a film of a photograph that we'd stuck up behaved like a cinematograph, and then we saw the treasure being hidden away."

"Then let's just go where that was—mark the spot, come home and then dig it up."

"It wasn't buried," Elfrida explained; "it was put into a sort of cellar, with doors, and we've looked all over what's left of the Castle, and there isn't so much as a teeny silver ring to be found."

"I see," said Dickie. "But suppose I just worked the magic and wished to be where the treasure is?"

"I won't," cried Edred, and in his extreme dislike to the idea he kicked with his boots quite violently against the stones of the tower; "not much I won't. I expect the treasure's bricked up. We should look nice bricked up in a vault like a wicked nun, and perhaps forgotten the way to get out. Not much."

"You needn't make such a fuss about it," said Elfrida, "nobody's going to get bricked up in vaults." And Dickie added, "You're quite right, old chap. I didn't think about that."

"We must do *something*," Elfrida said impatiently.

"How would it be," Dickie spoke slowly, "if I tried to see the Mouldierwarp? He is stronger than the Mouldiwarp. He might advise us. Suppose we work the magic and just ask to see him?"

"I don't want to go away from here," said Edred firmly.

"You needn't. I'll lay out the moon-seeds and things on the floor here—you'll see."

So Dickie made the crossed triangles of moon-seeds and he and his cousins stood in it and Dickie said, "Please can we see the Mouldierwarp?" just as you say, "Please can I see Mr. So-and so?" when you have knocked at the door of Mr. So-and-so's house and some one has opened the door.

Immediately everything became dark, but before the children had time to wish that it was light again a disc of light appeared on the curtain of darkness, and there was the Mouldierwarp, just as Dickie had seen him once before.

He bowed in a courtly manner, and said—

"What can I do for you today, Richard Lord Arden?"

"He's not Lord Arden," said Edred. "I used to be. But even *I'm* not Lord Arden now. My father is."

"Indeed?" said the Mouldierwarp with an air of polite interest. "You interested me greatly. But my question remains unanswered."

"I want," said Dickie, "to find the lost treasure of Arden, so that the old Castle can be built up again, and the old lands bought back, and the old cottages made pretty and good to live in. Will you please advise me?"

The Mouldierwarp in the magic-lantern picture seemed to scratch his nose thoughtfully with his fore paw.

"It can be done," he said, "but it will be hard. It is almost impossible to find the treasure without waking the Mouldiest-warp, who sits on the green-and-white checkered field of Arden's shield of arms. And he can only be awakened by some noble deed. Yet noble deeds may chance at any time.

And if you go to seek treasure of one kind you may find treasure of another. I have spoken."

It began to fade away, but Elfrida cried, "Oh, *don't* go. You're just like the Greek oracles. won't you tell us something plain and straight-forward?"

"I will," said the Mouldierwarp, rather shortly.

> "Great Arden's Lord no treasure shall regain
> Till Arden's Lord is lost and found again."

"And father *was* lost and found again," said Edred, "so that's all right."

> "Set forth to seek it with courageous face.
> And seek it in the most unlikely place."

And with that it vanished altogether, and the darkness with it; and there were the three children and Tinkler and the white seal and the moon-seeds and the sunshine on the floor of the room in the tower.

"That's useful," said Edred scornfully. "As if it wasn't just as difficult to know the unlikely places as the likely ones."

"I'll tell you what," said Dickie. And then the dinner bell rang, and they had to go without Dickie's telling them what, and to eat roast mutton and plum-pie, and behave as though they were just ordinary children to whom no magic had ever happened. There was little chance of more talk that day.

Edred and Elfrida were to be taken to Cliffville immediately after dinner to be measured for new shoes, and Dickie was to go up to spend the afternoon with Beale and 'Melia and the dogs. Still, in the few moments when they were all dressed and waiting for the dog-cart to come round, Dickie found a chance to whisper to Elfrida—

"Let's all think of unlikely places as hard as ever we can. And tomorrow we'll decide on the unlikeliest and go there.

Edred needn't be in it if he doesn't want to. *You're* keen, aren't you?"

"Rather!" was all there was time for Elfrida to say.

The welcome that awaited Dickie at Beale's cottage from Beale, Amelia, and, not least, the dogs, was enough to drive all thoughts of unlikely places out of anybody's head. And besides, there were always so many interesting things to do at the cottage. He helped to wash True, cleaned the knives, and rinsed lettuce for tea; helped to dry the tea-things, and to fold the washing when Mrs. Beale brought it in out of the yard in dry, sweet armfuls of white folds.

It was dusk when he bade them good night, embracing each dog in turn, and set out to walk the little way to the cross-roads, where the dog-cart returning from Cliffville would pick him up. but he dog-cart was a little late, because the pony had dropped a shoe and had had to be taken to the blacksmith's.

So when Dickie had waited a little while he began to think, as one always does when people don't keep their appointments, that perhaps he had mistaken the time, or that the clock at the cottage was slow. And when he had waited a little longer, it seemed simply silly to be waiting at all. So he picked up his crutch and got up from the milestone where he had been sitting and set off to walk down to the Castle.

As he went he thought many things, and one of the things he thought was that the memories of King James's time had grown dim and distant—he looked down on Arden Castle and loved it, and felt that he asked no better than to live there all his life with his cousins and their father, and that, after all, the magic of a dream-life was not needed, when life itself was so good and happy.

And just as he was thinking this a twig cracked sharply in the hedge. Then a dozen twigs rustled and broke, and something like a great black bird seemed to fly out at him and fold him in its wings.

It was not a bird—he knew that the next moment—but a big, dark cloak, that someone had thrown over his head and shoulders, and through it strong hands were holding him.

"Hold yer noise!" said a voice; "if you so much as squeak it'll be the worse for you."

"Help!" shouted Dickie instantly.

He was thrown on to the ground. Hands fumbled, his face was cleared of the cloak, and a handkerchief with a round pebble in it was stuffed into his mouth so that he could not speak. Then he was dragged behind a hedge and held there, while two voices whispered above him. The cloak was over his head again now, and he could see nothing, but he could hear. He heard one of the voices say, "Hush! they're coming." And then he heard the sound of hoofs and wheels, and Lord Arden's jolly voice saying, "He must have walked on; we shall catch him up all right." Then the sound of wheels and hoofs died away, and hard hands pulled him to his feet and thrust the crutch under his arm.

"Step out!" said one of the voices, "and step out sharp—see?—or I'll l'arn you! There's a carriage awaiting for you."

He stepped out; there was nothing else to be done. They had taken the cloak from his eyes now, and he saw presently that they were nearing a coster's barrow.

They laid him in the barrow, covered him with the cloak, and put vegetable marrows and cabbages on that. They only left him a little room to breathe.

"Now lie still for your life!" said the second voice. "If you stir an inch I'll lick you till you can't stand! And now you know."

So he lay still, rigid with misery and despair. For neither of these voices was strange to him. He knew them both only too well.

The Noble Deed

When Lord Arden and Elfrida and Edred reached the Castle and found that Dickie had not come back, the children concluded that Beale had persuaded him to stay the night at the cottage. And Lord Arden thought that the children must be right. He was extremely annoyed both with Beale and with Dickie for making such an arrangement without consulting him.

"It is impertinent of Beale and thoughtless of the boy," he said; "and I shall speak a word to them both in the morning."

But when Edred and Elfrida were gone to bed, Lord Arden found that he could not feel quite sure or quite satisfied. Suppose Dickie was *not* at Beale's? He strolled up to the cottage to see. Everything was dark at the cottage. He hesitated, then knocked at the door. At the third knock Beale, very sleepy, put his head out of the window.

"Who's there?" said he.

"I am here," said Lord Arden. "Richard is asleep, I suppose?"

"I suppose so, my lord," said Beale, sleepy and puzzled.

"You have given me some anxiety. I had to come up to make sure he was here."

"But 'e *ain't* 'ere," said Beale. "Didn't you pick 'im up with the dog-car, same as you said you would?"

"No," shouted Lord Arden. "Come down, Beale, and get a lantern. There must have been an accident."

The bedroom window showed a square of light, and Lord Arden below heard Beale blundering about above.

"'Ere's you coat," Mrs. Beale's voice sounded; "never mind lacing up of your boots. You orter gone a bit of the way with 'im."

"Well, I offered for to go, didn't I?" Beale growled, blundered down the stairs and out through the wash-house, and came round the corner of the house with a stable lantern in his hand. He came close to where Lord Arden stood—a tall, dark figure in the starlight—and spoke in a voice that trembled.

"The little nipper," he said; and again, "the little nipper. If anything's happened to 'im! Swelp me! gov'ner—my lord, I mean. What I meanter say, if anything's 'appened to *'im!* One of the best!"

The two men went quickly towards the gate. As they passed down the quiet, dusty road Beale spoke again.

"I wasn't no good—I don't deceive you, guv'ner—a no account man I was, swelp me! And the little un, 'e tidied me up and told me tales and kep' me straight. It was 'is doing me and 'Melia come together. An' the dogs an' all. An' the little one. An' 'e got me chuck the cadgin'. An' worse. 'E don't know what I was like when I met 'im. Why, I set out to make a blighted burglar of 'im—you wouldn't believe!"

And out the whole story came as Lord Arden and he went along the grey road, looking to right and left where no bushes were nor stones, only the smooth curves of the down, so that it was easy to see that no little boy was there either.

They looked for Dickie to right and left and here and there under bushes, and by stiles and hedges, and with trembling hearts they searched in the little old chalk quarry, and the white moon came up very late to help them. But they did not find him, though they roused a dozen men in the village to join in the search, and old Beale himself, who knew every yard of the ground for five miles round, came out with the spaniel who knew every inch of it for ten. But True rushed about the house and garden whining and yelping so piteously that 'Melia tied him up, and he stayed tied up.

And so, when Edred and Elfrida came down to breakfast, Mrs. Honeysett met them with the news that Dickie was lost and their father still out looking for him.

"It's that beastly magic," said Edred as soon as the children were alone. "He's done it once too often, and he's got stuck some time in history and can't get back."

"And we can't do anything. We can't get to him," said Elfrida. "Oh! if only we'd got the old white magic and the Mouldiwarp to help us, we could find out what's become of him."

"Perhaps he has fallen down a disused mine," Edred suggested, "and is lying panting for water, and his faithful dog has jumped down after him and broken all its dear legs."

Elfrida melted to tears at this desperate picture, melted to a speechless extent.

"We can't do anything," said Edred again; "don't snivel like that, for goodness' sake, Elfrida. This is a man's job. Dry up. I can't think with you blubbing like that."

"I'm not," said Elfrida untruly, and sniffed with some intensity.

"If you could make up some poetry now," Edred went on, "would that be any good?"

"Not without the dresses," she sniffed. "you know we always had dresses for our magic, or nearly always; and they have to be dead and gone people's dresses, and you'll only go to the dead and gone people's time when the dresses were worn. Oh! dear Dickie, and if he's really down a mine, or things like that, what's the good of anything?"

"I'm going to try, anyway," said Edred, "at least you must too. Because I can't make poetry."

"No more can I when I'm as unhappy as this. Poetry's the last thing you think of when you're mizzy."

"We could dress up, anyway," said Edred hopefully. "The bits of armor out of the hall, and the Indian feather head-dresses father brought home, and I have father's shooting-gaiters and brown paper tops, and you can have Aunt Edith's Roman sash. It's in the right-hand corner drawer. I saw it on the wedding-day when I went to get her prayer-brook."

"I don't want to dress up," said Elfrida; "I want to find Dickie."

"I don't want to dress up either," said Edred; but we must do something, and perhaps, I know it's just only perhaps, it might help if we dressed up. Let's try it, anyway."

Elfrida was too miserable to argue. Before long two most miserable children faced each other in Edred's bedroom, dressed as Red Indians so far as their heads and backs went. Then came lots of plate armor for chest and arms; then, in the case of Elfrida, petticoats and Roman sash and Japanese wickerwork shoes and father's brown paper tops. And in the case of Edred, legs cased in armor that looked like cricket pads, ending in jointed foot-coverings that looked like chrysalises. (I am told the correct plural is chrysalides, but life would be dull indeed if one always used the correct plural.) They were two forlorn faces that looked at each other as Edred said—

"Now the poetry."

"I can't," said Elfrida, bursting into tears again; "I *can't!* So there. I've been trying all the time we've been dressing, and I can only think of—

> *"Oh, call dear Dickie back to me,*
> *I cannot play alone;*
> *The summer comes with flower and bee,*
> *Where is dear Dickie gone?"*

And I know that's no use."

"I should think not," said Edred. "Why, it isn't your own poetry at all. It's Felicia M. Hemans. I'll try." And he got a pencil and paper and try he did, his very hardest, be sure. But there are some things that the best and bravest cannot do. And the thing Edred couldn't do was to make poetry, however bad. He simply couldn't do it, any more than you can fly. It wasn't in him, any more than wings are on you.

> "Oh, Mouldiwarp, you said we must
> Not have any more magic. But we trust
> You won't be hard on us, because Dickie is lost
> And we don't know how to find him."

That was the best Edred could do, and I tell it to his credit, he really did feel doubtful whether what he had so slowly and carefully written was indeed genuine poetry. So much so, that he would not show it to Elfrida until she had begged very hard indeed. At about the thirtieth "Do, please! Edred, do!" he gave her the paper. No little girl was ever more polite than Elfrida or less anxious to hurt the feelings of others. But she was also quite truthful, and when Edred said in an ashamed muffled voice, "Is it all right, do you think?" the best she could find by way of answer was, "I don't know much about poetry. We'll try it."

And they did try it, and nothing happened.

"I knew it was no good," Edred said crossly; "and I've made an ass of myself for nothing."

"Well, I've often made one of myself," said Elfrida comfortingly, "and I will again if you like. But I don't suppose it'll be any more good than yours."

Elfrida frowned fiercely and the feathers on her Indian head-dress quivered with the intensity of her effort.

"Is it coming?" Edred asked in anxious tones, and she nodded distractedly.

> *"Great Mouldiestwarp, on you we call*
> *To do the greatest magic of all;*
> *To show us how we are to find*
> *Dear Dickie who is lame and kind.*
> *Do this for us, and on our hearts we swore*
> *We'll never ask you for anything more."*

"I don't see that it's so much better than mine," said Edred, "and it ought to be *swear*, not *swore*."

"I don't think it is. But you didn't finish yours. And it couldn't be 'swear,' because of rhyming," Elfrida explained. "But I'm sure if the Mouldiestwarp hears it he won't care tuppence whether it's swear or swore. He is much too great. He's far above grammar, I'm sure."

"I wish everyone was," sighed Edred, and I daresay you have often felt the same.

"Well, fire away! Not that's it's any good. don't you remember you can only get at the Mouldiestwarp by a noble deed? And wanting to find Dickie isn't noble."

"No," she agreed; "but then if we could get Dickie back by doing a noble deed we'd do it like a shot, wouldn't we?"

"Oh! I suppose so," said Edred grumpily; "fire away, can't you?"

Elfrida fired away, and the next moment it was plain that Elfrida's poetry was more potent than Edred's; also that a little bad grammar is a trifle to a mighty Mouldiwarp.

For the walls of Edred's room receded further and further, till the children found themselves in a great white hall with avenues of tall pillars stretching in every direction as far as you could see. The hall was crowded with people dressed in costumes of all countries and all ages—Chinese, Indians, Crusaders in amour, powdered ladies, doubleted gentlemen, Cavaliers in curls, Turks in turbans, Arabs, monks, abbesses, jesters, grandees with ruffs round their necks, and savages with kilts of thatch. Every kind of dress you can think of was there. Only all the dresses were white. It was like a *redoute*, which is a fancy-dress ball where the guests may wear any dress they choose, only all the dresses must be of one color.

Elfrida saw the whiteness all about her and looked down anxiously at her clothes and Edred's, which she remembered to have been of rather odd colors. Everything they wore was white now. Even the Roman sash, instead of having stripes blue and red and green and black and yellow, was of five different shades of white. If you think there are not so many shades of white, try to paper a room with white paper and get it at five different shops.

The people round the children pushed them gently forward. And then they saw that in the middle of the hall was a throne of silver, spread with a fringed cloth of checkered silver and green, and on it, with the Mouldiwarp standing on one side and the Mouldierwarp on the other, the Mouldiestwarp was seated in state and splendor. He was much larger than either of the other moles, and his fur was as silvery as the feathers of a swan.

Everyone in the room was looking at the two children, and it seemed impossible for them not to advance, though slowly and shyly, right to the front of the throne.

Arrived there, it seemed right to bow, very low. So they did it.

Then the Mouldiwarp said—

"What brings you here?"

"Kind magic," Elfrida answered.

And the Mouldierwarp said—

"What is your desire?"

And Edred said, "We want Dickie, please."

Then the Mouldiestwarp said, and it was to Edred that he said it—

"Dickie is in the hands of those who will keep him from you for many a day unless you yourself go, alone, and rescue him. It will be difficult, and it will be dangerous. Will you go?"

"Me? Alone?" said Edred rather blankly. "Not Elfrida?"

"Dickie can only be ransomed at a great price, and it must be paid by you. It will cost you more to do it than it would cost Elfrida, because she is braver than you are."

Here was a nice thing for a boy to have said to him, and before all these people too! To ask a chap to do a noble deed and in the same breath to tell him he is a coward!

Edred flushed crimson, and a shudder ran through the company.

"Don't turn that horrible color," whispered a white toreador who was close to him. This is the *white* world. No crimson allowed."

Elfrida caught Edred's hand.

"Edred is quite as brave as me," she said. "He'll go. Won't you?"

"Of course I will," said Edred impatiently.

"Then ascend the steps of the throne," said the Mouldiestwarp, very kindly now, and sit here by my side."

Edred obeyed, and the Mouldiestwarp leaned towards him and spoke in his ear.

So that neither Elfrida nor any of the great company in the White Hall could hear a word, only Edred alone.

"If you go to rescue Richard Arden," the Mouldiestwarp said, "you make the greatest sacrifice of your life. For he who was called Richard Harding is Richard Arden, and it is he who is Lord Arden and not you or your father. And if you go to his rescue you will be taking from your father the title and the Castle, and you will be giving up your place as heir of Arden to your cousin Richard who is the rightful heir."

"But how is he the rightful heir?" Edred asked, bewildered.

"Three generations ago," said the Mouldiestwarp, "a little baby was stolen from Arden. Death came among the Ardens

EDRED OBEDYED, AND THE MOULDIESTWARP LEANED TOWARDS HIM
AND SPOKE IN HIS EAR.

and that child became the heir to the name and the lands of Arden. The man who stole the child took it to a woman in Deptford, and gave it in charge to her to nurse. She knew nothing but that the child's clothes were marked Arden, and that it had, tied to its waist, a coral and bells engraved with a coat of arms. The man who had stolen the child said he would return in a month. He never returned. He fought in a duel and was killed. But the night before the duel he wrote a letter saying what he had done and put it in a secret cupboard behind a picture of a lady who was born an Arden, at Talbot Court. And there that letter is to this day."

"I hope I shan't forget it all," said Edred.

"None ever forgets what I tell them," said the Mouldiestwarp. "Finding that the man did not return, the Deptford woman brought up the child as her own. He grew up, was taught a trade and married a working girl. The name of Arden changed itself, as names do, to Harding. Their child was the father of Richard whom you know. And he is Lord Arden."

"Yes," said Edred submissively.

"You will never tell your father this," the low, beautiful voice went on; "you must not even tell your sister till you have rescued Dickie and made the sacrifice. This is the one supreme chance of all your life. Every soul has one such chance, a chance to be perfectly unselfish, absolutely noble and true. You can take this chance. But you must take it alone. No one can help you. No one can advise you. And you must keep the nobler thought in your own heart till it is a noble deed. Then, humbly and thankfully in that you have been permitted to do so fine and brave a thing and to draw near to the immortals of all ages who have such deeds to do and have done them, you may tell the truth to the one who loves you best, your sister Elfrida."

"But isn't Elfrida to have a chance to be noble too?" Edred asked.

"She will have a thousand chances to be good and noble. And she will take them all. But she will never know that she has done it," said the Mouldiestwarp gravely. "Now—are you ready to do what is to be done?"

"It seems very unkind to daddy," said Edred, "stopping his being Lord Arden and everything."

"To do right often seems unkind to one or another," said the Mouldiestwarp, "but think. How long would your father wish to keep his house and his castle if he knew that they belonged to someone else?"

"I see," said Edred, still doubtfully. "No, of course he wouldn't. Well, what am I to do?"

"When Dickie's father died, a Deptford woman related to Dickie's mother kept the child. She was not kind to him. And he left her. Later she met a man who had been a burglar. He had entered Talbot Court, opened a panel, and found that old letter that told of Dickie's birth. He and she have kidnapped Dickie, hoping to get him to sign a paper promising to pay them money for giving him the letter which tells how he is heir to Arden. But already they have found out that a letter signed by a child is useless and unlawful. And they dare not let Richard go for fear of punishment. So, if you choose to do nothing your father is safe and you will inherit Arden."

"What am I to do?" Edred asked again—"to get Dickie back, I mean."

"You must go alone and at night to Beale's cottage, open the door and you will find Richard's dog asleep before the fire. You must unchain the dog and take him to the milestone by the cross-roads. Then go where the dog goes. You will need a knife to cut cords with. And you will need all your courage. Look in my eyes."

Edred looked in the eyes of the Mouldiestwarp and saw that they were no longer a mole's eyes but were like the eyes of all the dear people he had ever known, and through them the soul of all the brave people he had ever read about looked out at him and said, "Courage, Edred. Be one of us."

"Now look at the people on the Hall," said the Mouldiestwarp.

Edred looked. And behold, they were no longer strangers. He knew them all. Joan of Arc and Peter the Hermit, Hereward and Drake, Elsa whose brothers were swans, St. George who killed the dragon, Blondel who sang to his king in prison, Lady Nithsdale who brought her husband safe out of the cruel Tower. There were captains who went down with their ships, generals who died fighting for forlorn hopes, patriots, kings, nuns, monks, men, women, and children—all with that light in their eyes which brightens with splendor the dreams of men.

And as he came down off the throne the great ones crowded round him, clasping his hand and saying—

"Be one of us, Edred. Be one of us."

Then an intense white light shone so that the children could see nothing else. And then suddenly there they were again within the narrow walls of Edred's bedroom.

"Well," said Elfrida in tones of brisk commonplace, "what did it say to you? I say, you do look funny."

"Don't!" said Edred crossly. He began to tear off the armor. "Here, help me to get these things off."

"But what did it say?" Elfrida asked, helpfully.

"I can't tell you. I'm not going to tell anyone till it's over."

"Oh, just as you like," said Elfrida; "keep your old secrets," and left him.

That was hard, wasn't it?

"I can't help it, I tell you. Oh! Elfrida, if *you're* going to bother it's just a little bit too much, that's all."

"You really mustn't tell me?"

"I've told you so fifty times," he said. Which was untrue. You know he had really only told her twice.

"Very well, then," she said heroically, "I won't ask you a single thing. But you'll tell me the minute you can, won't you? And you'll let me help?"

"Nobody can help, no one can advise me," Edred said. "I've got to do it off my own bat if I do it at all. Now you just shut up, I want to think."

This unusual desire quite awed Elfrida. But it irritated her too.

"Perhaps you'd like me to go away," she said ironically.

And Edred's wholly unexpected reply was, "Yes, please."

So she went.

And when she was gone Edred sat down on the box at the foot of his bed and tried to think. But it was not easy.

I ought to go," he told himself.

"But think of your father," said something else which was himself too.

He thought so hard that his thoughts got quite confused. His head grew very hot, and his hands and feet very cold. Mrs. Honeysett came in, exclaimed at his white face, felt his hands, said he was in a high fever, and put him to bed with wet rags on his forehead and hot-water bottles to his feet. Perhaps he was feverish. At any rate he could never be sure afterwards whether there really had been a very polite and plausible black mole sitting on his pillow most of the day saying all those things which the part of himself that he liked least agreed with. Such things as—

"Think of your father.

"No one will ever know.

"Dickie will be all right somehow.

"Perhaps you only dreamt that about Dickie being shut up somewhere and it's not true.

"Anyway, it's not your business, is it?" And so on. You know the sort of things.

Elfrida was not allowed to come into the room for fear Edred should be ill with something catching. So he lay tossing all day, hearing the black mole, or something else, say all these things and himself saying, "I must go.

"Oh! poor Dickie.

"I promised to go.

"Yes, I will go."

And late that night when Lord Arden had come home and had gone to bed, tired out by a long day's vain search for the lost Dickie, and when everybody was asleep, Edred got up and dressed. He put his bedroom candle and matches in his pocket, crept downstairs and out of the house and up to Beale's. It was a slow and nervous business. More than once on the staircase he thought he heard a stair creak behind him, and again and again as he went along the road he fancied he heard a soft footstep padpadding-behind him, but of course when he looked round he could see no one was there. So presently he decided that it was cowardly to keep looking round, and besides, it only made him more frightened. So he kept steadily on and took no notice at all of a black patch by the sweetbrier bush by Beale's cottage door just exactly as if someone was crouching in the shadow.

He pressed his thumb on the latch and opened the door very softly. Something moved inside and a chain rattled. Edred's heart gave a soft, uncomfortable jump. But it was only True, standing up to receive company. He saw the whiteness of the dog and made for it, felt for the chair, unhooked it from the staple in the wall, and went out again, closing the door after him, and followed very willingly by True. Again he looked suspiciously at the shadow of the great sweetbrier, but the dog showed no uneasiness, so Edred knew that there was nothing to be afraid of. True, in fact, was the greatest comfort to him. He told Elfrida afterwards that it was all True's doing; he could never, he was sure, have gone on without that good companion.

True followed at the slack chain's end till they got to the milestone, and then suddenly he darted ahead and took the lead, the chain stretched taut, and the boy had all his work cut out to keep up with the dog. Up the hill they went on to the downs, and in and out among the furze bushes. The night was no longer dark to Edred. His eyes had got used to the gentle starlight, and he followed the dog among the gorse and brambles without stumbling and without hurting himself against the million sharp spears and thorns.

Suddenly True passed, sniffed, sneezed, blew through his nose and began to dig.

"Come on, come on, good dog," said Edred, "Come on, True," for his fancy pictured Dickie a prisoner in some lonely cottage, and he longed to get to it and set him free and get safe back home with him. So he pulled at the chain. But True only shook himself and went on digging. The spot he had chosen was under a clump of furze bigger than any they had passed. The sharp furze-spikes pricked his nose and paws, but True was not the dog to be stopped by little things like that. He only stopped every now and then to sneeze and blow, and then went on digging.

Edred remembered the knife he had brought. It was the big pruning-knife out of the drawer in the hall. He pulled it out. He would cut away some of the furze branches. Perhaps Dickie was lying bound, hidden in the middle of the furze bush.

"Dickie," he said softly, "Dickie."

But no one answered. Only True sneezed and snuffed and blew and went on digging.

So then Edred took hold of a branch of furze to cut it, and it was loose and came away in his hand without any cutting. He tried another. That too was loose. He took off his jacket and threw it over his hands to protect them, and seizing an armful of furze pulled, and fell back, a great bundle of the prickly stuff on top of him. True was pulling like mad at the chain. Edred scrambled up; the furze he had pulled away disclosed a hole, and True was disappearing down it. Edred saw, as he dog dragged him close to the hole, that it was a large one, though only part of it had been uncovered. He stooped to peer in, his foot slipped on the edge, and he fell right into it, the dog dragging all the time.

"Stop, True; lie down, sir!" he said and the dog paused, though the chain was still strained tight.

Then Edred was glad of his bedroom candle. He pulled it out and lighted it and blinked, perceiving almost at once that he was in the beginning of an underground passage. He looked up, he could see above him the stars plain through a net of furze bushes. He stood up and True went on. Next moment he knew that he was in the old smugglers' cave that he and Elfrida had so often tried to find.

The dog and the boy went on along a passage, down steps cut in the rock, through a rough, heavy door, and so into the smugglers' cave itself, an enormous cavern as big as a church. Out of an opening at the upper end a stream of water fell, and ran along the cave clear between shores of smooth sand.

And, lying on the sand near the stream, was something dark.

True gave a bound that jerked the chain out of Edred's hand, and leaped upon the dark thing, licking it, whining, and uttering little dog moans of pure love and joy. For the dark something was Dickie, fast asleep. He was bound with cords, his poor lame foot tied tight to the other one. His arms were bound too. And now he was awake.

"Down, True!" he said. "Hush! Ssh!"

"Where are they—the man and woman?" Edred whispered.

"Oh, Edred! You! You perfect brick!" Dickie whispered back. "They're in the further cave. I heard them snoring before I went to sleep."

"Lie still," said Edred; "I've got a knife. I'll cut the cords."

He cut them, and Dickie tried to stand up. But his limbs were too stiff. Edred rubbed his legs, while Dickie stretched his fingers to get the pins and needles out of his arms.

Edred had stuck the candle in the sand. It made a ring of light round them. That was why they did not see a dark figure that came quietly creeping across the sand towards them. It was quite close to them before Edred looked up.

"Oh!" he gasped, and Dickie, looking up, whispered, "It's all up—*run*. Never mind me. I shall get away all right."

"No," said Edred, and then with a joyous leap of the heart perceived that the dark figure was Elfrida in her father's ulster.

("I hadn't time to put on my stockings," she explained later. "You'd have known me a mile off by my white legs if I hadn't covered them up with this.")

"Elfrida!" said both boys at once.

"Well, you didn't think I was going to be out of it," she said. "I've been behind you all the way, Edred. Don't tell me anything. I won't ask any questions, only come along out of it. Lean on me."

They got him up to the passage, one on each side, and by that time Dickie could use his legs and his crutch. They got home and roused Lord Arden, and told him Dickie was found and all about it, and he roused the house, and he and Beale and half-a-dozen men from the village went up to the cave and found that wicked man and woman in a stupid sleep, and tied their hands and marched them to the town and to the police-station.

When the man was searched the letter was found on him which the man—it was that red-headed man you have heard of—had taken from Talbot Court.

"I wish you joy of your good fortune, my boy," said Lord Arden when he read the letter. "Of course we must look into things, but I feel no doubt at all that you *are* Lord Arden!"

"I don't want to be," said Dickie, and that was true. Yet at the same time he did want to be. The thought of being Richard, Lord Arden, he who had been just little lame Dickie of Deptford, of owning this glorious castle, of being the

"ELFRIDA!" SAID BOTH BOYS AT ONCE.

master of an old name and an old place, this thought sang in his heart a very beautiful tune. Yet what he said was true. There is so often room in our hearts for two tunes at time. "I don't want to be. You ought to be, sir. You've been so kind to me," he said.

"My dear boy," said the father of Edred and Elfrida, "I did very well without the title and the castle, and if they're yours I shall do very well without them again. You shall have your rights, my dear boy, and I shan't be hurt by it. Don't you think that."

Dickie thought several things and shook the other's hand very hard.

The tale of Dickie's rescue from the cave was the talk of the countryside. True was praised much, but Edred more. Why had no one else thought of putting the dog on the scent? Edred said that it was mostly True's doing. And the people praised his modesty. And nobody, except perhaps Elfrida, ever understood what it had cost Edred to go that night through the dark and rescue his cousin.

Edred's father and Mrs. Honeysett agreed that Edred had done it in the delirium of a fever, brought on by his anxiety about his friend and playmate. People do, you know, do odd things in fevers that they would never do at other times.

The red-headed man and the woman were tried at the assizes and punished. If you ask me how they knew about the caves which none of the country people seemed to know of, I can only answer that I don't know. Only I know that everyone you know knows lots of things that you don't know they know.

When they all went a week later to explore the caves, they found a curious arrangement of brickwork and cement and clay, shutting up a hole through which the stream had evidently once flowed out into the open air. It now flowed away into darkness. Lord Arden pointed out how its course had been diverted and made to run down underground to the sea.

"We might let it come back to the moat," said Edred. "It used to run that way. It says so in the *History of Arden*."

"We must decide that later," said his father, who had a long blue lawyer's letter in his pocket.

Lord Arden

There was a lot of talk and a lot of letter-writing before anyone seemed to be able to be sure who was Lord Arden. If the father of Edred and Elfrida had wanted to dispute about it no doubt there would have been enough work to keep the lawyers busy for years, and seas of ink would have been spilt and thunders of eloquence spent on the question. But as the present Lord Arden was an honest man and only too anxious that Dickie should have everything that belonged to him, even the lawyers had to cut their work short.

When Edred saw how his father tried his best to find out the truth about Dickie's birth, and how willing he was to give up what he had thought was his own, if it should prove to be *not* his, do you think he was not glad to know that he had done his duty, and rescued his cousin, and had not, by any meanness or any indecision, brought dishonor on the name of Arden? As for Elfrida, when she knew the whole story of that night of rescue, she admired her brother so much that it made him almost uncomfortable. However, she now looked up to him in all things and consulted him about everything, and, after all, this is very pleasant from your sister, especially when everyone has been rather in the habit of suggesting that she is better than you are, as well as clever.

To Dickie Lord Arden said, "Of course, if anything *should* happen to show that I am really Lord Arden, you won't desert us, Dickie. You shall go to school with Edred and be brought up like my very own son."

And, like Lord Arden's very own son, Dickie lived at the house in Arden Castle, and grew to love it more and more. He no longer wanted to get away from these present times to those old days when James the First was King. The times you are born in are always more home-like than any other times can be. When Dickie lived miserably at Deptford he always longed to go to those old times, as a man who is unhappy at home may wish to travel to other countries. But a man who is happy in his home does not want to leave it. And at Arden Dickie was happy. The training he had had in the old-world life enabled him to take his place and to be unembarrassed with the Ardens and their friends as he was with the Beales and theirs. "A little shy," the Ardens' friends told each other, "but what fine manners! And to think he was only a tramp! Lord Arden has certainly done wonders with him!"

So Lord Arden got the credit of all that Dickie had learned from his tutors in James the First's time.

It is not in the nature of any child to brood continually on the past or the future. The child lives in the present. And Dickie lived at Arden and loved it, and enjoyed himself; and Lord Arden bought him a pony, so that his lame foot was hardly any drag at all. The other children had a donkey-cart, and the three made all sorts of interesting expeditions.

Once they went over to Talbot Court, and saw the secret place where Edward Talbot had hidden his confession about having stolen the Arden baby, three generations before. Also they saw the portrait of the Lady Talbot who had been a Miss Arden. In rose-colored brocade she was, with a green silk petticoat and her powdered hair dressed high over a great cushion, but her eyes and her mouth were the eyes of Dickie of Deptford.

Lady Talbot was very charming to the children, played hide-and-seek with them, and gave them delightful and varied tea in the yew arbor.

"I'm glad you wouldn't let me adopt you, Richard," she said, when Elfrida and Edred had been sent to her garden to get a basket of peaches to take home with them, "because just when I had become entirely attached to you, you would have found out your real relations, and where would your poor foster-mother have been then?"

"If I could have stayed with you I would," said Dickie seriously. I did like you most awfully, even then. You are very like the Lady Arden whose husband was shut up in the Tower for the Gunpowder Plot."

"So they tell me," said Lady Talbot, "but how do you know it?"

"I don't know," said Dickie confused, "but you *are* like her."

"You must have seen a portrait of her. There's one in the National Portrait Gallery. She was a Delamere, and my name was Delamere, too, before I was married. She was one of the same family, you see, dear."

Dickie put his arms round her waist as she sat beside him, and laid his head on her shoulder.

"I wish you'd really been my mother," he said, and his thoughts were back in the other days with the mother who wore a ruff and hoop. Lady Talbot hugged him tenderly.

"My dear little Dickie," she said, "you don't wish it as much as I do."

"There are all sorts of things a chap can't be sure of—things you mustn't tell anyone. Secrets, you know— honorable secrets. But if it was your own mother it would be different. But if you haven't got a mother you have to decide everything for yourself."

"Won't you let me help you?" she asked.

Dickie, his head on her shoulder, was for one wild moment tempted to tell her everything—the whole story, from beginning to end. But he knew that she could not understand it—or even believe it. No grown-up person could. A chap's own mother might have, perhaps—but perhaps not, too.

"I can't tell you," he said at last, "only I don't think I want to be Lord Arden. At least, I do, frightfully. It's so splendid, all the things the Ardens did—in history, you know. But I don't want to turn people out—and you know Edred came and saved me from those people. It feels hateful when I think perhaps they'll have to turn out just because I happened to turn up. Sometimes I feel as if I simply couldn't bear it."

"You dear child!" she said; "of course you feel that. But don't let your mind dwell on it. Don't think about it. You're only a little boy. Be happy and jolly, and don't worry about grown-up things Leave grown-up things to the grown-ups."

"You see," Dickie told her, "somehow I've always had to worry about grown-up things. What with Beale, and one thing and another."

"That was the man you ran away from me to go to?"

"Yes," said Dickie gravely; "you see, I was responsible for Beale."

"And now? Don't you feel responsible any more?"

"No," said Dickie, in business-like tones; "you see, I've settled Beale in life. You can't be responsible for married people. They're responsible for each other. So now I've got only my own affairs to think of. And the Ardens. I don't know what to do."

"Do? why, there's nothing *to* do except to enjoy yourself and learn your lessons and be happy," she told him. "Don't worry your little head. Just enjoy yourself, and forget that you ever had any responsibilities."

"I'll try," he told her, and then the others came back with their peaches, and there was nothing more to be said but "Thank you very much" and goodbye.

Exploring the old smugglers' caves was exciting and delightful, as exploring caves always is. It turned out that more than one old man in the village had heard from his father about the caves and the smuggling that had gone on in those parts in old ancient days. But they had not thought it their place to talk about such things, and I suspect that in their hearts they did not more than half believe them. Old Beale said—

"Why didn't you ask me? I could a-told you where they was. Only I shouldn't a done fear you'd break your precious necks."

Of course the children were desperately anxious to open up the brickwork and let the stream come out into the light of day; only their father thought it would be too expensive. But Edred and Elfrida worried and bothered in a perfectly gently and polite way till at last a very jolly gentleman in spectacles, who came down to spend a couple of days, took their part. From the moment he owned himself an engineer Edred and Elfrida gave him no peace, and he seemed quite pleased to be taken to see the cave. He pointed out that the removal of the simple dam would send the water back into the old channel. It would be perfectly simple to have the brickwork knocked out, and to let the stream find its way back, if it could, to its old channel, and thence down the arched way which Edred and Elfrida told him they were certain was under a mound below the Castle.

"You know a lot about it, don't you?" he said good-humoredly.

"Yes," said Edred simply.

Then they all went down to the mound, and the engineer then poked and prodded it and said he should not wonder if they were not so far out. And then Beale and another man came with spades, and presently there was the arch, as good as ever, and they exclaimed and admired and went back to the caves.

It was a grand moment when the bricks had been taken out and daylight poured into the cave, and nothing remained but to break down the dam and let the water run out of the darkness into the sunshine. You can imagine with what mixed feelings the children wondered whether they would rather stay in the cave and see the dam demolished, or stay outside and see the stream rush out. In the end the boys stayed within, and it was only Elfrida and her father who saw the stream emerge. They sat on a hillock among the thin harebells and wild thyme and sweet lavender-colored gipsy roses, with their eyes fixed on the opening in the hillside, and waited and waited and waited for a very long time.

"Won't you mind frightfully, daddy," Elfrida asked during this long waiting, "if it turns out that you're not Lord Arden?"

He paused a moment before he decided to answer her without reserve.

"Yes," he said, "I shall mind, frightfully. And that's just why we must do everything we possibly can to prove that Dickie is the rightful heir, so that whether he has the title or I have it you and I may never have to reproach ourselves for having left a single stone unturned to give him his rights—whatever they are."

"And you, yours, daddy."

"And me, mine. Anyhow, if he is Lord Arden I shall probably be appointed his guardian, and we shall all live together here just the same. Only I shall go back to being plain Arden."

"I believe Dickie *is* Lord Arden," Elfrida began, and I am not at all sure that she would not have gone on to give her reasons, including the whole story which the Mouldiestwarp had told to Dickie; but at that moment there was a roaring, rushing sound from inside the cave, and a flash of shiny silver gleamed across that dark gap in the hillside. There was a burst of imprisoned splendor. The stream leaped out and flowed right and left over the dry grass, till it lapped in tiny waves against their hillock—"like sand castles," as Elfrida observed. It spread out in a lake, wider and wider; but presently gathered itself together and began to creep down the hill, winding in and out among the hillocks in an ever deepening stream.

"Come on, childie, let's make for the moat. We shall get there first, if we run our hardest," Elfrida's father said. And he ran, with his little daughter's hand in his.

They got the first. The stream, knowing its own mind better and better as it recognized its old road, reached the Castle, and by dinner-time all the grass round the Castle was under water. By tea-time the water in the moat was a foot or more deep, and when they got up next morning the Castle was surrounded by a splendid moat fifty feet wide, and a stream ran from it, in a zigzag way it is true, but still it ran, to the lower arch under the mound, and disappeared there, to run underground into the sea. They enjoyed the moat for one whole day, and then the stream was dammed again and condemned to run underground till next spring, by which time the walls of the Castle would have been examined and concrete laid to their base, lest the water should creep through and sap the foundations.

"It's going to be a very costly business, it seems," Elfrida heard her father say to the engineer, "and I don't know that I ought to do it. But I can't resist the temptation. I shall have to economize in other directions, that's all."

When Elfrida had heard this she went to Dickie and Edred, who were fishing in the cave, and told them what she had heard.

"And we *must* have another try for the treasure," she said. "Whoever has the Castle will want to restore it; they've got those pictures of it as it used to be. And then there are all the cottages to re-build. Dear Dickie, you're so clever, do think of some way to find the treasure."

So Dickie thought.

And presently he said—

"You once saw the treasure being carried to the secret room—in a picture, didn't you?"

They told him yes.

"Then why didn't you go back to that time and see it really?"

"We hadn't the clothes. Everything in our magic depended on clothes."

"Mine doesn't. Shall we go?"

"There were lots of soldiers in the picture," said Edred, "and fighting."

"I'm not afraid of soldiers," said Elfrida very quickly, "and you're not afraid of *anything*, Edred—you know you aren't."

"You can't be or you couldn't have come after me right into the cave in the middle of the night. Come on. Stand close together and I'll spread out the moon-seeds."

So Dickie said, and they stood, and he spread the moon-seeds out, and he wished to be with the party of men who were hiding the treasure. But before he spread out the seeds he took certain other things in his left hand and held them closely. And instantly they were.

They were standing very close together, all three of them, in a niche in a narrow, dark passage, and men went by them carrying heavy chests, and great sacks of leather, and bundles tied up in straw and in handkerchiefs. The men had long hair and the kind of clothes you know were worn when Charles the First was King. And the children wore the dresses of that time and the boys had little swords at their sides. When the last bundle had been carried, the last chest set down with a dump on the stone floor of some room beyond, the children heard a door shut and a key turned, and then the men came back all together along the passage, and the children followed them. Presently torchlight gave way to daylight as they came out into the open air. But they had to come on hands and knees, for the path sloped steeply up and the opening was very low. The chests must have been pushed through. They could never have been carried.

The children turned and looked at the opening. It was in the courtyard wall, the courtyard that was now a smooth grasslawn and not the rough, daisied grass plot dotted with heaps of broken stone and masonry that they were used to see. And as they looked two men picked up a great stone and staggered forward with it and laid it on the stone floor of the secret passage just where it ended at the edge of the grass. Then another stone and another. The stones fitted into their places like bits of a Chinese puzzle. There was mortar or cement at their edges, and when the last stone was replaced no one could tell those stones from the other stones that formed the wall. Only the grass in front of them was trampled and broken.

"Fetch food and break it about," said the man who seemed to be in command, "that it may look as though the men had eaten here. And trample the grass at other places. I give the Roundhead dogs another hour to break down our last defence. Children, go to your mother. This is no place for you."

They knew the way. They had seen it in the picture. Edred and Elfrida turned to go. But Dickie whispered, "Don't wait for me. I've something yet to do."

And when the soldiers had gone to get food and strew it about, as they had been told to do, Dickie crept up to the stones that had been removed, from which he had never taken his eyes, knelt down and scratched on one of the stones with one of the big nails he had brought in his hand. It blunted over and he took another, hiding in the chapel doorway when the men came back with the food.

"Every man to his post and God save us all!" cried the captain when the food was spread. They clattered off—they were in their armor now—and Dickie knelt down again and went on scratching with the nail.

The air was full of shouting, and the sound of guns, and the clash of amour, and a shattering sound like a giant mallet striking a giant drum—a sound that came and came again at five-minute intervals—and the shrieks of wounded men. Dickie pressed up the grass to cover the marks he had made on the stone, so low as to be almost underground and quite hidden by the grass roots.

Then he brushed the stone dust from his hands and stood up.

The treasure was found and its hiding-place marked. Now he would find Edred and Elfrida, and they would go back. Whether he was Lord of Arden or not, it was he and no other who had restored the fallen fortunes of that noble house.

He turned to go the way his cousins had gone. He could see the men-at-arms crowding in the archway of the great gate tower. From a window to his right a lady leaned, pale with terror, and with her were Edred and Elfrida—he could just see their white faces. He made for the door below that window. But it was too late. That dull, thudding sound came again, and this time it was followed by a great crash and a great shouting. The blue sky showed through the archway where the tall gates had been and under the arch was a mass of men shouting, screaming, struggling, and the gleam of steel and the scarlet of brave blood.

Dickie forgot all about the door below the window, forgot all about his cousins, forgot that he had found the treasure and that it was now his business to get himself and the others safely back to their own times. He only saw the house he loved broken into by men he hated; he saw the men he loved spending their blood like water to defend that house.

He drew the little sword that hung at his side and shouting "An Arden! An Arden!" he rushed towards the swaying, staggering melee. He reached it just as the leader of the attacking party had hewn his way through the Arden men and taken his first step on the flagged path of the courtyard. The first step was his last. He stopped, a big, burly fellow in a leathern coat and steel round cap, and looked, bewildered, at the little figure coming at him with all the fire and courage of the Ardens burning in his blue eyes. The big man laughed, and as he laughed Dickie lunged with his sword—the way his tutor had taught him—and the little sword—no tailor's ornament to a Court dress, but a piece of true steel—went straight and true up into the heart of that big rebel. The man fell, wrenching the blade from Dickie's hand.

A shout of fury went up from the enemy. A shout of pride and triumph from the Arden men. Men struggled and fought all about him. Next moment Dickie's hands were tied with a handkerchief, and he stood there breathless and trembling with pride.

"I have killed a man," he said; "I have killed a man for the King and for Arden."

They shut him up in the fuel shed and locked the door. Pride and anger filled him. He could think of nothing but that one good thrust for the good cause. But presently he remembered.

He had brought his cousins here—he must get them back safely. But how? On a quiet evening on the road Beale had taught him how to untie hands tied behind the back. He remembered the lesson now and set to work—but it was slow work. And all the time he was thinking, thinking. How could he get out? He knew the fuel shed well enough. The door was strong, there was a beech bard outside. But it was not roofed with tile or lead, as the rest of the Castle was. And Dickie knew something about thatch. Not for nothing had he watched the men thatching the oast-house by the Medway. When his hands were free he stood up and felt for the pins that fasten the thatch.

Suddenly his hands fell by his side. Even if he got out, how could he find his cousins? He would only be found by the rebels and be locked away more securely. He lay down on the floor, lay quite still there. It was despair. This was the end of all his cleverness. He had brought Edred and Elfrida into a danger, and he could not get them back again. His anger had led him to defy the Roundheads, and to gratify his hate of them he had sacrificed those two who trusted him. He lay there a long time, and if he cried a little it was very dark in the fuel house, and there was no one to see him.

He was not crying however, but thinking, thinking, thinking, and trying to find some way out, when he heard a little scratch, scratching on the corner of the shed. He sat up and listened. The scratching went on. He held his breath. Could it be that someone was trying to get in to help him? Nonsense, of course it was only a rat. Next moment a voice spoke so close to him that he started and all but cried out.

"Bide where you be, lad, bide still; 'tis only me—old Mouldiwarp of Arden. You be a bold lad, by my faith, so you be. Never an Arden better. Never an Arden of them all."

"Oh, Mouldiwarp, dear Mouldiwarp, do help me! I led them into this—help me to get them back safe. Do, do, do!"

"So I will, den—dere ain't no reason in getting all of a fluster. It ain't fitten for a lad as 'as faced death same's what you 'ave," said the voice. "I've made a liddle tunnel for 'e—so I 'ave—'ere in dis 'ere corner—you come caten wise crose the floor and you'll feel it. You crawl down it, and outside you be sure enough."

Dickie went towards the voice, and sure enough, as the voice said, there was a hole in the ground, just big enough, it seemed, for him to crawl down on hands and knees.

"I'll go afore," said the Mouldiwarp, "you come arter. Dere's naught to be afeared on, Lord Arden."

"Am I really Lord Arden?" said Dickie, pausing.

"Sure's I'm alive you be," the mole answered; "yer uncle'll tell it you with all de lawyer's reasons tomorrow morning as sure's sure. Come along, den. Dere ain't no time to lose."

So Dickie went down on his hands and knees, and crept down the mole tunnel of soft, sweet-smelling earth, and then along, and then up—and there they were in the courtyard. There, too, were Edred and Elfrida.

"I HAVE KILLED A MAN," HE SAID.

The three children hugged each other, and then turned to the Mouldiwarp.

"How can we get home?"

"The old way," he said; and from the sky above a swan-carriage suddenly swooped. "In with you," said the Mouldiwarp; "swan carriages can take you from one time to another just as well as one place to another. But we don't often use 'em—'cause why? swans is dat contrary dey won't go invisible not for no magic, dey won't. So everybody can see 'em. Still we can't pick nor choose when it's danger like dis 'ere. In with you. Be off with you. This is the last you'll see o' me. Be off afore the soldiers sees you."

They squeezed into the swan carriage, all three. The white wings spread and the whole equipage rose into the air unseen by any one but a Roundhead sentinel, who with great presence of mind gave the alarm, and was kicked for his pains, because when the guard turned out there was nothing to be seen.

The swans flew far too fast for the children to see where they were going, and when the swans began to flap more slowly so that the children could have seen if there had been anything to see, there was nothing to be seen, because it was quite dark. And the air was very cold. But presently a light showed ahead, and next moment there they were in the cave, and stepped out of the carriage on the exact spot where Dickie had set out the moon-seeds and Tinkler and the white seal.

The swan carriage went back up the cave with a wish and rustle of wings, and the children went down the hill as quickly as they could—which was not very quickly because of Dickie's poor lame foot. The boy who had killed a Cromwell's man with his little sword had not been lame.

Arrived in the courtyard, Dickie proudly led the way and stooped to examine the stones near the ruined arch that had been the chapel door. Alas! there was not a sign of the inscription which Dickie had scratched on the stone when the Roundheads were battering at the gates of Arden Castle.

Then Edred said, "Aha!" in a tone of triumph.

"*I* took notice, too," he explained. "It's the fifth stone from the chapel door under the little window with the Arden arms carved over it. There's no other window with that over it. I'll get the cold chisel."

He got it, and when he came back Dickie was on his knees by the wall, and he had dug with his hands and uncovered he stone where he had scratched with the nails. And there was the mark—19. R.D. 08. Only the nail had slipped once or twice while he was doing the 9, so that it looked much more like a five—15. R.D. 08.

"There," he said, "that's what I scratched!"

"That?" said Edred, "Why, that's always been there. We found that when we were digging about, trying to find the treasure. Quite at the beginning, didn't we, Elf?"

And Elfrida agreed that this was so.

"Well, I scratched it, anyway," said Dickie. "Now, then, let me go ahead with the chisel."

Edred let him: he knew how clever Dickie was with his hands, for had he not made a workbox for Elfrida and a tool-chest for Edred, both with lids that fitted?

Dickie got the point of the chisel between the stones and prized and pressed—here and there, and at the other end—till the stone moved forward a little at a time, and they were able to get hold of it, and drag it out. Behind was darkness, a hollow—Dickie plunged his arm in.

"I can feel the door," he said; "it's all right."

"Let's fetch father," suggested Elfrida; "he *will* enjoy it so."

So he was fetched, Elfrida burst into the library where her father was busy with many lawyer's letters and papers, and also with the lawyer himself, a stout, jolly-looking gentleman in a tweed suit, not a bit like the long, lean disagreeable, black-coated lawyers you read about in books.

"Please, daddy," she cried, "we've found the treasure. Come and look."

"What treasure?—and how often have I told you not to interrupt me when I am busy?"

"Oh, well," said Elfrida, "I only thought it would amuse you, daddy. We've found a bricked-up place, and there's a door behind, and I'm almost sure it's where they hid the treasure when Cromwell's wicked men took the Castle."

"There is a legend to that effect," said Elfrida's father to the lawyer, who was looking interested. "You must forgive us if our family enthusiasms obliterate our manners. You have not said good morning to Mr. Roscoe, Elfrida."

"Good morning, Mr. Roscoe," said Elfrida cheerfully. "I thought it was the engineer's day and not the lawyer's. I beg your pardon, you wouldn't mind me bursting in if you knew how very important the treasure is to the fortunes of our house."

The lawyer laughed. "I am deeply interested in buried treasure. It would be a great treat to me if Lord Arden would allow me to assist in the search for it."

"There's no search *now*," said Elfrida, "because it's found. We've been searching for ages. Oh, daddy, do come—you'll be sorry afterwards if you don't."

"If Mr. Roscoe doesn't mind, then," said her father indulgently. And the two followed Elfrida, believing that they were just going to be kind and to take part in some childish game of make-believe. Their feelings were very different when they peeped through the hole, where Dickie and Edred had removed two more stones, and saw the dusty grey of the wooden door beyond. Very soon all the stones were out, and the door was disclosed.

The lock plate bore the arms of Arden, and the door was not to be shaken.

"We must get a locksmith," said Lord Arden.

"The big key with the arms on it!" cried Elfrida; "one of those in the iron box. Mightn't that—?" One flew to fetch it.

A good deal of oil and more patience were needed before the key consented to turn in the lock, but it did turn—and the low passage was disclosed. It hardly seemed a passage at all, so thick and low hung the curtain of dusty cobwebs. But with brooms and lanterns and much sneezing and choking, the whole party got through to the door of the treasure room. And the other key unlocked that. And there in real fact was the treasure just as the children had seen it—the chests and the boxes and the leathern sacks and the bundles done up in straw and in handkerchiefs.

The lawyer, who had come on a bicycle, went off on it, at racing speed, to tell the Bank at Cliffville to come and fetch the treasure, and to bring police to watch over it till it should be safe in the Bank vaults.

"And I'm child enough," he said before he went, "as well as cautious enough, to beg you not to bring any of it out till I come back, and not to leave guarding the entrance till the police are here."

So when the treasure at last saw the light of day it saw it under the eyes of policemen and Bank managers and all the servants and all the family and the Beales and True, and half the village beside, who had got wind of the strange happenings at the Castle and had crowded in through the now undefended gate.

It was a glorious treasure—gold and silver plate, jewels and beautiful armor, along with a pile of old parchments which Mr. Roscoe said were worth more than all the rest put together, for they were the title-deeds of great estates.

"And now," cried Beale, "let's 'ave a cheer for Lord Arden. Long may 'e enjoy 'is find, says I! 'Ip, 'ip, 'ooray!"

The cheers went up, given with a good heart.

"I thank you all," said the father of Edred and Elfrida. "I thank you all from my heart. And you may be sure that you shall share in this good fortune. The old lands are in the market. They will be bought back. And every house on Arden land shall be made sound and weather-tight and comfortable. The Castle will be restored—almost certainly. And the fortunes of Arden's tenantry will be the fortunes of Arden Castle."

Another cheer went up. But the speaker raised his hand, and silence waited his next words.

"I have something else to tell you," he said, "and as well now as later. This gentleman, Mr. Roscoe, my solicitor, has this morning brought me news that I am not Lord Arden!"

Loud murmurs of dissatisfaction from the crowd.

"I have no claim to the title," he went on grimly; "my father was a younger son—the real heir was kidnapped, and supposed to be dead, so I inherited. It is the grandson of that kidnapped heir who is Lord Arden. I know his whole history. I know what he has done, to do honor to himself and to help others." ("Hear, hear" from Beale.) "I know all his life, and I am proudly that he is the head of our house. He will do for you, when he is of age, all that I would have done. And in the meantime I am his guardian. This is Lord Arden," he said, throwing his arm round the shoulders of Dickie, little lame Dickie, who stood the leaning on his crutch, pale as death. "This is Lord Arden, come to his own. Cheer for him, men, as you never cheered before. Three cheers for Richard Lord Arden!"

The End

What a triumph for little lame Dickie of Deptford!

*   *   *   *   *

You think, perhaps, that he was happy as well as proud, for proud he certainly was, with those words and those cheers ringing in his ears. He had just done the best he could, and tried to help Beale and the dogs, and the man who had thought himself to be Lord Arden had said, "I am proud that he should be the head of our house," and all the Arden folk had cheered. It was worth having lived for.

The unselfish kindness and affection of the man he had displaced, the love of his little cousins, the devotion of Beale, the fact that the was Lord Arden, and would soon be lord of all the old acres—the knowledge that now he would learn all he chose to learn and hold in his hand some day the destinies of these village folk, all loyal to the name of Arden, the thought of all that he could be and do—all these things, you think, should have made him happy.

They would have made him happy, but for one thing. All this was won at the expense of those whom he loved best—the children who were his dear cousins and playfellows, the man, their father, who had moved heaven and earth to establish Dickie's claim to the title, and had been content quietly to stand aside and give up title, castle, lands, and treasure to the little cripple from Deptford.

Dickie thought of that, and almost only of that, in the days that followed.

The life he had led in that dream-world, when James the First was King, seemed to him now a very little thing compared with the present glory, of being the head of the house of Arden, of being the Providence, the loving over-lord of all these good peasant folk, who loved his name.

Yet the thought of those days when he was plain Richard Arden, son of Sir Richard Arden, living in the beautiful house at Deptford, fretted at all his joy in his present state. That, and the thought of all he owed to him who had been Lord of Arden until he came, with his lame foot and his heirship, fretted his soul as rust frets steel. These people had received him, loved him, been kind to him when he was only a tramp boy. And he was repaying them by taking away from them priceless possessions. For so he esteemed the lordship of Arden and the old lands and the old Castle.

Suppose he gave them up—the priceless possessions? Suppose he went away to that sure retreat that was still left him—the past? It was a sacrifice. To give up the here and now, for the far off, the almost forgotten. All that happy other life, that had once held all for which he cared, seemed thin and dreamlike beside the vivid glories of the life here, now. Yet he remembered how once that life, in King James's time, had seemed the best thing in the world, and how he had chosen to come back from it, to help a helpless middle-aged ne'er-do-well of a tramp—Beale. Well, he had helped Beale. He had done when he set out to do. For Beale's sake he had given up the beautiful life for the sordid life. And Beale was a new man, a man that Dickie had made. Surely now he could give up one beautiful life for another—for the sake of these, his flesh and blood, who had so readily, so kindly, so generously set him in the palace that had been theirs?

More and more it came home to Dickie that this was what he had to do. To go back to the times when James the First was King, and never to return to these times at all. It would be very bitter—it would be like leaving home never to return. It was exile. Well, was Richard Lord Arden to be afraid of exile—or of anything else? He must not just disappear either, or they would search and search for him, and never know that he was gone for ever. He must slip away, and let the father of Edred and Elfrida be, as he had been, Lord Arden. He must make it appear that he, Richard Lord Arden, was dead. He thought over this very carefully. But if he seemed to be dead, Edred and Elfrida would be very unhappy. Well, they should not be unhappy. He would tell them. And then they would know that he had behaved well, and as an Arden should. Don't be hard on him for longing for just this "little human praise." There are very few of us who can do without it; who can bear not to let someone, very near and dear, know that we have behaved rather decently on those occasions when that is what we have done.

It took Dickie a long time to think out all this, clearly, and with no mistakes. But at last his mind was made up.

And then he asked Edred and Elfrida to come up to the cave with him, because he had something to tell them. When they were all there, sitting on the smooth sand by the underground stream, Dickie said—

"Look here. I'm not going on being Lord Arden."

"You can't help it," said Edred.

"Yes, I can. You know how I went and lived in King James's time. Well, I'm going there again—for good."

"You shan't," said Elfrida. "I'll tell father."

"I've thought of all that," Dickie said, "and I'm going to ask the Mouldiwarps to make it so that you *can't* tell. I can't stay here and feel that I'm turning you and your father out. And think what Edred did for me, in this very cave. No, my mind's made up."

It was, and they could not shake it.

"But we shan't ever see you again."

Dickie admitted that this was so.

"And oh, Dickie," said Elfrida, with deep concern, "you won't ever see us again either. Think of that. Whatever will you do without us?"

"That," said Dickie, "won't be so bad as you think. The Elfrida and Edred who live in those times are as like you as two pins. No, they aren't really! Oh, don't make it any harder. I've got to do it."

There was that in his voice which silenced and convinced them. They felt that he had, indeed, to do it.

"I could never be happy here—never," he went on; "but I shall be happy there. And you'll never forget me, though there are one or two things I want you to forget. And I'm going now."

"Oh, not now; wait and think, " Elfrida implored.

"I've thought of nothing else for a month," said Dickie, and began to lay out the moon-seeds on the smooth sand.

"Now," he said, when the pattern was complete, "I shall hold Tinkler and the white seal in my hand take them with me. When I've gone, you can put the moon-seeds in your pocket and go home. When they ask you where I am, say I am in the cave. They will come and find my clothes, and they'll think I was bathing and got drowned."

"I can't bear it," said Elfrida, bursting into sobs. "I can't, and I won't."

"I shan't be really dead, silly," Richard told her. "We're bound to meet again some day. People who love each other can't help meeting again. Old nurse told me so, and she knows everything. Goodbye, Elfrida." He kissed her. "Goodbye, Edred, old chap. I'd like to kiss you too, if you don't mind. I know boys don't, but in the times I'm going to *men* kiss each other. Raleigh and Drake did, you know."

The boys kissed shyly and awkwardly.

"I'VE THOUGHT OF NOTHING ELSE FOR A MONTH," SAID DICKIE.

"And now, goodbye," said Richard, and stepped inside the crossed triangles of moon-seeds.

"I wish," he said slowly, "oh, dear Mouldiwarps of Arden, grant me these last wishes. I wish Edred and Elfrida may never be able to tell what I have done. And I wish that in a year they may forget what I have done, and let them not be unhappy about me, because I shall be very happy. I know I shall," he added doubtfully, and paused.

"Oh, Dickie, *don't,*" the other children cried out together. He went on—

"I wish my uncle may restore the Castle, and take care of the poor people so that there *aren't* any poor people, and everyone's comfortable, just as I meant to do."

He took off his cap and coat and flung them outside the circle, his boots too.

"I wish I may go back to James the First's time, and live out my life there, and do honor in my life and death to the house of Arden."

The children blinked. Dickie and Tinkler and the white seal were gone, and only the empty right of moon-seeds lay on the sand.

*   *   *   *   *

"Shocking bathing fatality," the newspapers said. "Lord Arden drowned. The body not yet recovered."

It never was recovered, of course. Elfrida and Edred said nothing. No wonder, their elders said. The shock was too great and too sudden.

The father of Edred and Elfrida is Lord Arden now. He has done all that Dickie would have done. He has made Arden the happiest and most prosperous village in England, and the stream beside which Dickie bade farewell to his cousins flows, a broad moat round the waters of the Castle, restored now to all its own splendor.

There is a tablet in the church which tells of the death by drowning of Richard, Sixteenth Lord Arden. The children read it every Sunday for a year, and knew that it did not tell the truth. But by the time the moon-seeds had grown and flowered and shed their seeds in the Castle garden they ceased to know this, and talked often, sadly and fondly, of dear cousin Dickie who was drowned. And at the same time they ceased to remember that they had ever been out of their own time into the past, so that if they were to read this book they would think it all nonsense and make-up, and not in the least recognize the story as their own.

But whatever else is forgotten, Dickie is remembered. And he who gave up his life here for the sake of those he loved will live as long as life shall beat in the hearts of those who loved him.

* * * * *

And Dickie himself. I see him in his ruff and cloak, with his little sword by his side, living out the life he has chosen in the old England when James the First was King. I see him growing in grace and favor, versed in book learning, expert in all noble sports and exercises. For Dickie is not lame now.

I see the roots of his being taking fast hold of his chosen life, and the life that he renounced receding, receding till he can hardly see it anymore.

I see him, a tall youth, straight and strong, lending the old nurse his arm to walk in the trim, beautiful garden at Deptford. And I hear him say—

"When I was a little boy, nurse, I had mighty strange dreams—of another life than this."

"Forget them," she says; "dreams go to the making of all proper men. But now thou art a man; forget the dreams of thy childhood, and play the man to the glory of God and of the house of Arden. And let thy dreams be of the life to come, compared to which all lives on earth are only dreams. And in that life all those who have loved shall meet and be together for evermore, in that life when all the dear and noble dreams of the earthly life shall at last and for ever be something more than dreams."

EXPLICIT